The Bakery on Main

Welcome to Woodsburrow

Book Two

J.R. Cook

First paperback edition February 2024

ISBN 979-8-9898991-2-8 (paperback edition) 979-8-9898991-3-5 (eBook edition)

To my beautiful daughters, may you always be as fierce as Hannah in your lives as you grow and navigate this crazy world, we live in. I love you both more than anything.

Chapter 1

Hannah

"Hannah! That's the third complaint I've had about you today!" Pierre had hollered as the customer stuck up her nose, turned on her heels, and walked out the front door.

Hannah took a deep breath and closed her eyes. This particular customer had come in to complain that the flowers on the cake she had just spent hours and hours perfectly piping were too red. *Too red? This woman has lost her mind.* Hannah had thought as she bit her tongue until her teeth drew blood while the woman berated her for being too incompetent to make her vision come to life in an accurate manner. She announced loudly that she would not be paying for the atrocity Hannah had just created and would need a new one with the proper shade of red roses made promptly, and ready for her bridal shower at 11:00 tomorrow. Pierre had been watching her and sneering during the entire interaction. He had enjoyed watching her be humiliated. Hannah wanted to tell the woman she was acting like a fool, and it was virtually impossible to match the exact red shade that she saw only in her mind, but she stood silently until she left. When the door closed, Pierre unleashed his condescending remarks in rapid fire on her. She held back tears as Pierre proceeded to humiliate her in front of the entire staff. He had always had an obsession with trying to make her feel small.

Golden Goose Bakery had a clientele that was made up of the richest and most prominent humans in the city. They catered all their events from club meetings to weddings and were frequently featured in the press. Pierre, the owner of the Golden Goose had won multiple baking competitions and expected nothing, but the absolute best from his employees. They only created items that their clientele would buy. Anything that was out of the box or considered a classic would never be baked and sold there. The hours were long and brutal, and every day was full of complaints.

It wasn't that Hannah didn't think that complaints were never warranted. Of course, you wanted timely service, the writing done correctly on your cake, and high-quality customer interactions, but these humans seemed to complain, just to complain. Sometimes, cakes were re-baked and decorated, only to look identical to their prior version. Hannah had taken photographs with her phone to prove that point. While the satisfaction of the buyer had changed from disgusted to proud, the product had remained indistinguishable from the original. These people just liked to make noise to have the upper hand, to remind the staff that they were the ones in charge.

Hannah had begun sneaking the wasted cakes out of the bakery, saving them from a trip into the dumpster, and bringing them to the homeless shelter that was in her neighborhood. Pierre never would have approved if he found out, and she knew she risked getting fired each time she smuggled in a cake from its way to the trash into the back of her Bug. Had he known his prestigious cakes were being fed to the lowly homeless of the city, he would have blown a gasket. He would rather continue to waste beautiful cakes and frankly his money in the toilet, than have such a tarnishment be brought against his brand. He relished the limelight his baking afforded him. His name was everything to him, and he was not shy about informing anyone who surrounded him of that fact.

Hannah had wanted to be a baker ever since her first Easy Bake oven she received for Christmas as a child. She used it constantly until her mother deemed her old enough to use the real oven. She treasured the joy that baking brought to others around her. She loved to spread happiness and see smiles on the faces of people she loved. She marveled at the pure magic that was created with some eggs, flour, and sugar. Every holiday and important event was smattered with baked goods of significance. Birthday cakes were the center of birthday parties, wedding cakes the crown jewel for brides and grooms, Christmas cookies covered trays upon trays during the holiday season, pumpkin pies were baked with love for Thanksgiving feasts, and chocolate was deemed the healing hand for broken hearts. Each one elicited an emotional response, and some came with deep-seated memories and tradition. One could be transported to another place and time with just a bite of a well done classic.

Hannah attended a program to become a bakery chef, despite the teasing of her two older sisters who held master's degrees and considered baking to be a housewife's hobby and not a career. When she graduated, she held various jobs around the city and had many excellent mentors and teachers who taught her techniques she would have never seen anywhere else. She finally was working at the finest and most elite bakery in the city. She had achieved an important goal she had strived for, and it was miserable.

After she began working at the Golden Goose and discovered that her dream job was more like a nightmare, Hannah started planning for a new dream. She began by saving money. It was why she rented a studio apartment near the homeless shelter and the reason she had gone from wearing designer clothing to thrifting for outfits. And now, that was what she preferred. She could pull together an outfit that was much more unique and accentuated her bright personality more accurately with a carefully thrifted outfit than any pre-styled piece she had bought at a high-end boutique. She had scored her first vintage Chanel coat thrifting, and it had been her favorite for years now. She never ran into anyone who looked quite like she did on any given day.

So, day after day she went to work, reminding herself of the goal she had in mind, and returned to her little nook of an apartment at the end of the day to retreat and find herself a bit of hope. The dollar amount she needed to illicit her two-week notice was the constant reminder in her mind. Hannah was determined to open her own bakery, and the final check she was going to be receiving on Friday, would be the one that made her savings equivalent to the number she had been waiting for.

Her hours spent at the shelter were the only time Hannah felt that feeling of spreading joy with the magic of baking anymore, the entire reason she had started baking, to begin with. She loved people. She was an outgoing personality who thrived on being around others. She didn't care about money, prestige, or power. She just wanted to bake. She wanted to be able to use her creativity, to make something other than the same tarts on repeat. On weeks she didn't have cakes that she was saving from the trash, she baked cookies at her house on her time off and would bring them into the shelter. She would sit and talk and laugh with the people that were there that week. They looked forward to her visit, and the atmosphere always shifted from tense and rundown to hopeful when she arrived, Hannah enjoyed their company immensely.

Hannah was relieved her rotten day finally ended, and she was headed home. A text buzzed on her phone from her mother reminding her of family dinner that evening. Her relief had quickly dissipated with the reminder. Her fiancé Mark would be joining her.

Hannah had always been the girl who could date any man she wanted. They had flocked to her in droves. She had been Prom Queen in high school and had dated the quarterback on the football team. Throughout the years she had been with semiprofessional athletes, business types, and hot servers. Every man she dated was disappointing. None of them were exhilarating enough and could keep up with her sense of adventure.

Currently, she was engaged to the perfect fiancé. He worshiped her. He told her she was beautiful every day. He bought her gifts regularly. He told her everything she ever baked was divine, even if that wasn't true, and she had tested his insistence on this. One time, she had baked brownies until they were almost so chewy and tough that you could break a tooth, and he had claimed it was the best he had ever eaten. He had a good cooperate job that he loyally attended every day without fail. He had worked for the same company for years. Her mother and sisters loved him. He wasn't a drinker. He was handsome, but he was also boring.

Hannah had loved the flattery at first. It was nice being with someone who wasn't afraid to show their affection. Hannah and her friend Abby had been out on a Friday night when he had approached her. He was confident, and well-dressed and made her feel like she was the most beautiful woman in the world. Abby had just finished telling her she needed to be with someone who grounded her. Hannah had never considered that before, and Mark had seemed like the perfect opportunity to give that type of man a try. For a while, things had gone well.

After the engagement became official, however, she began to see the problems that she hadn't noticed before, and once she noticed, she couldn't go back to that place where she didn't see them. Mark had no personality of his own. When they went out together, he didn't add much if anything, to conversation. Hannah would do all the talking. She would even throw him lead-ins to conversations like a slow-pitched softball, and he would stand proudly at her side, smile, and revert the conversation back to her. When they needed to decide where they were going out to eat, Hannah was the one who always made the decision on which restaurant they would go to. Mark would say, "Wherever you want to eat, babe." It became insanely annoying that the man couldn't make a decision for himself. Even if it were a choice she didn't agree with, she wished he would just make one.

He constantly seemed to be along for the ride. Hannah felt like she was dragging him along on his leash. His only hobby was collecting old game cards of games he had never and would never play. The man was a straight snooze. Hannah wanted him to take chances, make a decision once in a while, and have a little spirit of adventure. Even if he might spark a disagreement, that was better than the way they had been living so far.

Of course, her sisters loved him and thought he was Prince Charming. They would tell her often how lucky she was. When Hannah would roll her eyes, they would remind her that he was so handsome, so attentive, and constantly in an agreeable mood not everyone got that lucky. He was always pleasant, never too happy, never too sad, and even-tempered. Hannah however had been seriously doubting that she had ever loved him and dreaded their time together. Mark might be the dream man for a woman out there, but he wasn't hers. She couldn't share their excitement of his presence.

She arrived home grabbed one of her emergency pies from the freezer and preheated the oven. Blueberry pie would be her rescue for this forgotten dinner. "Perfect!" Hannah remarked to herself. She glanced at the clock and quickly jumped into the shower.

Hannah was a beautiful bombshell. She had long luscious blonde hair. She was curvy with a bit extra in all the right places and none in the wrong ones. Her stride consistently was full of confidence, and she almost always had a smile on her face. That smile was beautiful bright and genuine. Her green eyes glistened when she beamed, and it was impossible not to return her smile with one of your own. Everywhere she went, Hannah would leave with new lifelong friends. Anyone could sit with Hannah without knowing her prior to that encounter and share their most intimate secrets. They would look up at the clock and hours would have passed in what felt like minutes. She was enjoyable to spend time with. There was something so infectious about her energy.

Everyone loved Hannah, which might have been why her sisters were always so critical of her. Her sisters were both plain. They were smart. They were Type A personalities. Both had risen to management level positions in their careers, and both were married to their own predictable men. They owned their own homes and had one child or one on the way. They were both akin to Plain Janes and had sandy brown hair and dressed to hide their figures, not because they needed to, but because they wanted to be seen as equal to men instead of sexy or womanly. Hannah loved her sisters, but she couldn't relate.

She knew that despite being so different, she never would have grown up being unapologetically herself without her sisters fighting off any battle that came in her way. Even though they had very few interests in common, and they frequently tried to counsel her on her life decisions, Hannah treasured them which made it hard for her to voice her disagreement aloud to them with their opinion on Mark.

Hannah had never stopped following her own heart and her true self. She was bold and felt proud of all the parts of herself. She loved pink, and neon yellow. Hannah dressed to feel beautiful and confident and match her moods. She was proud to be a woman, and although she didn't dress scandalously by any means, her curves made anything she wore look voluptuous and sexy. Men stared at her everywhere she went, and more than once she had had to prove that she had talent and not just beauty.

Hannah slipped on her tight cheetah print dress with thin straps and a frilly hemline and slipped on some black heels. She heard her oven ding as it alerted her to the preheat being complete. Hannah slipped the pie inside and finished her hair and make-up as she waited for Mark's arrival. As she waited, she reflected on her day.

She hated letting Pierre treat her the way she did. In her entire life, she had never allowed a man to speak down to her. Keeping her job at the Golden Goose had been the quickest way to build her savings account, and according to her count, she wouldn't be stuck there much longer.

She hadn't told anyone about this goal, including Mark and her mother. It wasn't that she cared what anyone's opinion might be. She was opening her own place whether anyone supported the idea or not. It felt like a bright piece of hope inside her that burned brighter when she didn't speak the words out loud. A special secret that was all hers. It felt like if she shared it, the light would flicker. Hannah knew she couldn't go on living the life that she was living now. Her dream of her own place, the smell of her own creations, and the company with her own clients was what kept her going.

She heard Mark knock on the door. It always drove Hannah crazy that he didn't say anything when he knocked. They had been dating for years and he still knocked on the door like a scout delivering cookies. "Come in, Mark." She called from inside. She slipped on her pink oven mitts and carefully removed the pie from the oven.

Mark stiffly walked in through the door and moved to kiss her. Hannah gave him her cheek. "You look wonderful. Are you ready to go, babe?"

She smiled. "Yes, of course."

Hannah slipped the pie into her carrier, grabbed her purse, and walked out of her apartment. Mark spoke about his day and asked Hannah about hers. Hannah would tell him about the projects she worked on and the things she created, but she never shared how much she hated working at the Golden Goose or how horrible Pierre could be, and how tense the environment was. It made her feel embarrassed, and she didn't want to have to justify her decision to stay.

Hannah's mother, Katherine, met them at the door and scooped Hannah into a giant hug before greeting Mark with a friendly hug as well. Hannah was her mother's favorite, and she bragged about her job at the Golden Goose at every book club and bingo game she attended. She had always supported Hannah's wild ideas and impulsive plans. They regularly went shopping together, and Hannah often came over for dinner for alone time with just her parents. It had only been just recently that Mark, at her mother's insistence had begun attending, too.

Hannah and Mark moved to the table, and Hannah unloaded her pie onto the center. Her mom had made pot roast. The scent permeated the air. The table had been set and her dad moved back and forth from the kitchen bringing out the pot roast and rolls. Her dad said hello to Mark and shook hands with him. He had always been kind to Mark, but his demeanor was always indifferent. Like Hannah, he didn't have much in common with him, so the conversation quickly fell flat.

"So, Mark, how are things?' Her mother asked and Hannah listened to the same boring story she had just heard in the car as she focused on her food. He grabbed her knee and her body stiffened. His touch felt foreign. She needed to find a way out of this engagement, and soon.

Luke

"Summer always brings the most ridiculous calls." Luke grumbled as he flopped down into his desk.

"Long night?" Tori asked from the next desk over.

"You could say that. I had three noise complaint calls, a brawl over at the brewery, and vandalism over at the park and zero time to fill anything out. I'm going to be swimming in paperwork the next two hours." He yawned. "I just want to go home to my bed."

"I'll make a pot of coffee for us." Tori patted his shoulder and went to fill the Mr. Coffee pot.

Luke drained the entire pot while he finished the stack of reports he had started earlier in the night but had been interrupted by a new call nearly every time he was almost finished. The summer brought tourists into town which made the population of Woodsburrrow double in size. Whatever a normal shift might look like in the dead of winter, was the exact opposite of what you might expect in July, and no one seemed to be on their best behavior while on vacation. He was scheduled to be on nights through the rest of the summer and would swap with Tori come the fall. The night shift was relentless and without backup. In the morning, he tended to be over the drama.

Regardless of the tough situations people were in when he met them though, he loved being a police officer. He had always been very articulate, and he enjoyed people. In general, he could quickly diffuse situations, and make people who were hysterical, calm themselves. He took his job seriously and at the end of the day, he was proud to be an officer of Woodsburrow.

Luke had lived in Woodsburrow his entire life. He had grown up an only child. His parents Bob and Becky were farmers. They had instilled in him the value of hard work. Despite being in sports year-round, farming was a family affair. Luke was always expected to complete his chores and do them well. He didn't get a free pass because of a game or practice. When they weren't working on the farm, his family tended to volunteer at every possible opportunity. His mom enjoyed her time socializing at these events, so it was rare that they missed an opportunity to help lend a hand. Even as an adult, he attended every event. He had never wanted to live anywhere else. Woodsburrow would always be what his soul called home.

Luke enjoyed assuming positions that required him to lead, and entertaining people. He also enjoyed the sense of brotherhood that being on sports teams had given him. Becoming a cop had seemed like the most logical career choice, and it fit him like a glove. He worked long rotating shifts but frequently had days off that he spent doing whatever it was that he wanted.

Two hours after he had drunk twelve cups of coffee, Luke fumbled into his house and went straight to his room. He had three days off starting today, and tonight he was meeting with his dad and Steele to go on their overnight fishing trip. He pulled his black-out curtains closed and stripped down to his boxers tossing his uniform in a crumpled mess on the floor. No amount of tired could compare to a night shift tired, but it was worth it to be a police officer in this town. Despite the coffee, he crashed hard and scarcely moved all day.

He woke up at four with an ungodly urge to pee. He blindly ambled to the bathroom let out a huge sigh and shivered. He knew that it wouldn't matter if he tried to go back to sleep, he was awake. Luke got in the shower and let the water run over his body until it changed from steamy to ice cold. After he dressed, he packed his hiking pack and checked over his fishing gear. This was his favorite part of the entire summer. They had been doing this trip every year since Luke and Steele were kids. Steele and Luke were never into Boy Scouts, and they wouldn't have had the time to allot to it anyway. So instead, they had learned all their survival skills, fishing skills, and map reading skills from their fathers. Eddie had to stop going after his stroke and insisted that they keep going to keep the tradition alive. They always missed his stories around the campfire, nonetheless, it was still one of their favorite parts of summer.

Luke was eating an overloaded plate of scrambled eggs with whatever groceries he still had left in his fridge when Steele walked in.

"Luke man, you really need to learn how to cook something other than eggs. What did you put in that gross mixture?"

He had ham sandwich slices, pepperoni, mozzarella cheese, and his pickled jalapeños. "Everything in my sandwich drawer. I didn't have time to go shopping, and we are leaving anyway. It wasn't worth it."

Steele shook his head and pulled a chair out to sit in. "How was work this stretch?"

Luke shrugged. "It was fine. I've had worse. I kept getting repetitive calls of Jesse starting fights down at Gearshift. His old lady must have kicked him out again. He always hits the booze too hard when they aren't living together."

Steele nodded. "Jesse was like that in high school too. He won't ever change."

"What did Stacey have to say about the camping trip this year?" Luke asked.

"That is a giant waste of my time, and I should be using it to take a trip to the Rocky's like she has been asking for all year and last. She keeps telling me I have to start traveling if I want this to work. She doesn't get that the store is mine now. I can't just move to another city and live like someone with no responsibilities."

"How are you guys going to get past that? She has been begging you to move since graduation day. I think you have had that same fight a million times."

Steele shrugged. "I don't think we will. I thought I could make her see how important staying is to me, but she doesn't hear any of that. She doesn't hear most of what I say. She is too busy talking; it drives me crazy. It's hard to make a change when you have been living the same way for years, though. It's that habit that keeps us together."

"Is that worth it? I mean, I'm not one that is qualified to give relationship advice. I haven't even found a woman I like being with for more than a few months, but is something better than nothing?"

Steele shook his head and shrugged. "I don't know."

Luke knew he was ready to change the subject, and he happily obliged. Stacey was a beautiful woman, but she strode around like she knew it, and she was a huge chatterbox. Luke and Steele had always been like brothers, but when Stacey was around, Steele changed. He shut down and clammed up looking odd and uncomfortable. He was looking forward to having some time with his friend without her constant interruptions.

Steele and Luke grabbed Luke's gear and loaded it into Steele's truck as Bob pulled into the driveway. "Yahoo! Ready to go boys?" He called excitedly.

"Waiting on you old man." Luke teased as he pulled open the passenger door and grabbed his dad's stuff. Luke took his jacket from his recliner as his dad settled into Steele's front seat. "Let's go boys!" He cried as they headed off for the woods. Nothing could be better than two nights with his favorite people off the grid, campfires, and fishing. Luke couldn't wait.

<h1 style="text-align:center">Chapter 2</h1>

Hannah

Today was the day, and Hannah could hardly believe it. She arrived at work early and was extra cheerful. Pierre was the only one there. He looked up at her and huffed a "Morning," under his breath. Pierre had ended her day yesterday by chastising her and screaming that he couldn't afford any more of her mistakes. She had spent the entire day making hundreds of pink cupcakes that were adorned with delicate handmade sugar unicorns. They were done perfectly and delivered on time with Hannah's magnificent smile. She had wished she had gotten to see the look of surprise and delight in the pretty little princess' face. She was proud of the work she had done and exhausted from the hours and hours of intense focus it had required to get them exactly right.

But the mother of the little girl who was turning three, had called Pierre to complain that she had wanted milk chocolate cake, and the cupcakes seemed to be a dark chocolate. She was just going to have to "deal with the variation, but she wasn't pleased." The complaint made no sense at all, and Hannah had used Pierre's chocolate cake recipe, just like she was always required to. They were never allowed to deviate from his recipes, and Hannah wasn't interested in rocking the boat any more than what was necessary. Pierre didn't care or listen to what she had to say. He interrupted her to remind her the customer was always right and followed it by telling her how worthless and embarrassing her baking emphasizing what a disgrace she was to his name. He ended the reprimanding session by telling her there was no more room for her mistakes. Hannah had left the bakery holding back tears from his beratement. She had gotten into her Bug and drove away as fast as she could without looking back. Pierre had always been mean and nasty to her, and Hannah had vowed long ago that when she became an owner, she would never treat her employees so poorly. There was no excuse to be such a horrible human being.

She was following that terrible night, with an early morning and a bright smile. Pierre was a terrible control freak, and it drove him wild that for starters, Hannah had refused to sleep with him when he first hired her. He had inappropriately cornered her and tried to convince her that the only reason she had gotten the job, was so he could hook up with her. After all, he had said, what was a blonde Playboy bunny thinking she could bake here? She immediately declined his advances and from that time forward, Pierre had been acting like she was a worthless pebble in his shoe that would never be able to do anything right and caused him great annoyance with every step. It was more than the fact that she had refused to sleep with him though, he was a bully who wanted to break her wild happy, and carefree spirit.

He wanted to see her unhappy, to dominate her soul in a sick and twisted way. She wasn't going to let him, and it killed him inside. She hummed when she baked and greeted her coworkers, and their customers warmly. She was everyone's favorite person to have around. The dynamic of the bakery that she had molded around her was welcoming. Pierre didn't want welcoming. He wanted exclusive, cutthroat. He wanted his employees to compete against each other. To Hannah, this made no sense. They should all be coming together on a common goal and reaching heights they could never reach on their own, teaching each other and bouncing ideas off each other, but they weren't allowed to use their creativity or ideas in any capacity.

Pierre told the customers what they wanted, and the customers ordered as such. He oversaw every order consultation so that he knew all the ins and outs of each encounter. Hannah was not competing for anything here and wouldn't be participating in any of his sick and twisted games. She was buying her time and hoarding away her paycheck. So, despite the despicable way she had been treated the evening before, she gave him a sweet Hannah smile and walked over to her station while Pierre swam in his disgust.

The day went along like every other. She baked an order of croissants that were warm, flakey, and crispy and the perfect shade of light brown. That croissant order had included their famous tarts, blueberries, and strawberries over a lemon cheesecake. They were fresh, decadent, and crunchy. The perfect combination. Hannah loved tarts and croissants. There wasn't anything she didn't enjoy baking, but what she didn't love was that croissants and these tarts, and a few orders of cupcakes were all she had made for the last few months, on repeat. Despite easily being one of Pierre's best bakers, she constantly was assigned the easiest orders. The customers always ordered the same items anyway, but when there was an important cake or stunning dessert ordered, it didn't get assigned to Hannah. You could add it to all the other ways that Pierre tried to break her down piece by piece. She regularly ate Ben and Jerry's before bed now, but otherwise, she hadn't broken and didn't intend to.

By four o'clock, the workday had ended. She handed Pierre her two-week resignation like she was handing him a coupon for $1 off toilet paper and walked out the door. She let the door fall shut behind her as she strode towards her car feeling freer with every step. While she was unlocking the door to her yellow Volkswagen Beetle, she was already thinking about putting the top down as she rode home and celebrating that she had made it to today.

She heard an angry shriek behind her. "How dare you! No one quits the Golden Goose!"

She turned and saw Pierre's face red and angry. She swore she could almost see smoke pouring out of his ears. "I'm sorry, Pierre. This just isn't the right fit for me long term." She replied nonchalantly while studying his face with a neutral expression plastered on hers.

"Not the right fit? You were always too lazy and lacking in talent. You only got the job because you have a nice rack. I'll ruin you in this town you little slut!"

"Excuse me? You know this qualifies as workplace harassment and probably worse things than that."

"This isn't your workplace anymore. You are fired, Hannah Jones!"

She smiled at him sweetly. "Okay. See you around then." Hannah turned away and got into her car. She stared him down as she belted herself in and rolled the top down of her convertible. She gave a little wave as she drove out of the parking lot. "Later weasel." She mumbled to herself as she merged onto First Avenue.

When Hannah got home, she celebrated. She drank three giant glasses of Port, made a delicious dinner of shrimp linguine, and ate her last piece of raspberry chocolate cheesecake. She knew that opening her own bakery would be the most challenging thing she had ever done, and there were no guarantees she would succeed, but after being suppressed under Pierre for far too long Hannah was ready for the challenge and whatever obstacles might come her way.

When she had finished her cheesecake, she settled on the couch to watch her favorite film, *Eat, Pray, Love.* Hannah loved Julia Roberts. She was beautiful witty and down to earth. She considered watching her all weekend since she had nowhere else to be. *My Best Friend's Wedding, Pretty Woman,* and *Erin Brockovich* were up on deck next. She was right in the middle of watching her eat the best pizza Hannah had ever seen when someone knocked on her apartment door transporting her back to reality. She threw off her plush white blanket and walked in her pink fluffy slippers to the front door.

"Hello, Mark." She said with her flushed cheeks and loose smile. He gave her a peck on the cheek and entered her apartment. She looked at the clock, 8:00 pm. *Great, he would want to spend the night.* She thought. "What brings you by? I wasn't expecting you tonight." In fact, she had been avoiding him as much as she could the last few weeks. He looked around her apartment.

"Have you been drinking alone?" He asked as he studied the empty Port bottle and her flushed red face.

"Absolutely." She smiled.

"A special occasion?"

"Yes, I was fired today."

"You were what?"

"Fired. I tried to put in my two-week notice, and Pierre decided he would rather I not work there at all effective immediately."

"You did this without telling me?" He asked.

Hannah looked shocked. "I don't need your permission." She replied firmly.

He looked at her like she had lost her mind. "Why would you quit your job? That's the top-tier bakery in the city. There isn't a better one out there."

"I'm going to open a better one." She said beaming. "You think you can open your own bakery? What makes you think you are qualified enough to do that? You have no management or business skills to speak of. All you know how to do is bake." He asked looking at her.

Hannah stared him down. He had never spoken doubt in her ability to do anything before. "You don't think I can do it?"

"Look Hannah, I know that you believe you can do anything you desire all the time, but life isn't like that. You had a good job. Now what are you going to do?"

"Exactly what I just told you I was doing. I think you should leave." Hannah said as she opened the door and gestured him out.

"Hannah don't be upset with me. It was your poor choice that put us here."

"Leave. Now." She said bluntly.

He looked puzzled, but finally turned and left. She slammed the door shut behind him and turned the lock. She didn't need his approval to chase her dreams, and if he was going to try to create doubt, she was better off alone.

Luke

When the boys returned home from their camping trip, Luke was tired, smelled like campfire, and his cup was full. They had come home with enough Perch to split among themselves and had caught some of the largest Walleyes and Northern Pike that they had ever caught on their yearly trips. He glanced at the clock, nine, he could get a solid sleep in before his scheduled shift tonight. He was too tired to eat and too tired to run to the store. He put his fish into the fridge and headed to his room to catch some shut-eye.

Luke's shifts that week were extra-long with calls almost back-to-back. The twelve-hour shifts had stretched from thirteen to fourteen hours. When he pulled up to the rink for their hockey game, he was looking forward to being just plain Luke. "Steele! Wait up." He called as he hustled to catch up with his friend.

"Did you ever get groceries you bum?" Steele asked with a grin.

"Nope. I've had a well-rounded week of scrambled eggs, pizza, and fish, supplemented with some of my mom's cooking."

"Dude I'm telling you. Learn to cook something other than eggs. The next place you will end up is my kitchen to mooch my food." Steele said.

Luke shrugged. "It's just not one of my talents."

The essence of the ice rink sharply permeated his face. Luke always enjoyed being on the rink. The constant chill in the air, the bright lights, and the crisp shiny ice, all brought him back in time to his high school days when they won state two years in a row. He knew he wasn't good enough to play professionally, but like every other young man, he had wished that he could. Steele did have that special talent that few possessed, but he never would have left his family to travel with a team. Family had always been foremost to Steele. He had settled for coaching at the high school level, and they had had excellent teams ever since he had taken over. It was more than just about wins for Steele though. He had told Luke many times about the boys' personal growth. He had led them through volunteering, helped one who had gotten his girlfriend pregnant, and more than once tutored a few so their grades maintained a C average.

Hockey was an important place where they could come together like brothers. Tonight though, superstar Steele was acting off. They had been like Goose and Maverick through the years, and it shined especially bright on the ice. They had been undefeated the last five years in intramurals, but today Steele had missed several passes and had caused more than a few turnovers. They hit the lockers with a solemn team.

"What happened tonight man? You seemed like something is off." Luke said with concern.

"Don't blame the team's loss on me! It wasn't like I was the only one not having their best night out there." Steele said defensively.

Luke put his hands up. "Hey. Not trying to throw blame. You know me better than that." Luke said.

Steele was the most levelheaded person he knew. It wasn't like Steele to blow up a situation into something it wasn't.

Steele sighed and placed his head on his locker. Without looking up he spoke. "I broke things off with Stacey today. It was harder than I thought it would be. I had to make it clear that we were breaking up and that was that. She told me no less than five times that she wouldn't allow me to break up with her. What kind of psycho says that? I am certain this is for the best. But even with all that, I feel off without her. She has been there for so many years, I just feel lost. That sounds ridiculous. I feel like a wimp."

Luke slapped a hand on his back. "Let's get a drink." He said simply.

They drove to Gearshift Brewery. It was buzzing with the usual crowd for a midweek night. They each ordered an IPA and found a place to sit at the end of the bar.

"It's alright to be a mess for a bit you know. I know you are always the responsible one, and the one who always has it together, but you guys have been together for years. I think it's pretty normal to feel like you have cut off a foot. Even if it was the right thing to break things off."

"It's infuriating that she acted like I didn't get a choice in the matter. I have been letting her talk and take up space for so many years that she thinks I am a pushover who doesn't get a voice. I've been telling her for ages that I'm not moving, and she honestly thought I would just change my mind and go, even with my dad's stroke and the store!"

Luke shook his head. "You deserve better, bro. This town is lucky to have you. If she doesn't want to be a part of it, it's better this way." Steele nodded.

When Luke arrived back at his apartment, he parked and sat quietly in the car before going inside. Stacey had always been an exuberant personality, and Steele was a more patient and softer-spoken one. He didn't know if they had stayed together for love, or because it had been easier, but he felt upset at seeing his friend hurt. At least he had given a long-term relationship a try, that was more than Luke could say for himself. It wasn't that he was a womanizer. He loved women, but he had never met one that he wanted to have that kind of time commitment with. None of them enjoyed his wit or shared his sense of adventure. He didn't know where his undeniable pickiness had come from, but his mom and his aunt Molly were forces to be reckoned with, and they were beautiful. His dad and mom were always going off on adventures together. They had been together since they were twenty and had been faithful and happy together all these years. He wanted that, or he wanted nothing at all.

<h1 style="text-align:center">Chapter 3</h1>

Hannah

Hannah spent Saturday morning tucked into her cozy blanket with Julia Roberts and hunted for business properties to view. She had reached out to an agent she had known through mutual friends, and Jeremy was going to show her as many properties as possible on Monday morning. Each one had its positive and negative qualities, but Hannah was giving any property she had interest in a chance. She knew that how something appeared online, might not compare to how it looked in person, and although she wasn't in a hurry to rush through the process, her funds didn't support her being extra fussy.

Her oldest sister, Jenny was having a birthday party for her niece who was turning one. Since it was July, they were having a backyard BBQ for her that afternoon. Jenny had asked Hannah to make the cake, and she was thrilled. This would be the most important item she had baked all week. It was vanilla confetti with sprinkles and drizzled chocolate forming a ring on the outside. She had used rainbow colors to frost the cake, and the filling inside had cream cheese ganache. It was beautiful and matched her niece's colorful personality perfectly. She had made Little Piper her own pan-sized cake. Smash cakes were adorable and honestly took little effort when she already had all the ingredients whipped up for the full-sized version. Her apartment smelled of vanilla and cream cheese. She inhaled and smiled. *Paradise*, she thought.

Hannah threw on her favorite full-length floral mint-colored sundress and grabbed her brown floppy hat. She had been ignoring Mark all day and felt lucky that she had forgotten to mention this event to him. She was beginning to feel resentful when he was around. He made her feel heavy and claustrophobic. Not to mention she was angry with how had had spoken to her, addressing her like she was a silly woman. She didn't want to hear her sisters tell her again today how she "shouldn't mess this one up." Even with the annoying comments, she knew she would be receiving; she wouldn't miss the BBQ. She loved Piper and knew she would get to be the cool aunt as she grew. She was not about to miss out on that and that meant risking the comments. She loaded the cakes into the back of the Bug along with the tricycle she had bought. She had gotten Piper her first tricycle. It was flashy pink with pink tassels floating out of each of the handles. She checked her make-up in the rearview mirror and drove over to her sister's house.

She jammed loudly to Taylor Swift as she danced and sang fearlessly as she drove with the top down. She didn't care if people saw or looked. She hoped they would join in if they did. Hannah was riding a high. She was chasing down her dream. She was only going to bake to spread happiness again, and not only that, but she was going to be able to experiment and flex her creative side. Her bakery would be a reflection of herself and not some arrogant man. *What could be better?*

She carefully carried the cakes one at a time into Jenny's kitchen and placed them on the counter.

"Oh, Hannah they are so sweet." Jenny came around the corner looking flustered, and they kissed each other's cheeks. "Thanks for coming."

"I wouldn't have missed it," Hannah said. "Where should I put her gift?"

"There is a table set up in the back off the porch." Jenny shuffled away attending to the next task, and Hannah went to retrieve the bike. She set the tricycle down next to the mountain of presents and walked over to say hello.

Her brother-in-law was holding Piper. She swept her up in her arms from his embrace and tickled her until she giggled.

Piper settled into Hannah's chest with her thumb in her mouth as her mom walked over. "Hannah my baby, you look so good today! You are absolutely glowing, and that baby looks perfect in your arms. Where is Mark today?" She looked around as if she thought he would appear out of the bushes on cue.

"He couldn't come. You know, work." She shrugged.

Her mom nodded. "His dedication to his job is so impressive. I really like how persistent he is. Such a steady and stable man is good for you."

Steady was one way to put it, Hannah thought. He was predictable. He worked, and he sat at home waiting for Hannah to call him while he organized his useless card collection.

Hannah settled into a lawn chair with Piper and waited for lunch to be ready. Jenny grabbed Piper and slipped her into her highchair. Their other sister Amanda had sat down next to Hannah, her big belly making her obviously very uncomfortable in the July heat. "This baby is trying to kill me." She muttered as she adjusted her dress and shifted to find a position of comfort. "I'm sweating bullets under this thing Nothing feels good on my skin, and there is even less that fits or makes me feel like I am not a whale." Hannah giggled at her.

Amanda looked great for being seven months along, and she knew despite her grumblings, she was thrilled to be pregnant after her fertility struggles. Amanda and Kyle had tried to become pregnant for seven years. They had used countless fertility doctors and even tried a Shaman, and although they didn't share all of the details, they quit trying a year ago. The stress of it was mounting on their marriage, and they had accepted the fact that they may never have a child. Not long after this, they took a long two-week cruise and came back with a miracle baby on board. Their mom was in heaven at the thought of being a Grammy to two babies. She had been asking Hannah when she was going to be next. Hannah had been avoiding the topic. Babies came up often along with the question about her wedding date. They had been engaged a year, and Hannah felt like Mark was more of a stranger than when they had first met. She had no intentions of setting a date and definitely didn't see Mark as the father of her children.

The potato salad, homemade baked beans, Mexican street corn on the cob, strawberry fruit salad, and grilled cheeseburgers were delicious. The women in Hannah's family could cook. Her mom had dedicated hours when they were all little to teaching them her beloved recipes in the kitchen. It was her favorite way to bond with them, and all three of the girls, despite their different interests, enjoyed it thoroughly. Amanda, Hannah, and Jenny all cooked in their own households regularly and weren't afraid of a challenge. This menu was mild for the Jones sisters, but a complicated recipe wasn't always needed to make a delicious meal.

Jenny brought out Hannah's cakes, and they all sang Happy Birthday and clapped for little Piper. Hannah took as many pictures as she could of Piper's expression after her first bite of cake, and the mess that exploded after her third one. Jenny served the cake, and Hannah listened and watched as people began eating it. She could hear quiet moans being let out as everyone took bites of their slice of cake. The feeling of satisfaction after serving an item that was well-executed and well-loved never got old. This was what baking was all about.

When she got home that evening, she threw her heels off as soon as she got through the front door and went directly to the shower. She had gotten sticky sitting in the sun, and Hannah had just wanted to get out of the dress that clung to her with heavy sweat spots and be cool and comfortable in her air-conditioned bed. The feeling she got when she slid into her sleek shiny light pink pajamas made her let out a huge sigh. She crawled under the sheets and shivered. Hannah glanced at her phone, five missed calls from Mark and twenty text messages. The man was lost without her. Hannah just wanted him to go away. She put her phone on silent and went to sleep.

***

Monday morning arrived and Hannah was beyond excited to meet with Jeremy. He had been able to set up showings for them at five different locations. She put on her lucky black fedora with her red V-neck and a jean skirt. She felt powerful in this outfit, and she knew she would need a little bit of added confidence to give her luck.

She met with Jeremy outside of building number one. They exchanged pleasantries, and she strode inside. The interior was small, smaller than she had anticipated. It hadn't had any identity in its previous life besides an office for a private investigator, so it would need quite a bit of renovating to make it usable. The location was great, but the lack of size and renovation requirements made the property impractical. She crossed it off her list.

The second property was eye-catching at first glance. It was on a street with a steady traffic flow and had been used as a restaurant. It was, however, within a block of another bakery. Hannah wasn't sure she wanted to start learning the ropes of owning a business and building a customer base with the competition right next door. It was also larger than she needed and at the top end of her budget. It was too risky to take that kind of chance.

Property number three was a good price. She could easily mold it into what she envisioned, but it was in a bad part of town and on the outskirts of an even worse neighborhood. There was no way she would be able to get enough foot traffic into her store here. Hannah could see a business here folding within two years. That would not be worth her time and would crumble what she was trying to build right from the start.

She was feeling stress creeping into her chest and starting to tighten when they saw the fourth property. Again, the location was good, and the building was cute, but she could immediately tell there were problems in the bathroom and the kitchen that would be costly to fix. It would blow her budget, and that was without all the equipment she needed to purchase as well. Number four was a no go.

"This last place is for rent, not purchase, but I don't see anything else within the city limits to add to our list so I figured we should give it a chance," Jeremy said.

Hannah agreed. She wouldn't be able to move forward without having a location decided upon. They walked up the curb. This place was a former bakery that had gone out of business. It had shelves in the window to display your fresh goods. There was an obvious area for a new sign to be hung. The location was clean. The traffic was good. There weren't any red flags that Hannah could see. "I'll take it. Can we contact the owner?"

Two hours later Jeremy was on the phone with Hannah apologizing. "I'm so sorry, but the owner said he had already had a signed contract when I called this morning."

"But why did he let us view it then?"

"Some people continue to show rentals until the background is cleared so they have a backup tenant if they need one. It is odd, but not completely uncommon. I did another look around, but I don't see anything else to show you today. Let me know if you see something new pop on the market, and I'll be asking about up-and-coming properties as well."

Hannah thanked him but hung up the phone feeling discouraged.

Step one of establishing her bakery was becoming a flop. She couldn't even find a location that would work. The longer she waited, the more she would be gambling her savings that should be spent on the bakery itself and not her survival until she finally got the opportunity to sign her name on a dotted line. She needed a new plan.

That evening she expanded her search to include surrounding areas. There was no reason that she needed to stay in the city. She had seen all the most promising properties and neighborhoods today anyway. They just didn't seem quite right. She had to expand her thought process and think creatively. Hannah looked at the suburbs surrounding the city. All of the businesses were new, and most neighborhoods already had a bakery. She combed through the listings looking for that needle in the haystack.

A generated ad appeared on her computer of a beautiful old brick building. It was in a charming downtown, and the inside was an open canvas. The photographs in the ad showed plenty of size and exposed beams. The flooring was aged wood that matched the ceiling beams, and Hannah was immediately in love. She had to have this building. Her intuition told her this was what she had been waiting for. *Where was it located?* She thought as she scanned through the listing. "Woodsburrow. Hmm." She murmured to herself.

A quick Google search showed her that Woodsburrow was located a few hours North. She hadn't ever considered moving out of the city before. She was raised in Greenleaf which was a nearby suburb. She had always loved the excitement the city held and being close to family, so she attended her baking program here and had only ever held jobs in this area, but a few hours wasn't that far away. She could use a chance to start fresh. She would be able to reach an entirely new set of customers and reinvent herself as a confident and successful small business owner instead of the silly clueless blonde baker she seemed to be considered here. The more she thought about it, the more excited she became.

As she continued to research Woodsburrow, she saw that it was a quaint vacation town. There were a few bed and breakfasts, a hotel chain, campgrounds scattered around the lakes and river, a strong local farming presence, a coffee shop, a brewery, and a diner, but no bakery. The population was a fair amount and with the tourists they received during the summer and fall, she would be able to generate enough customers to be moderately successful. She could also develop the intimate relationships were her customers she had been craving. The opportunities and ideas began to run through her brain. She could become a designated tourist destination stop. She might even be able to convince the coffee shop or other local businesses to sell a few of her items so she could reach a broader area. The ideas seemed endless. Not to mention, there wasn't already a bakery in existence that she would be battling for business. Hannah was too excited to wait any longer and called the realtor on the listing.

***

Shannon was waiting at the curb when Hannah arrived. She was a petite woman who wore a white matching pantsuit. She was chipper and Hannah was pleased to see how direct, knowledgeable, and organized she was. "It's so great to meet you! I'm Hannah Jones. I've been looking for a location to open my bakery."

"A bakery? That would be just darling. I am glad you called today. A big corporation has been trying to buy it. They have been putting heavy pressure on the seller, even offering over the listing price. The town and the city council don't want her to sell to them though. I'm not sure how long she will hold out before she caves. It will be just a headache for her if she goes in that direction though."

Hannah did a mental eye roll. She had just gone from one drama fest to another. "I don't want to be paying too far above listing. Is it even worth me seeing it?"

"Oh, I think it is. If we told Merri what your business plan is, it might sway her in your direction." Hannah couldn't imagine why that would make a difference, but Shannon had more experience in this town than she did.

"Let's take a look then. Hopefully, this place is worth going to war with a big business." Hannah said a silent wish to the universe that her search would end today.

Hannah and Shannon walked over to the building. It was even more stunning in person. The brick walls were original but in great condition. Vines swept along the right side of the building. The large windows allowed sunlight to flood the structure. Hannah turned around. They were located in the same direction the sun rose in the morning, and there would be sunrises to enjoy during the best parts of the day when she would be baking and seeing customers.

They walked through the door and Hannah was blown away by the natural beauty of the building. The exposed beams were magnificent. Wooden floors spread throughout the entire room. There was space for tables and chairs by the one window and room to make a bakery case by the other. She could see exactly where she wanted the counter and in the back of the giant open space, was the beginning of a small kitchen. It would have to be tripled in size, but at least the structure and space was there to do just that. She was smitten with this location. She could picture herself here. Even in its blank canvas state, it felt like entering your grandparents' home and being greeted with genuine smiles and warm hugs.

She envisioned the colors she wanted on the walls and the light fixtures that would hang down among the exposed beams. If she could get it for the listing price, even with the additions she would need to do, it would be under her budget. "Oh," said Shannon as she scurried over. "I forgot to mention an important feature. Let's head out the back door." A small door exited from the left of the kitchen into the back alleyway. Hannah couldn't imagine what it was that Shannon wanted to show her back there but appreciated her thoroughness all the same. "Over here," she said as she led Hannah over to a set of metal stairs that ascended the backside of the building. "It comes with an upstairs apartment," Shannon announced with a wide smile.

Hannah's jaw dropped. *The cost would cover her business and a place to live, and it was under budget?* She hurried up the flight of stairs into the apartment. The apartment that sprawled out before her was at least double the size of the shoebox she lived in in the city. The windows and ceilings were large. There were three bedrooms, a huge living room, and an open kitchen with plenty of counter space. The walls had brick accents and beams just like the downstairs had. She walked down the hall that led to the bedrooms. There was a master with a giant walk-in closet and attached bathroom. The bathroom had been recently renovated, and there was fresh shaggy carpet that covered the floor with a new carpet smell. The window was narrow, but floor to ceiling like the living room had been. The other bathroom was also recently renovated, and the other two bedrooms had fresh carpeting just like the first. Hannah whirled around to look at Shannon. "I need you to help me get this place."

Shannon grinned. "That's what I do best."

They sat down at Shannon's office and drew up the strongest offer Hannah was willing to give. She typed up a document about her envisioned bakery and why she wanted to open it Woodsburrow. She told Merri how in love with the place she was and how she would be only renovating to make it function as a bakery, but also would be preserving the character of the building. She talked about adding to the small business owners of the community, and the spreading of joy that bakery would create. She shared how long she had been baking and how she had wanted to open Drury Lane as a little kid. She asked her to help make her dreams come true. "I hope Merri likes doughnuts," Hannah said. "Mine are the best in the state and if she accepts, I'm giving her free doughnuts for life!"

Hannah thanked Shannon, and Shannon promised she would be in touch as soon as she had gotten the news. She drove home praying to the universe to let her have this break. Hannah was in love with that building. The town was incredibly charming. She had driven around the streets to see all the businesses and realized each one was locally owned. They all had the utmost pride in their four walls and laced the streets in such a way that made the little city look like it was straight out of a snow globe. There was a décor and clothing shop called Driftwood that Hannah had gone into and came out with bags of dresses, and outfits and a new lamp that had been upcycled from a bright pink flamingo. It was the coolest thing she had ever seen and had to have it. She was smitten with the building and the town of Woodsburrow. She wanted to root herself down right here in this magical place and never leave.

When she arrived back in the city limits, her mind was still dreaming of the bakery location. She absently took her bags upstairs and tried to keep busy while she waited for word on her location. She unloaded the lamp and set it up by her couch. Nervous energy filled her entire being. She was too antsy to sit still. Waiting was not in her vocabulary. Hannah was an action person and did not do well in situations where she was required to be patient. She decided to busy herself making some cookies to bring down to the shelter. She blared Beyoncé from her phone as she danced along in her kitchen. As the cookies baked, she ate her chicken salad sandwich and debated if she should go out for a new outfit or ice cream when she went to drop off the cookies. She had to keep busy or she was going to lose her mind. She got lost in the process of whisking and tasting like she had hoped she would and made four dozen lemon sugar cookies with a drizzled lemon glaze on top.

After the cookies were cool enough to stack and transport, she grabbed her gym bag along with the cookies and headed to her Bug. She wanted to spend some time in the pool to get out some of her pent-up energy. She wasn't much of a runner nor did she like to lift weights or do organized workout sessions, but in the water, she was a natural. She tried to get there most days of the week. A day with baking and swimming in it was the best kind of day there was.

She was welcomed into the shelter when she arrived, and her cookies were immediately placed out for everyone to share. There were a few familiar faces that had missed her visit the week prior. She gave hugs to everyone she knew, and everyone expected it, even the previous self-described non-huggers. A few single moms had gotten jobs, some had custody hearings in their future, and the news was celebrated no matter how big or little it seemed. There were new people that she hadn't seen before who quickly became like old friends. Hannah had that magic about her that made everyone feel at home. She had always loved being around people and loved how everyone's personalities and lives made them so unique. She supported everyone she knew on their achievements and mourned their losses beside them during their lows. It was one of her strengths. She had a cup of coffee with the residents and, they scarfed up the cookies.

"Hannah, girl you have talent! When are you opening up your place? Stop working for that brainless French man."

"Hopefully soon Shawna."

"I'm rooting for you. Us women are going to rule the world."

They high-fived. Hannah loved Shawna's energy. "When do you start at the new salon?"

"Next week Monday. I have an interview with the low-income housing building on State next week too."

"I'm so proud of you." The women hugged.

Shawna was a wonderful high-spirited cosmologist who had ended up homeless after she left her abusive ex. Thankfully, he had been arrested for armed robbery, and she would be able to move on without looking over her shoulder. Hannah gave Shawna her number. "Give me a call when you have a schedule to fill. I'll come in for an appointment."

Hannah entered the pool at the YMCA two hours later and let out a huge sigh. She hadn't heard anything from Shannon yet, and it felt good to focus on only the water and not the uncertainty of her future. She swam her laps. The consistent sounds of her strokes and the even lengths of the laps made Hannah relax and go to a blank place. She wasn't thinking of anything but the next stroke. By the time she left the pool with her wet hair draped down her back, her faith was restored in trusting the process and her Zen had once again been found. She knew she had been made to do this; the universe would provide.

That night she had heard nothing from Shannon, and she decided she should say something back to Mark before he had an aneurysm. "I'm not ready to talk," was all she sent to him in a text. Immediately her phone dinged with a message back begging her to let him see her so they could figure it out together. She put her phone down and decided it was just time to go to sleep. Despite the light still pouring in from the sun, Hannah pulled her curtains settled into her bed, and went to sleep.

A vibrating hum was coming from the table in the dark. Hannah swatted for it and looked at the clock, it was 7:00 AM. Hannah was not used to sleeping in and usually woke up early even on weekends, but she had been sleeping hard. *What was that noise?* She fumbled for her phone. Shannon's name flashed on the screen. "Hello?" She said in a hoarse voice. Shannon was too polite to ask if she had been sleeping and ignored the hoarseness completely. Hannah didn't care what she sounded like. She felt like she was going to burst with anticipation of what Shannon might say next.

"Hannah! Good morning! I have excellent news. Merri accepted your offer. Welcome to Woodsburrow!"

Hannah screamed into the air. "For real? She chose my offer over all that money she was getting from the corporation?"

"Qdoba was going to cause her such a headache it wasn't worth the risk. Merri was just ready to get that building off her hands. She was absolutely thrilled that you wanted to keep the business as is. She said as soon as we can get the papers together, you will be able to close and move in. I'll be in touch."

"Shannon you are a dream maker! Thank you!"

"It's what I do. You are very welcome." She said in a sing-songy voice.

They disconnected. Hannah was moving to Woodsburrow. "Yes!" She shouted. She was finally going to make her dream a reality.

Luke

Knock, knock, knock. Luke was in a dead sleep when he heard the insistent knock on his front door. "Luke!" Someone called. In a daze, he stumbled into the bathroom, threw water on his face, and pulled on the wrinkled t-shirt and jeans from the floor. His brain was still not functioning as he walked down the hall to answer the door. *Was he expecting someone? What day was it?* He pulled open the door and saw Molly standing there. Her face was plastered with a smirk and her arms were crossed. "Hey, little buddy." She said teasingly. "Did you forget I was coming today?"

"Maybe." He answered. *Shoot.* Molly was coming for the week. He had completely forgotten. He had told her the days that he had off this week, and they were going out to lunch at Gearshift. He looked down at the wrinkled clothes he had grabbed from the heap on the floor. "Do you mind if I shower before we go?"

Molly laughed as her red hair shined in the sun. "I'm in no hurry. I'll just wait for you." She sauntered in and sat down on his couch.

Molly always looked put together no matter the day or situation. Her long red hair always seemed to be perfectly straight and sleek. She always chose outfits that complimented her porcelain skin and wore every classy getup with confidence. If Luke didn't know Molly as well as did, he never would have known that something was wrong in her world. She had been visiting more frequently and despite her husband Travis also being from Woodsburrow, Luke hadn't seen him in two years. Molly pulled out her latest Sandra Brown novel as Luke went to get into the shower.

Fifteen minutes later he emerged with his hair properly styled, cologne applied and a fresh black t-shirt and jeans free of wrinkles. "Ready, Auntie?" Luke and his aunt Molly had always been close. Becky, his mother, was Molly's older sister by a solid twelve years, and he had grown up with Molly and her sons living with them. Molly had gotten pregnant in high school and while she finished her schooling, his parents had helped with her childcare. Luke saw her more like a sister than an aunt.

She smiled at Luke. "Let us go."

They arrived at Gearshift during the lunch rush and found a table on the patio to eat. It was a beautiful summer day, and it was stuffy inside with all the customers that were swarming the bar. "So how did the camping trip go this year?" Molly asked. Luke told her the long version about how they had gotten soaked the first night, and the exact encounters when they had caught each and every fish that had beaten their previous records. Molly listened intently and laughed when he told the story about his dad falling into the lake after a misstep had been taken when throwing a fish back.

"Every year you come back with the best stories."

"How is everything going back in the city?"

"Oh, you know, fine."

He narrowed his eyes and raised his eyebrows. "Fine, huh?"

She shrugged. "Well, Logan graduates next year. He is pretty sure he wants to go to college with his older brother, and Noah is good. He loves being on the hockey team. He has been keeping up his grades and is on track to graduate on time."

Luke was proud his cousin had taken to hockey like he had, despite Travis being a college football star. It took a lot of skill to be able to be drafted into college right out of high school. Noah had always been better than he ever was. Logan wasn't interested in sports, but he had a mind for building and wanted to be an engineer. "Those boys make me proud. But what about you?"

Molly shrugged. "I think a big change is in my future. I hardly see Travis, and when I do there is either silence or arguing, nothing in between. We have been telling the boys that he has been taking more travel commitments for work, but he is staying somewhere else when he is in town. We are trying counseling, but..." She trailed off and shrugged. Luke didn't know what to say.

His uncle had constantly seemed to have other priorities, and Molly had always been independent. She had been visiting more often this summer, and he had known something wasn't right. "You know Mom and Dad are always willing to have you around when you need it. You are welcome in my spare bedroom too. I am not an expert host, but it's yours if you need it."

Molly smiled. "Thanks, bud. What about your love life? Did things go anywhere with that Amber?"

Luke shook his head. 'I just didn't have that connection. She was pretty, but there wasn't any depth to our conversations." She sighed.

"I know you think I'm too picky, but maybe I'm just too different to have a woman well-suited to me out there. I'm fine on my own. I get to wear blue, sleep until noon if I want to, and do the things that make me happy when I'm off duty."

"I know you are happy alone, and if you are content then I'm happy for you," Molly said with a tone in her voice that Luke recognized as her not being totally convinced.

They ordered the house burger and fries, enjoyed the music playing from the speakers, and felt the breeze that gave the air just enough movement to ease the staleness. "What are you doing the rest of the week?" Luke asked between bites of burger.

"I'm going to spend a few hours with Mom. I promised I'd take her shopping and do a few things around the house for her. Becky and I are going to the farmers' market on Saturday. I'll probably meet up with a few friends from high school on Saturday or Friday night, and then I'm back to work on Monday. I am planning to be up here pretty frequently this summer and fall. Logan will be here next time. He is at an engineering summer camp this week."

"That kid is a miniature freaking Einstein," Luke said with a chuckle. "Who would have thought there was an engineering camp?"

"I know, and he was so excited about it. I'm just happy to get him involved with other kids. He did pick up a summer job, so he hasn't been as cooped up as he was last year."

Luke nodded. "Does he like it?"

Molly shrugged. "It's hard to tell with him, but I think he has a crush on one of the girls that work there with him, which seems to be enough to keep him showing up. However, he needs to learn that responsibility is fine with me."

"Does he need a talk about women and their inner workings?"

Molly laughed. "From you and your infinite relationship knowledge?"

"Well maybe not for that, but we could at least have the safe sex talk and how to think with your head."

"You could try. Goodness knows he doesn't talk with Travis. They couldn't be more different people, and the boys have always had a stronger relationship with me than him. Despite my hardest efforts, they just never built that bond."

"Well, you tell him I want to take him fishing just us when you come next."

"Are you coming to the market this weekend?"

"I haven't decided yet. I don't have to work, and I do enjoy the BBQ brisket from the Fat Hippo."

"Well let me know if you do, and we can have lunch." She said as they paid for meals. "I'd love to spend some more time together before I go back home." Molly pulled her nephew in for a hug, and Luke squeezed her tight.

"I'd like that, too. Love you, Molls."

"Love you too, bud."

Chapter 4

Hannah pulled out her tattered business plan notebook. She had been planning this bakery for years, and the notebook had been well-used. It held good ideas and terrible ones. There were lists and random scribbles. The cover was blanketed in different drawings that had inspired her. Pages had been ripped out and very few were left untouched. She reviewed her last entries and then got to work sketching out the store in the final open pages of the notebook. She had a real location and her vision just clicked into place. She wanted it to have bright colors on the wall and accent pieces to play off the huge windows and a large amount of natural light. She wanted to find some eclectic tables and chairs, nothing sterile or matching. The lighting would become hanging pendants that harmonized with the rustic look of the rest of the property. She needed to buy ovens and a much larger sink.

She wanted a huge display space installed around the front that continued into the storefront window. The name she had come up with when she was eight and had received that Easy Bake oven from her mom, Drury Lane. It was a representation of where she had started and how much she had grown. A whimsical place that all could enter searching for a reprieve from whatever their day might bring next or whatever burden they might be shouldering, and they could find something to spark joy within themselves and make everything a little bit sweeter.

By the end of the day, Shannon and Hannah had a rough closing date down. She would be in her Drury Lane location by the beginning of August. It would be closer to September before she would be selling items out of the shop, and she needed to make some money in the meantime, so she didn't squander all the savings that she had.

The first stop was the coffee shop. She hoped to make an appointment with the owner of Woods and Brew. She planned to woo them with her fresh doughnuts, apple turnovers, blueberry muffins, and cheese danishes. No one could resist any of those items. The world's best diet would be ruined in seconds of smelling any of those goodies filling the air.

The next thing she needed to consider was a type of outdoor market. That was something she could start attending now. A few clicks on the city's tourism page showed that they in fact did have a farmers' market on Saturday mornings, and it was a huge deal. She had been to the one in the city with her mom and thought it was a pretty decent setup. Its turnout had been respectable. This one put that to shame. It had food trucks rows of vendors, and live music every weekend. It was hosted at the fairgrounds so the room they had to continue expanding was always present. Hannah would need to develop a sign this week and invest in a table and tent, not to mention trays for serving and paper bags for customers, but she wanted in. She was jumping into this journey full speed ahead. She emailed the coordinator for the event and asked if she could participate as a vendor for the remainder of the summer.

Hannah couldn't believe her good fortune with all the pieces that were clicking into place. She would open Drury Lane, and Pierre could kiss her butt. The sound of knocking came from across the kitchen. Hannah groaned. She knew it would be Mark. With that uniform cadence and stuffy silence. He just couldn't wait any longer for her to take space. *A conversation had to be had some time. It might as well be now.* Hannah thought. She strode over to the door and opened it to let him in. He entered carrying a huge, oversized bouquet of red roses.

After two years together, he still didn't remember that she thought roses were cliche and her favorite flowers were pink peonies. "Hannah my angel, let's not fight anymore." He said in a baby voice handing her the roses. "I already talked to Pierre. He is willing to give you your job back. I know that's what's been bothering you and making you so distracted."

"You what? I don't want that job back, and I'm not distracted. You had no right to do that." Hannah responded angrily.

"Hannah if you need to take some time off to relax, we could take that vacation to Hawaii we talked about last winter. We could take two weeks in the sun, and then come back and you can get back to business as normal, refreshed and ready to go."

"Who vacations to Hawaii in July? I don't have a lack of sun. Listen, Mark, this isn't going to work." Hannah had been waiting years for Mark to get a backbone and have a unique thought and this is what had come from that? She set the bouquet down on the table. "I'm moving." She announced.

"Moving apartments? Hannah we are supposed to be moving in together when your lease is up in September. It doesn't make sense to move now. Though, understandably, you might feel cramped here." He said looking around with a tone of disdain in his voice that Hannah had never heard before.

"We aren't going to be doing that. Mark, I bought a building. It's in another town. I'm opening up my own bakery."

"What? You bought a building in another town without consulting with me?"

Hannah felt like she was seeing only red as her anger grew. "Why do you always make it sound like I need your permission?"

"You didn't even think that I might have some concerns with moving? We are supposed to be getting married and starting our own family. I am not interested in leaving my job." He moved to take her hands. Speaking softer now he added. "I don't know how you think you will be able to handle all that. Being a business owner requires a special grit and intelligence that not everyone has."

She dropped her hands from his and stepped backward. *Did he just insinuate she was dumb?* "Mark, we have been engaged for a year, and we've done no wedding planning. We have no date set, and I have no desire to do any of that. We aren't getting married, not now, not soon, not ever."

She slipped off her engagement ring which had a classic oversized single square stone in the center. She handed it to Mark. "It's over."

"You are being rash. Hannah this is just a fight. People fight. You always think that things are like they are in the movies." He just continued sinking his own ship with every word he spoke.

She shook her head. "It isn't a fight. We aren't compatible. We have been together too long, and you know nothing about me. I hate red roses, and this engagement ring was not created for me. I have wanted to own my own bakery since I was eight, and the minute I started pursuing it, you tried to backpedal me and tell me I couldn't do it successfully. I am not in love with you and frankly, our personalities don't jive. It's over." Hannah said annunciating the words so he wouldn't miss what she was saying.

She flung the bouquet into his arms leading him towards the door. "Get out of my apartment and leave me alone." She could tell that Mark was stunned. He stood firmly planted in place. He hadn't considered the possibility that they wouldn't be together. "Please leave." She repeated. He looked up at her with sad puppy dog eyes and left.

Hannah couldn't muster up any sympathy for Mark. He hadn't been listening to her. He had pushed her to go back to her old job, and more than that, had disrespected her by setting up exactly that without her input at all. Instead of being excited or asking questions, he just told her she was being silly. "Silly woman." She muttered to herself. To be fair, she thought in retrospect, she hadn't considered him at all when she bought her building. He hadn't crossed her mind once during that transaction. Hannah had known she just wanted their relationship to end. She should have said that to him earlier.

Hannah shook her head. Mark was a person that she wouldn't miss. She couldn't believe she had made the mistake of staying with him as long as she had. She had seen how happy her engagement had seen her mom, and she had loved seeing her proud. The only regret she had about the breakup was the disappointment and shock her mom would feel. She was thankful she hadn't made any wedding plans, or it could have been much worse. This wasn't love, and her sisters could enjoy their lives with their husbands who liked to live monotonously, but Hannah needed jazz, excitement, and adventure. She wanted a partner whose spirit matched her own. She loved to be big and bold and inviting to all and wanted someone whose energy would match hers. Hannah liked to be spontaneous and generous. She wanted someone who could keep up and maybe even keep her on her toes as well. She needed someone who remembered she would only eat toast warm, that she thought mac n' cheese was best with gouda, knew she didn't like olives, and remembered that her favorite holiday was Valentine's Day. She didn't know if that kind of man existed, but she certainly wasn't going to settle in the meantime for someone who didn't fit that description whatsoever.

Her mother's favorite dessert was tiramisu. It had been one of the first desserts Hannah had mastered after cookies and cakes because of this. She assembled the chocolatey deliciousness as Frank Sinatra sang his soul through her phone speaker. She sang into her whisk and twirled around the room. She dunked her leftover lady fingers into her expresso and nibbled as she prayed this would be enough to soften the blow for her mom. She would need to be bearing gifts when she told her mother her baby was moving and was no longer engaged or working at the Golden Goose.

Her parent's house in the suburbs was only 45 minutes farther from her new bakery than it was to her current apartment, but she knew her mother wouldn't see it that way. All she would hear was that her baby was moving away, and no longer working at the top bakery in town, and that didn't even cover the breakup with Mark, whom she adored. She called her mom and asked if she could join them for dinner.

"Of course, sweetheart! We are having pork chops with mashed potatoes and corn on the cob for dinner at six. Will Mark be joining as well?"

"No, it will just be me. I'll bring the dessert."

At 6:00 PM sharp, Hannah pulled into her parent's driveway. She had the tiramisu and was wearing her light blue dress with darker blue polka dots. It was free-flowing and fun. Hannah prayed it would give her the courage she needed tonight. She hoped she could deliver the news without her mom missing out on the exciting part of why all this was happening. She didn't need her mom's approval, but she did want her support. She loved her, and the thought of making her sad broke her heart.

Hi, Mom!" She called as she entered the house.

"In here, Sweetie!" Her mom called back from the kitchen. Her mom and dad were in the kitchen together finishing dinner. Her dad gave her a kiss on the cheek as he manned the porkchops. Her mom was mashing the potatoes.

"We are almost done, Hannah." Her dad said. "Why don't you set the table?"

"Ooh, is that tiramisu?" Her mom asked. "You can put that right out on the table when you set it." She added.

Hannah grabbed the dishes and set the table while her dad talked about his insurance business. He had had the same clients for years and knew almost everything about their lives. Her mom listened and shared her results from the BINGO game the night before and how it was rumored that Ethel had been cheating. An argument had broken out among the regulars and a few had been tossed out. It was all very scandalous. Hannah had always suspected the drama was part of the reason she kept going back every week. She giggled as she told the story with arms flailing and eyes wide with shock on her face.

They sat down to dinner while her dad's pork chops were still sizzling on their plates. They were all quiet as they filled their faces with the hot pork chops, buttery corn on the cob, and creamy mashed potatoes. "Mom, I actually wanted to talk to you about something," Hannah said between bites.

"Did you finally set a date for the wedding? That would be great because dates are already filling up for next summer. I think one of your cousins is getting married in July, of course, it is his second wedding." She trailed off.

"No, Mom. There isn't going to be a wedding. I broke it off with Mark this morning." *Ugh*, that wasn't the lead-in that Hannah had wanted to do. Starting with the calling off the engagement had set her up for failure in delivering the rest of the news.

Her mom dropped her fork and stared up at her wide-eyed. "What?" She said in barely a whisper.

Her dad wordlessly placed his hand on hers.

"What happened?" She asked.

"Mark isn't the one. We aren't interested in the same things. Our personalities just don't match. We've never had that same zing that you and Dad have. We aren't missing pieces from the same puzzle. I'm a puzzle piece, and he's a video game cartridge."

Her dad broke out in laughter.

"Well, honey you know every day doesn't come easy for us. Successful marriages and relationships are about consistency and hard work."

Hannah nodded. "I know that. You and Dad always have put your marriage first. But for goodness sake we have been engaged a year and the only thing planning a wedding with him makes me feel is fear and entrapment. I don't love him."

"I'm proud of you." Her dad said as he gave her a grin.

Hannah was shocked at this response and by the looks of it, so was her mother.

"You could not make a bigger mistake than staying with someone who isn't a match with yourself just for everyone else or a big party. It's important your partner is somebody you can see yourself maneuvering ups and downs with and if you don't feel a spark now, you won't feel it in five years."

"Thank you, Dad. There is more news." Her mom's face was as white as a sheet, and she looked like she was going to have a stroke. "I bought a business building, actually it comes with a huge apartment as well. I'm opening my own bakery."

"How will you have time for that while working at the Golden Goose?" Her mom asked.

"I quit the Goose. I have been planning to leave there for a long time. I've been careful to continue working until I was ready to take this step. I've been saving money. I created a safety net, and my time at the Golden Goose always had an expiration date. Thank God for that too because that job was horrible." Hannah said blurting it all out.

"I thought you loved the Golden Goose! That job is highly desired by bakers all over the state."

Hannah shook her head. "I've never liked it there. At first, I learned a few new techniques, but the customers are ungrateful and snooty. The bakery items are unoriginal. I've never been allowed to use any of my own creativity or recipes. The competition between co-workers reminds me of a bake-off challenge on the Cooking Chanel every day, and Pierre is an ass who hired me to try to get into my pants and spent every day he didn't get that luxury reminding me of my constant incompetence."

Her dad started laughing again, this time uncontrollably.

"How come you never mentioned this?" Her mom asked with a bewildered look on her face.

Hannah shrugged. "None of that mattered. I was making good money at a quicker rate than I would have somewhere else. I needed to keep going until I met my goal. Now that I have, I'll be opening up Drury Lane this summer in Woodsburrow." Her mom suddenly fainted. "Mom!" Hannah called as she rushed for her mom.

She awoke seconds later while Hannah and her father fanned her. "You ok, Mom?"

"Yeah, I think so. Gosh, I am so dizzy. Maybe my blood sugar is low."

"Great! Let's break out the dessert then! I'll help you up, Mom." Hannah gave her mother a hand and carefully made sure she was sitting safely in her chair. Hannah served everyone a large slice of tiramisu and a tight silence spread over the room.

After ten minutes had passed her mom looked up at her. "Are you sure you want to do this, Hannah?" Hannah nodded.

"Positive. I have put hours of thought into this. I want to bake to spread joy and happiness. I haven't done that in any of the years I've been at the Golden Goose. When I told Mark, he told me I couldn't do it, and I had made a huge mistake. He went and begged Pierre to allow me to return to my old job behind my back. I might be a happy-go-lucky person, but I am not a fool."

Her dad looked up suddenly and made eye contact with her. "I didn't raise any fools. I raised girls who turned into women who could rule the world. Hannah, you use your gifts wisely, and you know yourself well. I'm excited to see where this next chapter will lead you. You have always had excellent intuition when it comes to all things baking. I've never known you to accept defeat either. This challenge will be a good thing for you."

Hannah's smile widened, and she looked over at her mother. She sat pale faced with uncertainty written in her expression. "It's only 45 minutes farther from the house. Plus, I have three bedrooms now. You can help me decorate a guest room for you so it's cozy when you come to visit. I'm not trying to run away. I tried to find a place in town first, but there aren't many options for businesses to buy that will work and even fewer to rent. I'm certain Mark isn't the one, and I know I can do this."

"Hannah there is something about you that no one I know has. You have always been so bright and vivacious. I have always been worried someone would break your spirit. I never wanted to lose that piece of you. It's not something that I possess myself. I have always wanted to protect you from that. I know when you make up your mind, you are all in. There is no changing it. Let me know what I can do to help. I won't let you fail. I'm sorry I didn't recognize that Mark didn't make you happy. He seemed so attentive and loving."

"He was attentive, Mom. He also had no personality of his own. It was always just so dull, and when he did finally open his mouth, I found that I didn't like what he had to say. He didn't bring anything to the relationship that I didn't have all by myself."

Her mom smiled at her dad. "We did raise them well, didn't we?" They kissed.

Hannah smiled. She loved her parents like crazy. They had given her the best childhood. They supported every one of their daughters and encouraged them to be all that they could be, and they showed them exactly what love looked like.

Her parents completed each other like a pair of socks. They each had their own set of skills and complimented one other so beautifully. Her dad made the coffee for her mom every day and brought her a fresh cup to her favorite chair while she read her devotions to start the day. They bowled together every Wednesday night and had for years and years. They kissed every morning before they went to work and every night before bed. When they went out to events, they always held hands.

Her mom was a librarian at the Quincy High School and ran an afterschool program on Friday evening called Game Night. She was late every Friday due to this, so her father for years had made homemade pizza and bought her favorite wine on Fridays, sometimes with chocolate and flowers. Her dad loved to fish on the weekends, and her mother would lay out his favorite fishing outfit complete with his bucket hat, so he didn't have to search for it. She always packed him his favorite sandwich, pastrami, salami, ham, and provolone with spicy peppers and mayo.

They did those extra things that made the other's days better and showed their love. Everyone had always commented on how sweet they looked together. Even though they had been married for years, they looked at each other like newlyweds. Hannah wanted time spent with her partner to be like that. She wasn't willing to compromise for anything less.

When Hannah shut the door to her apartment, she threw off her shoes and dropped her purse on the floor. She sighed loudly and felt a huge amount of relief. She had already felt freer after breaking it off with Mark. He had been nothing but a weight over her shoulders. She wondered how much holding back from life she had been doing with him by her side. She was eager to face the world without him holding her down. She felt stronger from her parent's support, and she was ready to take on this new adventure at full speed.

Hannah received an email from the farmers' market confirming her spot as a vendor for this Saturday. There were only a few days to the market, and she had plenty to do. She would need to spend the entire next day baking. It had been a while since she had made some of the recipes she was planning, and she wanted to make her mark in Woodsburrow in a big way. This was her first step in her journey to becoming a business owner, and there was no way she would allow herself to fail. By the end of the day, she had narrowed down her menu. Hannah had decided on sourdough bread loaves, her famous doughnuts, cinnamon rolls, chocolate eclairs, and blueberry cheesecake. She wanted to show her customers that she had range. After the first market, she could decide what had been the most popular items and adjust from there. She was thrilled to feel the heat of a challenge again.

Luke

News spread around town like wildfire that Merri's building had been bought. Last week Luke had been worried that people would be picketing her building against a possible Qdoba purchase, and he had responded to calls about an egging of her house and toilet papering her trees. Merri was a kind lady, and Luke felt awful for the poor treatment she had been getting. Her husband had died from a long battle with cancer, and the little shop had been his. She had no reason to keep it, so it only made sense to list it for sale. There hadn't been an overwhelming market for a downtown space, so it had been sitting for much longer than she had anticipated, and she needed to get it off her hands. She hadn't even had an agreement with Qdoba when the gossip had trickled all over town, and people began to behave like fools. An unknown person from the city had purchased the building from out of nowhere and people excitedly spoke about what might be planned for it.

"I heard it was a photographer who is using the space for a studio." A woman whispered at the diner's front counter. "I don't think so." Someone else replied. "I thought it was a clothing designer." "You are both wrong." Someone else interrupted. "Lindsey from the farmers' market just said a baker asked to join the venues this weekend. That has to be the new owner." Luke shook his head and grinned over his coffee.

The sleuthing in this town never ended. Gossip could be a curse or a blessing depending on what was going on. He finished his cup of coffee and breakfast sandwich with hash browns and left a generous tip with Dawn. She had worked here for years and had become a staple in the diner. Everyone knew that a large tip was the easiest way to ensure you would get the best of anything that was on the menu that day and in the future. Dawn always took care of her favorite customers. "Thanks Dawn!" He waved as he left the diner. She waved back at him from behind the counter. He couldn't help but be curious as to who the baker was that was coming on Saturday to the market. He already had an invitation from Molly, and he would love some doughnuts that weren't wrapped in plastic. *Maybe he would go, it wouldn't hurt to show his support.*

"Hey, Brett." He said as he approached him on the sidewalk.

Brett fidgeted with his glasses. "Hi there Luke."

"How's business at the coffee shop?"

He shifted uncomfortably. "A bit slow, but I'm sure it will pick up."

Luke nodded "A lull happens to everyone. I hope the rest of your summer picks up. Fall is around the corner. I hope you have enough pumpkin spice ordered for the leaf peepers!" Brett smiled weakly in return. He gave Brett a pat on his back. "See you later." He called back to him as he walked away.

Brett had never been much of a talker, but he was extra quiet today. He must have had a huge drop in customers to be as stressed as he appeared. Luke hoped the business would pick up for him. Woodsburrow had been lucky to almost have all of their shops on Main Street consistently filled. It drove tourists to their town instead of visiting some of the other towns in the area that were similar. Brett's coffee shop was just the right addition to Woodsburrow. The reality was over half of small businesses didn't last five years. Brett would undoubtedly come across challenges that would make or break his. Luke made a mental note to do what he could to help support him. This town had always felt like they were a part of Luke's family, and as an adult, he felt that pride and love of his town deeply. Family pulled together through hard times. It was the beauty of living in a place like Woodsburrow. He ascended the steps into the police station to begin his shift.

Chapter 5

Hannah

Hannah called her friend Abby to invite her to join in on some evening shopping together. When Abby heard she would be leaving, she was heartbroken, but Hannah knew she would be fine though. Her relationship with Tim had been heating up, and things were getting serious. Abby had gradually been spending more and more time with Tim and had been less available to do things together. She beamed with total happiness when she spoke about him. Hannah knew an engagement was not far around the corner. She would be too busy to worry about Hannah's home address.

"Abby let's get a pretzel. Do you want to share a large one?"

"I never turn down a pretzel, you know that." Abby smiled. "Aren't you freaked out about moving to the middle of nowhere?"

Hannah shook her head. "Woodsburrow is absolutely adorable. It's really not that far, and I could use the change of scenery. It will force me to adapt fully to the locals."

"You are so brave. I've always admired that about you. I wish I had some of that courage."

"You are braver than you think," Hannah said as she squeezed her tight. "Now do you want the bigger half or the smaller one?"

They bopped in and out of stores and left with a folding table that fit in Hannah's car, a tent, a stand that she could set her items out on for display, and a bag to store her money. She had bought supplies to create a sign announcing her store and her prices. Abby and Hannah hugged goodnight, and Hannah headed home.

Hannah woke with the sun to try to complete her bakery list for the day. She had less than twenty-four hours before she had to load up her Bug and publicly declare that she was an entrepreneur. Her counters quickly became overloaded with ingredients, bowls, cooling goods, rising dough, and softening butter. She had never baked more than one item at a time in the tiny kitchen, and it certainly felt every inch its size. She couldn't believe when night fell that she had gotten everything done. Everything had taken much longer than it would have taken with the correct tools and space. Her kitchen was trashed, but her mission was accomplished.

***

When Saturday arrived, Hannah was so excited she could barely contain herself. She loved meeting new people and just knew her baking would be a hit. She couldn't wait to watch the happiness on her customer's faces while they ate her doughnuts or inhaled the smells through the brown paper sacks. She loaded the car with freshly baked everything and sat in the smells of her favorite foods while she played "Fearless" on repeat. This was her day.

Hannah struggled immediately on arrival though, while she tried to get her tent up. It wasn't as if she was an outdoorsman, and she certainly hadn't had time to attempt to assemble it before today. A rush of doubt flowed through her. *What if she had pushed this whole thing? Who did she think she was that she could open her own business? Maybe Mark had been right after all. She couldn't even organize her closet.* That atrocity had only been worsening year after year. She had squeezed out every bit of time in the last couple of days and had stayed up late and woken up early to even be here today. *It was ridiculous of her to think she could pull this off.* She thought. "Do you need some help?" She heard from over her shoulder. She stood up and turned around.

A very handsome and tall man with vibrant blue eyes and sun-kissed skin that made her appear that he spent most of his time outside, was standing there smiling.

"Are you laughing at me?" Hannah asked with feistiness in her voice.

The man shook his head. "No not laughing, just wondering how many times you are going to attempt to erect that tent before you ask someone for help."

She immediately broke out laughing. "I'm not good with tents, okay? I'm even worse at asking for help."

"That is evident. Let me help you. No asking involved." The man took the poles and inserted them. He had the tent up within two minutes.

Hannah was impressed. "That would have taken me all day. Any chance you want to help me grab the rest of the stuff out of my car since you are already assisting? This is my first time at this market, and now I've spent nearly all my set-up time on that evil thing."

The man shrugged. "Sure. I am here way too early anyway. I heard from Diane that there might be fresh doughnuts today, and I had the day off."

"You are in luck. I definitely have fresh doughnuts, among other things." She flashed him a smile.

They worked together to get the tables set up, and the baked goods displayed perfectly on her stands. The Drury Lane sign was attached to the tent with a whimsical picture of a giant floppy baker's hat and a few oversized muffins. Drury Lane was written in her best calligraphy in an arc over the top of the image. Hannah was so happy with how it had turned out and couldn't wait to see it in full scale hanging above her new building. She propped the sign-up that contained her prices and was ready with ten minutes to spare.

"Can I thank you with some doughnuts?"

He shook his head yes. "Absolutely."

She filled a paper bag and handed it to him. "Thank you by the way. I don't think I caught your name."

"It's Luke." He put his hand out to shake hers. She grabbed his hand and felt the warmth from his touch spread from her fingers into the rest of her body. She held back a shiver. "And you must be the muffin man that lives on Drury Lane. There was a twist to that poem the whole time. I knew it. The muffin man is a woman. Welcome to Woodsburrow."

Hannah laughed. "It's nice to meet you, Luke. The secret muffin man's name is Hannah."

"I'll see you around Hannah." He smiled back and opened his paper sack to give it a big inhale. "Ugh. That's my favorite smell." He had two of the doughnuts devoured before he even walked away.

She smiled big until her cheeks began to hurt and felt her heart swell. *Perfect. Let the joy-giving begin.* She thought to herself.

The rest of the morning was a blur. Everyone was incredibly friendly. Her lines were long and contained both tourists and locals. It was obvious from the conversations she was having, and the way people were dressed, who was who. Some of the locals who came through the line introduced themselves. A few of the farmers with booths had snuck curiously over between customers to say hello. By 11:00 AM, she had sold out all of her products and still had an hour left to go. That didn't help her narrow down her offerings for the next market, and she would need to bake more of almost everything, an excellent problem to have.

Luke

Luke was stunned when he saw the gorgeous blonde struggling through setting up her tent. She looked like she had walked right out of a magazine ad. He hadn't expected the new baker to be a woman. Despite being frustrated, she held herself with confidence and was full of energy. Luke had tried to think of something to say to extend their time together but ended up feeling like his words were tangled up with each other.

The slight touch that had occurred when they bumped into each other had made him feel like he needed more.

And then, she had handed him the biggest bag of doughnuts that were soft and pillowy, and perfect. He had eaten the entire bag before he even made it to the food trucks. He could have polished off another bag easily. "Hannah." He said to himself quietly as he walked away. *Wow.* He thought. He wasn't sure what Hannah had planned as she worked to open her new business, but he had to see her again. The new owner of Drury Lane had him hooked.

Luke bought his coveted BBQ brisket from the Fat Hippo and grabbed extra napkins. He went to sit with Molly and his mom by the live music and listened as they talked excitedly about their new matching jewelry, they had picked up from one of the vendors, and some of the people Molly had seen that week. "Did you see the baker, Luke?" Molly asked with a twinkle in her eye.

"I did, Molly." He said mockingly back.

"Did you talk to her?"

"I welcomed her to the town and helped her set up her tent."

"That was nice of you, son. I am so proud of how hospitable you are." His mom said with a smile.

"Thanks, Mom" He answered. His mom might be sincerely complimenting his people skills and oblivious to the fact that there may be chemistry between them, but he couldn't hide anything from Molly. She was onto him. She had the eerie ability to know himself better than he did sometimes. *Had she been watching them?* He could bet that this conversation would come up again. He sighed and devoured his brisket like he hadn't been fed in a week.

Chapter 6

Hannah

After fumbling through and taking the tent down, Hannah loaded up her car and headed into town. She wanted to set up a meeting with the owner of the coffee shop before she left Woodsburrow. She would have a few more weeks of markets before she closed on her bakery and wanted to get moving on a partnership.

Woods and Brew was staffed that afternoon by a high schooler who said that Brett, the owner, wasn't there that day, and she didn't expect him to be there the rest of the weekend. She took down a message with Hannah's name and number to hang up in his office.

Hannah had nothing else to do after that but drive around and check out the area. A few people had mentioned a lake that was just north of town. It had been a hot morning and if there was a lake around here, Hannah was going to swim in it. She was pleasantly surprised by how close to the city limits it was.

Lost Lake was in full dazzling mode this afternoon. The sun shone at its highest peak and sparkles danced across the water. There were various people off in the distance fishing in boats. Otherwise, it appeared that most everyone else had retreated for their lunch. Hannah stripped off her shirt and shorts and jumped into the water. It was instantly refreshing and made her body temperature drop to a level that was not so miserable. She felt pure bliss in the water, and she began to swim laps like she did at the pool. There was something different about the sensations you experienced in a lake.

It wasn't something she had observed before, but she found it exciting and peaceful. The smells of the lake were more inviting than the chlorine that filled the air in an indoor pool. She could see herself swimming here the rest of the summer. *Today was a perfect day.*

When she finally decided she had had enough, she emerged from the water and walked back to her car dripping like an overloaded sponge. Her shoes squished as she walked, leaving water puddles where her feet had stepped. She opened her car door and began to look for something to wear. She shuffled through the random items that had been in her backseat for what felt like an eternity.

Hannah eventually found an old blanket that was fraying and a t-shirt that she bought at a Taylor Swift concert when she was 18. She dried herself off with the blanket and pulled the old t-shirt over her head. She was able to get her shorts back on without the feeling that they had become hardened plaster on her body. Satisfied, she wrapped her long hair up in her pink t-shirt and headed back into town.

After a full morning's work at the farmers' market and a long swim, Hannah was starving. She didn't want to make the drive back to her apartment without stopping for lunch, so she pulled into the Cozy Kitchen. The lunch crowd had left for the day, and there seemed to be a lull.

She was seated by a woman named Dawn; whom Hannah struck up a conversation with immediately. Dawn had lived in Woodsburrow all of her life and knew everyone. According to Dawn, the word on the street about the bakery opening was overall positive. Everyone was relieved that Qdoba wouldn't be moving in, but they felt cautiously optimistic about Hannah's intentions.

Dawn talked about her two kids who attended the local school and how her shifts this summer had been much busier than in years past. She seemed to spend most of her waking hours picking up shifts at the restaurant. The words poured out of Dawn, and Hannah had heard her entire life story before she wrote down her order on her notepad.

"You know what?" Dawn said as she scribbled down Hannah's order of a chicken bacon ranch wrap with chilled cucumber soup and tapped her pen on the edge of her writing pad thoughtfully. "Now that you mention all that, I think we may need someone to make pies. We used to have someone who brought some periodically, and we have talked about bringing it back. I could give Charlene your number if you are interested."

"Really? That would be so great! I'd love to supply your pies!"

Dawn smiled at her. "I think you are going to be the perfect addition around here." She went into the back to place her order with the cook.

Hannah sat at the window table with a seemingly permanent smile on her face. She let the sunshine flow over her and warm her soul. She felt like she was finally getting a chance to prove that she could make something big. Hannah had always been considered the frivolous one by her sisters. Her friends never knew she had ambitions and a high work drive. They all thought everything came easy to her because she was beautiful. No one knew how much time she put into making plans and channeling her creativity behind the scenes. In reality, her beauty made it more difficult to be taken seriously instead of giving her a leg up. She wanted to earn her way through life. Here she was making something tangible with her bare hands. She finally had a place to showcase her skills and creativity.

Woodsburrow, although an unexpected place for her to land, felt so homey and welcoming. Everyone at the farmers' market had offered to visit her shop soon and help with whatever needed. Hannah thrived with meeting new people and had been soaking that up today, and she couldn't wait to continue to meet all the faces that would become as familiar as her sisters someday soon.

Luke

Luke started his second shift in his stretch exhausted. He was distracted. He had spent his free time coming up with reasons to hang out with Steele without him thinking he was hovering over him. They had worked on a project in his parent's garage that had been put off for months and would have been just fine being put off for longer. They had gone golfing, and of course, played hockey. It was worth it though. Steele seemed to be adjusting to the space that Stacey left in his life, and he felt more confident his friend would reach out when he needed help or wanted company, instead of wallowing internally. The last night's shift had been long and combined with all the extracurriculars he had been involved with outside of work, his fuse was short.

By the time the shift ended, he was too wired, and too geared up to go to sleep. He had arrested a high school classmate for drinking and driving, for a third time. He had spent hours with a sexual assault victim, leading to the arrest of her attacker, and he had a call for a man naked running around the gas station talking to himself about the devil's shoes. Thankfully, he was able to catch the man bring him to the Emergency Room and have the medical staff check him over.

His shifts seemed to always be this way during the summer. That was the part of his career he disliked. He enjoyed the sense of keeping his community safe and being there for people in their time of need. It was hard to see someone like Jesse, who had been one of his classmates growing up, having a hard time consistently with life. His heart ached for them, and it caused him to focus on the gifts in his own life and be grateful for them. He was lucky that he had such a great bunch of friends and family around him. He always knew it was important to live for the moment. Luke pulled out of the parking lot and drove to somewhere he could decompress and think. He parked at the trailhead for the Lost Lake trails and followed the first path he saw.

The sunlight was flooding the trail in front of him from the sky and his brain throbbed with how tired he was. He pushed his body to move quickly along the trails listening to the simplicity of nature. The birds seemed to echo one another, and their calls rang out through the sky. He watched the squirrels jumping from tree to tree. He heard the sound of something large rustling and looked to his left. A flock of fifteen turkey scampered off in the opposite direction and flew into the trees. Luke stopped and sat down on a large rock that sat on the edge of the trail. He inhaled and closed his eyes.

Being in nature gave him the feeling he was connected to something bigger. Your piece of the puzzle was important, just as the oak trees to the squirrels. He knew that despite wanting the best for everyone, that people were on their own journeys. They made their own choices, good or bad, and walked their own path. He hoped that the interactions that he had with people made a positive influence in their lives. Sometimes, it felt like he saw the same people repetitively without seeing them make change of any kind in a better direction for themselves.

He sat there silently until he slowly let go the stress of the day, of the things he couldn't change. He reflected on his own life and the choices he made on a daily basis. *Did he think he was really being the best version of himself he could be? Was he trying new things and forcing himself to think outside the box?* He always regarded himself as an adventurer and a risk taker, but when was the last time he made a decision that was outside of his day-to-day routine? Maybe it was time that he kept his eyes open for a new something that might force him to have some growth of his own.

Chapter 7

Hannah

When the farmers' market came around the next week, Hannah felt more prepared than she had the week before. She had decided to bring her sourdough bread loaves again. She doubled her total amount of doughnuts and cinnamon rolls. Instead of eclairs, she baked ten raspberry kringles, and blueberry cream cheese danishes. She wanted to add in more savory elements as well, so she had made large sourdough pretzels and everything flavored sourdough bagels, along with jalapeno cheddar ones. She was certain that she could set up her booth by herself this time without needing help like some damsel in distress.

She had been looking forward to the drive to Woodsburrow. After being back in the city all week, she had begun to feel claustrophobic. The air wasn't as fresh, and the spaces weren't as open. She had swum at the pool daily, and every time she sunk herself into the water, she pictured her swim last week at Lost Lake. She wanted to spend her time exploring the different shops and meeting the people who worked on Main Street not cooped up in her studio. Now that she knew where life was taking her, she was ready to get started on that new life. These markets were the closest thing she had to that right now. They were a small taste of life to come. The weather was comfortable enough to have the windows down, and she felt pure happiness as the trees became thicker outside and the traffic thinned.

She arrived at the market and was able to assemble her tent within fifteen minutes. She was so proud that she hadn't needed the help of some random knight in shining armor this time. She set her items out on display, so the savory and sourdough items were on one half and the sweet covered the other. She had fifteen minutes to spare and wandered over to the other tents nearby to say hello to some familiar faces and introduce herself to some new ones.

Zack and Emily, a couple from a nearby town, remembered Hannah from last week. "Hi Hannah! It's great to see you again! How was your week?"

"So good! I've been spending most of my time planning for the opening of Drury Lane. I'm so excited for the move. How about you guys?"

"It was great! We were really productive and were able to spend lots of time outside since the weather was so nice! We are going camping this next week, so you won't see us next weekend. Do you camp?"

"I have never gone, but I love a good adventure! Maybe someday!"

Zack and Emily sold signature furniture and décor pieces. They repurposed and made anything from end tables to light fixtures and everything in between. They called themselves Whiskey Leather. They had a completely different selection from last week and as always, let any interested customers know that they could custom make anything they might need.

As Hannah browsed their items and complimented them on their attention to detail, she got an idea. "Have you guys ever done renovation type work?"

"I used to work in construction prior to doing this, so I've done just about everything." Zack said.

"What are the chances I could hire you to renovate my bakery? The space I bought downtown has just gorgeous wood and brickwork. I am wanting to in cooperate some whimsy into its style while maintaining that rustic look."

"What kind of renovations are you needing?" Zack asked.

"Well, I need a display case. I wanted to change out some lights into pendants. I also need to change the location of the wall in the kitchen to give it more space and then I'll need to install some seating space in there, appliances and a commercial sink set up."

"If you are willing to hire us plus another guy, we would take it on. I used to work with a man named Gary who is excellent with electric along with basic renovating. I could handle the rest of the job."

"That would be amazing!" Hannah replied.

"When do you need us to start?"

"I close on August 3rd. Maybe we could do a walk through that day, and you can give me an estimate on time and cost?"

Zack stuck his hand out, and they shook on it. "Absolutely, we'd love a new challenge."

Hannah described the table and chair set up she was looking for to Emily. "I think I'll need six tables and varying chairs. Seating at each should be two to six depending on the size of the table, with a combination of large and small."

"I could find you those tables and chairs easy and repurpose them whatever color you would like. Zack could build a built-in bench or counter that we could add some colorful stools to as well. I also have some really cool ideas for the light fixtures you are describing."

Hannah hugged Emily. "You guys are so amazing! I can't wait to get started! In the meantime, that standing lamp and nightstand belong in my new apartment. How much?"

Hannah hustled back to her stand with three minutes to spare. People had started to drift in and amble around. She was excited to have the feeling like she belonged there. Talking to people about her bakery items over warm sunshine and a cool breeze was a dream come true. She had never considered a farmers' market for sales before, and now she knew she wouldn't want to miss a weekend. The music last week had been folk, and this week it was jazz. The music seemed to set the mood for everyone at the market, and the atmosphere was serene.

"Hannah!" Someone called from her left. She turned to look and saw her knight from last week. She had forgotten how tall he was, or maybe she had been too distracted last week with the excitement, and how broad his body looked.

The man could have been a professional sports' player. Hannah thought. He had medium brown hair that he kept long enough to style. He had not a hair out of place and his facial hair was trimmed meticulously. He was wearing a faded blue t-shirt and his blue eyes shone vividly. Hannah's involuntary smile was just a touch brighter than her usual high-wattage greeting.

"Luke! Hey!"

"I see you got the tent up this week." He observed with a smirk.

"Hilarious." She replied. "See if you get any doughnuts from me with that attitude."

"I don't believe you have a right to refuse service to anyone and must treat everyone with equal rights here." Luke teased.

She smiled. "Oh? Are you going to tattle on me to the authorities?" She teased.

"I am the authorities." He replied. "Well, one of." He said with a shrug. "I am on the local police force."

"Fitting that you love doughnuts then." She giggled.

"Hey now! No stereotyping. Listen, what if I buy some of those jalapeno cheddar bagels with the doughnuts? Will you reconsider that judgment? I am a man who likes some spice with his sweet." He grinned.

Hannah couldn't believe how she was being pulled into this man. Hannah Jones did not chase men. She also did not have an interest in dating a pretty boy who might be charming but could be a super dull by-the-book rule follower. She needed to restrain herself and get a grip. If she was going to even consider dating again, she needed to make sure the man she was interested in had a true sense of adventure. "Let me throw in a cinnamon roll, and you have yourself a deal. You are limiting your breakfast horizons if you stick with the typical cop doughnut." She smiled as she handed over his two bags.

He pulled out his wallet and handed her a twenty-dollar bill. "It was a pleasure doing business with you Miss Hannah. I'll be seeing you next week. It's going to be a problem when you finally move to town." He said patting his hand to his skintight abs.

"I'm sure pretty boy." She razzed back. "See you later Luke."

"Later, muffin man." He said with a sexy smirk and walked off towards the food trucks.

***

Hannah was left with a dozen doughnuts and six giant cinnamon rolls when the market closed. She hadn't heard from Woods and Brew, so she stopped to drop off some samples. She told the new face working the counter that she had been trying to get a hold of Brett and had thus far been unable to reach him. "I'm leaving these free samples for staff to enjoy. Feel free to let him know I stopped in. Oh, and one more thing." She reached into her pocket to pull out a business card she had printed that week. "If you can put it on his desk somewhere he will find it. It would be much appreciated."

While she was there, she ordered a chai latte and looked around at the coffee shop. It seemed rather quiet for a Saturday, and the mood of the staff seemed solemn. *What was the deal with this Brett guy?* She thanked the barista for her drink and was soon out the door.

She only had a few more weeks left in the city, but she couldn't believe how much it pained her to leave for the drive back home. She was able to put her top down in her Bug to enjoy the wind in her hair, but she was starting to feel like she had one foot in two entirely different worlds. Even with the tourist industry, Woodsburrow was at a slower pace. It was more inviting. Everyone was friendly, and although there were not as many bustling shops and restaurants, there was plenty to do. Hannah had exchanged numbers with some hairstylists, a teacher, and a few other artisans who she couldn't wait to start building relationships with.

Woodsburrow was like any small town on television. Friday nights were spent at the football games, Sunday mornings at church. There were festivals frequently throughout the year and each one was done up bigger than the last. It would be autumn soon, and the Harvest Festival was the talk of the town. She had already been asked to do some baking for it, and her ideas were churning about what she would bring.

People had been approaching her to ask about her doing birthday cakes or baby showers. She had promised that once she closed on the bakery, she would immediately start doing cakes regardless of the state of the construction job. She could see the relationships she had craved coming naturally, but the distance was putting on the breaks. It was driving her crazy. She could have easily been a lifer here, and no one would have been the wiser. She loved how the town was nestled in the trees, and it seemed to sit in the middle of a forgotten island, with its magic tucked safely inside.

***

The city might have held magic for Hannah at one time, but now it felt foreign. There were noises everywhere, and

Hannah craved the depth of conversations she had had with people in Woodsburrow. In the city, people were always thinking or even doing something else while they spoke to you. It was not as satisfying to have conversations that didn't have genuine connections attached. The distracted air made you feel like an annoyance or an afterthought. It took away from the enchantment of the experience. She spent much more time than usual alone as she waited, and her mind swam with ideas for the next market and upcoming holidays. Her creativity pulse was bounding and all of this stuff that surrounded her here, was merely a distraction. Because she was craving interactions with people, she was excited when she received a message from Shawna. She had sent her the name of the salon she had been hired at, and Hannah immediately booked a time for a cut and a manicure at Elemental Beauty.

Hannah arrived at Elemental Beauty and was immediately impressed. The building had a very chic look. Everyone was dressed professionally and the music inside was all instrumental and nature sounds. Shawna had her own "room" for appointments Each stylist had their own "room" to give their clients a comforting and immersive experience. Shawna spoke excitedly about how much she loved working here. The clients tended to tip well, and because of the individual corners, the gossip was easier to stay away from. Her new apartment was perfect, and she was thrilled to be back on her feet again. She had even started dating a new man who had his life together.

"I'm telling you, Hannah, if I can catch myself a good man then you can too."

"I can't say I've been trying to catch one. After breaking it off with Mark, I just have a bad taste in my mouth."

Shawna shook her head. "It's that feeling you get after wearing a pair of shoes that just don't fit how they should. Your feet are sore, and you want to walk barefoot for a while, but eventually, you will have to wear shoes again. This time though, you will choose a style that feels better on." Shawna said.

"I have never thought of it that way, but that was a dang good analogy," Hannah added. "I just want to choose better this time. I want someone who can keep up. It's not even that there is a lack of men to pick from, it's that they all are missing something that I can't live without."

"I met Troy in the egg aisle at the grocery store. Just let it happen naturally. The best things in life play out organically."

"So true," Hannah said. "It's best to let fate lead the way." She relaxed as she enjoyed the massage on her scalp. When she said goodbye, she hugged Shawna extra tight.

"Girl, I've got a good man, an excellent job, and a place that's all mine. It's your turn to crush it!"

***

Hannah had finally arranged a time to meet with each one of her sisters to break the news. That had been just about impossible to schedule between her farmer's markets on Saturdays and busy lives. She had begged her mother not to say anything until she had time to tell them in person. She had agreed but had already almost forgotten twice.

Both of her sisters were shocked by the news when they heard she wanted to own her place.

"I thought you liked your freedom to leave at night, to work your scheduled hours and go home." They had said.

"Freedom is not the word I would use to describe my past employment. I felt like a caged bird. This will be great for me! You guys can come stay whenever you would like. I have a very roomy place and will be upgrading from my studio to three bedrooms!" "

What does Mark have to say about moving? I thought he enjoyed his work." They had followed with.

"Mark and I ended our engagement. He didn't feel like he could support my dreams of becoming a bakery owner."

Hannah didn't go into further details. She had surprised herself with how little sadness she had felt to have Mark gone from her life, and although her sisters had liked Mark, they were too engulfed in their own lives to spend much time missing him. Despite being her first serious relationship in quite a while, and almost planning a wedding with him, she hadn't once felt like eating a carton of Ben and Jerry's, and she didn't feel like laying on her bed and crying. She also wasn't rushing into the arms of other men to fill a gaping hole inside of her. She just felt at peace with her choice. Hannah wished him well in life, that life just didn't include her. She knew in time her family could get to the same place.

Saying goodbye to her friends at the homeless shelter proved to be the hardest. They seemed to be the only area in the city that had let go of the busyness of life and clung to genuine conversation and human connection. Hannah cried when she left. It felt like she was leaving friends. After that goodbye, she was ready to move on and go forward.

Luke

Luke just couldn't stay away from Hannah Jones. After meeting her at the farmers' market the week before, he had convinced himself he would be able to keep their interactions casual. It would be no different than running into any other acquaintance on the street. *Who had he been kidding?* Despite having a week filled with busy shifts, and extra time with Steele, his thoughts kept drifting to the gorgeous witty blonde and the way her eyes shone when she smiled. He usually wasn't a weekly attendee of the farmers' market. The only time he went was to see his favorite artist Nikki Stevens, or the first and last ones of the year. Those were always a big deal and everyone in the community attended like it was a county fair. Now it seemed, he was a regular. Even though he had worked the night before, he set his alarm for three hours after his shift had ended so he could shower and be there to buy some of Hannah's doughnuts.

Hannah's line was long and constant. He stalled and chatted with friendly faces as he glanced at her stand every ten minutes to see if the line was getting shorter. When he had finally approached her, his mind had gone blank. He had ordered jalapeño cheddar bagels. He hated spicy things. *What on earth was he thinking?* The fact of it was, that he wasn't. He would have to pawn those off on Steele. Hopefully, he wouldn't pry into the details of how and why he had them.

The cinnamon rolls however had been delicious. Luke was sure he hadn't ever had any besides the ones that came in the Pillsbury cans. They got hard and crispy fast, and they always tasted like fake cinnamon if there was such a thing. Those had never been his favorite. These, however, were a whole other beast entirely. They were fluffy and soft. The filling made a caramel-like texture that was chewy and sweet in between the decadent swirls. It was the best thing he had eaten in quite a while. *Damn, he would marry her for her baking alone.*

But she wasn't just an incredible baker. She had spunk, and she was gorgeous. She had enough courage to start a brand-new business in a new city, and she was confident doing it. There was something so enticing about Hannah. Luke knew he had no experience with women like her. He could imagine her in his daily life, and he had never had that thought before.

Here he was all worked up and waiting for the next time he could run into Hannah, but she would be moving here full-time in the coming weeks. *Then what? Would he tell her how he felt? Would he be able to avoid her or lean into his temptation?* His feelings were running him into a hole he didn't know how to get out of. Maybe it was time he started reconsidering his self-described chronic single life, or maybe he needed to get out and relax more. He was straddling a line that separated the life he had chosen from the one he was running from. Hannah Jones was making him reconsider everything he had previously thought was just not changeable.

That evening Luke felt like a caged rat. He had spent the day trying to distract himself from the constant fantasies that kept creeping into his brain. Those full lips and curves were driving him mad. He was liable to lose his mind tonight. He decided it was best if he got out of the house. After a couple of drinks, maybe a few dances, he wouldn't be swimming so deeply in his thoughts. There would be a Yankee game on as well that he could catch. He grabbed his keys and shut the door behind him.

He walked into Gearshift and picked a seat at the bar where he could see the Yankees on the big screen. Kyle and Matt sat nearby. "Hey, cowboy! How's life been on the night shift?"

He grinned. "Always busy. Summer just seems to constantly have something going on with all the out-of-towners, and the kids out of school."

They nodded. "Good for business, but it's always harder to get out fishing with all those boats on Lost."

"I hear you," Luke replied. "The best fishing, I usually get is some of the remote lakes, and they are not always an option."

"It's almost not even worth attempting unless no one else is out there, but even when the fish aren't biting, a cold beer on the lake is the best way to end a work week."

"Here, here," Matt added as the three raised their beers in agreement.

"Did you hear about that woman opening up the bakery at Merri's place?' Matt asked.

Luke nodded. "I've tried her stuff. Everything I have tried is better than anything I've had before."

"I heard she is a hottie," Kyle said. Luke smiled but said nothing and instead took a swig of his beer. "Well? If you tried her stuff, then you had to have gotten a look at her." He added.

"She is easy on the eyes no doubt," Luke answered. There was no way Kyle would let the conversation continue in any other direction without him commenting on her looks.

The thought of other men thinking about Hannah in that way, made him feel possessive. He usually could care less about those things. In fact, having a woman that others were interested in made him feel like he had won a prize. But Hannah Jones wasn't a prize. She was so much more than that.

"Everyone is talking about her catering for birthday parties, baby showers, and weddings already. Apparently, people are really excited. Lexi mentioned she was thrilled to have someone doing her daughter's birthday cake other than Barb." Matt added.

"Barb has been doing the same three different cakes on repeat since she was forty," Luke said chuckling. They turned their attention back to the game. Luke was relieved to have the topic changed. He hadn't come to the bar to talk about Hannah.

A woman with brown hair looked over across the bar and grinned at Luke. "Looks like you are getting more bites here than on the water," Matt said with an elbow nudge. "That brunette at three o'clock will be walking over here any minute." As he said those words, the woman sauntered over.

"Hey." She said to Luke as she gave him a big smile.
"Hi." He answered.
"Want to buy me a drink?" She asked forcefully.

He smiled tightly. This woman was confident and pretty, but she had read the signs wrong and came on way too strong. He didn't want to be rude, but he did not plan on having this interaction last longer than it needed to. "Only if you are a Yankee fan." He said playfully back.

"I could be a Yankee's fan." She winked.

He waved over to the bartender. "One Redd's for the lady." He quickly uncapped the drink and slid it over "Here you go, Miss?" He asked expectantly.

"Aimee." She said as she flashed a huge smile.

"Nice to meet you, Aimee. Luke." He said as she shook his hand weakly. *Ugh.* Limp handshakes were a pet peeve of his.

He turned his attention back to the game. Aimee tried to engage Luke in conversation, but Luke had little interest. He smiled and nodded a few times. Eventually, Kyle gave him a look that said, "What are you doing man?"

He returned the look with a "Not for me man, you go ahead." From there, Kyle steered the conversation with Aimee towards himself, and before long, Aimee was sitting inches from Kyle completely engrossed in conversation with Luke long forgotten.

Another woman with blonde hair made eye contact repeatedly with him across the room, but never got up and moved to make herself closer to him. When the game was over, he was ready to leave. He had found himself unconsciously comparing both of these women to Hannah. Her confidence and the way she could glide around a room was indescribable. She knew how to talk to truly engage people and never would have pretended to watch a game she had no interest in. Nor would she have avoided having a conversation with someone she felt attracted to. Hannah was definitely the type of woman who wouldn't think twice about making her feelings known. Avoiding thoughts of Hannah wasn't working, and he needed to get some sleep. The three hours he was running on was making his brain function a bit rough. He told Kyle and Matt good night and gave Kyle an attaboy high five. He wanted to get home. Apparently, there was no escaping Hannah today.

Chapter 8

Closing day came fast. Hannah had gotten lucky and all her stars had aligned. By the beginning of August, she was signing the closing documents. She entered the building with a giant bag of doughnuts to give to Merri, as promised. When she left the title company, she felt the complete silence around her like the calm before a storm. She had a big mountain to climb to convert the space into what she needed it to be. Her parents were helping her move out of her apartment this weekend. Today, she was limited in her actions. It was a day to explore.

As she went to unlock the door to her bakery, she saw a small 3x5 notecard had been slipped into the door pane. "We don't want women without class running the stores in this town." was scribbled on the front. She knew there were people in Woodsburrow who had a hard time adjusting to outsiders. It was a tight-knit community and people protected it fiercely. Although the words stung, she didn't let it bother her. She would just have to turn up the charm factor a bit more and meet more faces. She knew in time; everyone would come to respect her and her business.

She unlocked the door to her new bakery and stepped inside. She walked through the space in awestruck excitement as ideas churned in her head. Zack and Emily would be arriving in an hour, and she was bursting with ideas she wanted to bounce off them. Hannah finished her walk-through and walked around the back of the building. She wondered if there was a way to get up to her apartment from the inside as well as the outside of the building. She opened a closet door and the store bathroom. She walked further down the hall around the corner. To her luck, there was a door on the left that led up to the apartment. It entered the apartment behind a door in the open kitchen space that she had previously thought was a pantry. She loved that she could walk down into her bakery without even needing to leave the building. This would come in handy in the wintertime when the outside metal stairs would be prone to getting slippery.

She walked through the secret door into her apartment. Hannah had brought some basic cleaning supplies and cleaned up countertops in the kitchen. The cupboards were navy blue with butcher block countertops. There was a hanging rack for her pots above the stove. The large ceiling-to-floor window shone natural light from the far brick wall into the kitchen. The top floor of this building was taller than the others downtown, and she could see beyond the trees into the horizon through it. There were trees as far as the eye could see, and Lost Lake appeared as a puddle within the forests that went on forever. She could see a glimpse of the river that flowed from the lake down to the neighboring towns.

Hannah couldn't believe that owning an apartment and a business downtown could have provided her with that slice of heaven to enjoy. She paused to adore the view before walking down into her master bedroom. She had never in her life had a bedroom this large. The fresh shaggy carpet was brand new, and the closet was giant. Hannah laid down on the new soft carpeting and ran her fingers through it. She inhaled the smell. She could almost sleep here. She studied the closet from the floor. She could hang her entire wardrobe in a way that she could see everything at the flip of a light switch. That would be a huge change from the way they were shoved like sardines in her dresser and piles on the floor, not to mention the clothes that pop out of her closet like snakes in a can every time the door is opened.

The bathroom was accessible through the closet. The giant soaking tub was the first thing she was going to try out after her things were moved in. The vanity was navy like the kitchen but had a bright white quartz top instead. The lights framed the mirror in a way that would make her feel like she was a movie star as she applied her makeup in the morning. She clapped her hands together. "Welcome home, Hannah." She said to herself.

She glanced at her watch, Emily and Zack would be there any minute. Hannah hurried down the stairs to the front of the building. She watched as they got out of their cars and walked over to greet her. "Congratulations Hannah! This building is gorgeous! What character! Thank you for inviting us to do this. It's going to be such great buzz for our business." Emily said as she hugged her. "Oh, I brought a little housewarming gift."

A handcrafted recipe stand engraved with the words Drury Lane bold and beautiful on the front, and the images of the floppy baker's hat and muffins were on the back. Hannah's eyes welled up with tears. "You guys! This is amazing, and so thoughtful. I knew you were the perfect one for this job! Come on in! I want your thoughts and ideas. Zack don't be afraid to be harsh and specific on prices and things that may not be possible or if you have a better way to get it done. I am very much a creative, so I don't always have a good feel for that stuff."

Zack nodded. "Got it."

They walked through slowly as they all bounced ideas off each other. Zack had suggested she do some carving into the sides of her bakery case to add to the whimsical atmosphere. Emily loved the idea of a bold color for the front door. Emily and Zack immediately knew they had previously made repurposed lights that were almost exactly what could be installed throughout this building and with speaking only partial sentences, had agreed on what they would look like. Emily had already collected most of the tables and chairs and showed the pictures to Hannah in their raw states. "Ugh! The ornate detailing is amazing." "I figured once we know wall colorings we could go ahead and paint them."

"Did you decide if you wanted bench seating or a counter?" Zack asked.

"Bench seating. I don't want any dry spaces in here. I want it to be warm and inviting like you are sitting around the table at your grandmother's house around the holidays."

"I love that," Emily replied.

Zack nodded. "Understood. I think here is the place then." He said moving his hands to simulate the location. "We could build a table that could slide right in between the benches. I could engrave it with a Nordic style engravement."

Hannah nodded wildly. "I love all of these ideas. Let's go back to the kitchen, and you can tell me the damage there."

They went through the list of appliances that would be coming and pulled out the tape measure to mark off the sizes. Thank goodness Hannah had had the foresight to scribble them down. The kitchen would be exactly how she wanted and have a set of swinging doors within a partial wall that led out into the front of the bakery. She couldn't wait to start baking in an area that had only the sky as the limit. She had goosebumps as she saw herself singing in her kitchen while the sun rose in the big windows out front.

"So, how long before we can have this done?" Hannah asked after shuffling through Zack's scribbles and price estimates. The building cost plus renovations plus her housing was still falling way under her budget. *Why hadn't she thought about searching outside the city limits initially? She could have quit months ago.* She thought. Hannah was anxious to finally have her shop up and running.

"I think we should have it completely finished by Labor Day weekend." He estimated.

Hannah reached out to shake his hand. "You are hired." Hannah walked her friends out and said goodbye. Zack would start two days from now after he had gotten his tools and materials in alignment. Hannah had told him to come in at any point when he was ready to begin working. His friend would come in to help with the plumbing and electrical wiring when he had time in his schedule. The appliances, pots, pans, sheets, and items that would fill the kitchen would be arriving in two weeks. Things were quickly becoming a reality that made her extremely proud. She hoped to announce a Labor Day weekend opening in the near future.

After Emily and Zack left, Hannah unloaded the objects that she had managed to stuff into her tiny car. She had her lamp and table she had gotten from Whiskey Leather stacked on top. She had her suitcases that were full of her clothing and bags of shoes. She hauled them up the stairs and into her bedroom one by one. The last items that had fit were bowls from her kitchen, some blankets, standing framed pictures of her and her family, and a watercolor supply.

She carefully brought up her easel and a brand-new set of paints and set them up on the side of the large window in her room. She had found her watercolor supplies in the back of her closet collecting dust. She had loved painting all her life and had stopped almost the moment she had started at the Golden Goose. It seemed ironic now that she had never noticed how much her happiness working there had cost her, but she was determined to live her entire life exactly the way she wanted from here on out.

With the painting easel always set up and in front of this gorgeous view, she would be able to paint every dang time she felt like it. Satisfied with the location, she went back down to grab the final boxes. A man in uniform walked up to the back of her car.

"Well, look who is becoming a local." He said as he approached her.

Hannah smiled. "And a proud one, officer." She added.

Luke reached into her car and pulled two boxes out. "Lead the way, Ma'am. It's only proper that I welcome you with some moving assistance." He said standing at attention beside her. She grabbed the bags she had shoved under the passenger seat and led him upstairs. "You have no furniture." He observantly stated as he placed the boxes down.

"My parents are helping me move the bigger things this weekend, and I only live in a studio in the city, so I don't have much furniture to begin with."

"There is a furniture store about thirty miles away that will deliver. They have some good quality stuff, too. It's the one my family always uses. I can send you a link to their website if you would like."

Hannah smiled. "Yes, please. I'd like that."

Hannah liked that Luke seemed to have different sides to him. Today, his teasing personality seemed to be replaced by this helpful neighbor persona, and oh my God did he look sexy in that uniform. "Here," he said putting out his hand. "Give me your phone."

Hannah took her phone out of her pocket and placed it in his hands. Their fingers touched and a heightened awareness zapped through her. "I sent a message to myself." He said handing the phone back to her and taking his out.

Hannah heard her phone vibrate and looked down at the link and an unknown number. "Thanks, Luke."

"Let me know when you are moving in this weekend. I can swing over and help move stuff. Steele would probably help, too. Don't try to yank a bed up these stairs with your dad. I'll end up escorting you both to St. Joe's."

Hannah laughed. "If you are sure it isn't messing up your weekend."

"Nope. I play in a few softball leagues during the summer, but those are mostly done for the year." He said nonchalantly.

"We are loading up my parent's truck and trailer Friday night, and on Saturday we will be unloading after the farmers' market. It will be officially my first night here."

"We are ready to have you. Everyone is talking about you baking for their events and how good your doughnuts are. It's the buzz of the town."

Hannah's face beamed. "Really?"

Luke nodded. "Oh yes. We are lucky to have someone besides the ladies who cater the church funerals baking for us. We have been pretty limited in our options around here. It'll be nice to have something new. Well, I should let you go." He said putting his hands in his pocket and leaning back on his heels.

"Any requests for the market this weekend?"

"Actually, yes. Those cinnamon rolls changed me. They made me a believer. I might have a new favorite."

"Really? I have converted you from a doughnut-loving cop?"

"Yes. I'm a whole new man now. Who knows what could happen next? I might even join a bluegrass band and tour the southern states."

Hannah laughed until her side hurt. Luke grinned wide clearly satisfied with himself.

"You should consider some cookies too. I've always been partial to my grandma's chocolate chip. I think everyone loves themselves a cup of hot coffee and some cookies. I swear I could eat one every day."

"Speaking of coffee, I've tried to get in touch with the man who runs the coffee shop, and I haven't had any luck. Do you know why he wouldn't want to talk to me, or how I could get a hold of him?"

"Really? That's strange. Brett usually isn't like that. He isn't the most outspoken man I know, but he doesn't usually ignore business opportunities either. I'll ask around. See you this weekend Hannah."

"See you then," Hannah said as he walked down the steps and entered the street.

She looked at the empty room around her with the boxes and bags that they had just brought up and stacked to the side. This place was hers now. She felt stunned by the thought. She had no other plans for the day, but she didn't want to leave yet. Hannah grabbed the boxes meant for the kitchen and started unpacking. *Who said she had to go back to that stuffy apartment and sit?* Hannah was tired of sitting in that little place dreaming she was here. She would do everything she could to extend her time here today, starting with organizing the silverware. She unpacked every bag and box she could in the apartment and then headed to the grocery store.

While at the store, she bought ingredients that she would need for baking for the market this weekend. She had mounds of butter, eggs, and flour. Next, she grabbed ingredients for cooking for herself for the next few days after she moved in. She kept it simple, but delicious. Late summer and fall always had the best produce in season, and her favorite recipes both to bake and to cook, were ones she could access the best ingredients for now. The grocery store had a section of locally grown items from the Grant farm.

She bought tomatoes, zucchini, corn, green bell peppers, and a watermelon. She made a mental note to try to pick some up at the last few markets if she could find time to steal away. She took all the items up to her apartment and put them away. The sight of things in her refrigerator gave her delight. Hannah was beginning to mix pieces herself with the property, and it made her heart happy. The person she was just months ago with a dead weight fiancé and pleasure-sucking job, was no longer. The caged bird was no longer locked in a cage and could spread her wings and sing without sadness.

There wasn't much more she could do that day, so she drove to Lost Lake Beach. It was late in the day, and the air had started to develop a chill with the sinking sun. She didn't bring her suit again, but this time she had a bath towel. She stripped and jumped into the water. Hannah could not believe how different and freeing it was swimming in the lake compared to the pool. It was just how she had been imagining it. You didn't have chlorine stinging your eyes or your lungs, and the cool air brushed your skin heightening your senses. The sun sunk lower in the sky and set off a fan of peach-colored lights that reflected a mirror image into the lake. She swam until her arms ached and forced herself to leave the lake. She still was the only person on the beach, so she wrapped herself in a towel and sat down. The lake was as smooth as glass, and the stars had begun to pepper the sky. The crickets and frogs were increasing in volume, and the silence around their chorus was deafening.

Hannah hadn't spent much time outside of the city, and when she had traveled with friends or family, she traveled to other large cities, like Boston or Minneapolis. This type of silence she hadn't heard before and the pleasure of being outside, wasn't something she had experienced to this degree. She had always loved the details that plagued your senses with you started to look around you. Her idea of getting into nature was a backyard BBQ, golfing with her dad, or a walk in the park. She hadn't camped or hiked or done anything daring and adventurous in the outdoors. It felt like such a shame because jumping in and being spontaneous was what Hannah did best. She had always loved the energy of the fresh air, the vibrant colors, and the melody of the birds and crickets. She looked around her at the abundance of places to explore.

She realized that this experience wasn't just about opening her own bakery or having her own power in the creativity process. It wasn't just about the connections she would make and lasting relationships she would build. It wasn't just about the happiness that came from delivering wedding cakes, or special sugar cookies with royal icing. She wanted to continue to grow and challenge herself in other aspects of her life as well. Hannah wanted to try hiking or camping. She wanted to learn to fish and start painting regularly again. Who knew? Maybe she would start doing some dating as well.

Based on how far Hannah had gotten into her relationship with Mark before she even recognized that they weren't right for each other, Hannah felt like she might not even know what her type was. *How could she have been completely blind for that long?* She wanted to date someone daring and challenging, someone who wasn't passive and liked to venture into new places and encounter challenging goals. She wanted someone who wouldn't change their commitment to her while she evolved as a human and tried new things. She wanted to be treated as an equal and seen as a human with depth and interests.

If she woke up one day and wanted to go all in as a ukulele player? She wanted someone who would join the band with her. She didn't want a partner who would spend the next 48 hours reminding her she didn't know how to play guitar, and the degree of unlikeness it was that she would be successful at that venture. She wanted someone who was audacious and unique and wasn't afraid of failure. She knew that she liked to tell stories and be around large groups of people, and she wanted an extrovert at her side that felt the same. She didn't want to have to exert extra effort to include them or make sure they were having fun too.

She wanted a man who would also be comfortable sharing stories and meeting new people with or without her there. Maybe someone like that didn't exist, and that was fine with her. She would rather be alone and date when she needed some company than spend her life with someone who tried to make her fit in a little box.

Relaxed and hopeful about the future, she watched the moon begin to glisten in the sky, and the stars start to gleam one by one above her. Their glow intensified and the lake looked like it had been decorated in jewels. She sat there, no longer thinking, but connecting to the cold sand beneath her and pure air around her, just being. Eventually, her body insisted that she get to warmth, and she got up and went to her Bug. She pulled on her oversized faded blue sweatshirt and black sweatpants as she blared the heat in her car. On the ride home, she quietly played Justin Bieber while she drove away from the place that she never knew that she needed or how desperately she had needed it.

***

It felt like it was much later than nine when she climbed the stairs to her studio. The day had been exhausting, and she was starving. She dropped her purse on the ground and tossed a box of Thai takeout into the microwave. As it reheated, she ran a hot bath. She threw in some lavender bath bombs and lit her favorite pumpkin pie candle. She grabbed her box of takeout and a glass of Merlot and got into the bath. She shivered as she stepped into the bath water. Hannah had run the water as hot as she could, but her body was still chilled from her time at the beach. She shivered from the shock of the difference in her internal temperature and the one that surrounded it.

She sat in silence in her dark bathroom and contemplated the next two days. She needed to pack, and she needed to bake. Those were the only things on her priority list. She considered how long it would take her to pack what she had left. *Really, it shouldn't take that much time.* She thought. She only had one full room and a bathroom. She wanted to be sleeping in her spacious apartment with the high ceilings and bright night skies, not this dingy studio that had one window that barely constituted as such and frequently flooded with smells from the nearby pub. She had worked hard not to identify what those odors were from. Tomorrow, she would see if she could pack up everything and load her parents' truck and trailer in the evening. Her parents didn't drive the truck to work anyway, so it was possible she could be sleeping in Woodsburrow tomorrow night. Even if she were laying directly on the carpeting, it sounded worth it.

After she settled into bed, she furniture shopped at the store that Luke had suggested. She found a beautiful wooden table and chairs set that would fit perfectly under the large dining room light and navy-blue couches with a matching chair covered in beautiful velvet upholstery. They had a bohemian-style rug with navy accents that would fit perfectly between them. Because she lived in a studio that came with a Murphy bed, she didn't have a true bed either. Hannah would be moving into a three-bedroom apartment owning zero beds. The furniture store was running a sale on queen beds and frames, and she bought three of various combinations. She thought that would be enough to start with.

While checking out, she saw that all of the items were in stock, and the day the store delivered to Woodsburrow was Friday. *How could she have gotten that lucky?* Hannah placed the order and turned off her phone. It took her much longer to fall asleep due to her excitement, but eventually, her tired brain complied.

Luke

When Luke walked downtown after lunch at the Cozy Kitchen, he had planned to walk past Hannah's future bakery, but he didn't plan to see her there. He saw her tiny car packed to its roof haphazardly with bags, boxes, and loose items. He chuckled at the sight. Then his mind became scrambled at the vision of her long hair flowing behind her as she grabbed handfuls of odd objects and carried them up her stairs. She looked determined and in her own world. There was a touch of happiness in her step, and he thought he had heard her humming. *Should he say hello, or did that make him look like a stalker?* If he didn't stop to help, it looked like she would be emptying this overloaded teacup by herself. *Would she be upset with him offering to help without being asked a second time? Why was he overthinking this?*

He saw Hannah walk over to her car again, and he made his move. He said hello. Before he knew it, he was helping her unload and behaving like Woodsburrow's own welcoming party. He didn't know what had come over him, but eventually, he relaxed and offered his help to move furniture when she returned in a few days. He had volunteered to meet her parents before he had even made any kind of move. It was crazy. He was behaving crazy. He hadn't even met any woman's family that he was dating before and here he was jumping in with a woman he was infatuated with, but he was curious at what type of people had created such a woman. It felt natural to offer his help regardless of the details, not to mention, it was the only way to ensure he would see her again, and soon.

She had seemed thrilled to hear that everyone was excited to have her open Drury Lane. *She had to be nervous.* It was risky to be a business owner, and despite her sunny disposition, he knew that everyone worried sometimes. The question she had asked him about Brett was odd. *Why would he avoid Hannah?* If business had been slow, he should have been open to any opportunity that might increase his business, at least the conversation of that opportunity. Hannah wasn't exactly aggressive although she was persistent. Not to mention he could imagine why a man like Brett wouldn't enjoy a conversation with a beautiful woman. Everything about it just set off warning bells in his head, but he didn't know why.

He made sure to stop in at the coffee shop the next day he had off. Brett always opened the shop on Friday mornings. He walked in with a cheerful demeanor. "Morning Brett!"

Brett looked up from the glass that he had been cleaning with more vigor and precision than was absolutely necessary. "Hi, Luke."

"How have things been going? Has business picked up?"

"It has started to. I was worried for a while, but I am back to where I normally am this part of the year."

"That's great to hear," Luke answered. He didn't think he should directly ask him about ignoring Hannah. Hannah wouldn't appreciate him fighting her battles like that. He would have to be more subtle. "Did you happen to meet your new neighbor yet?" He asked hitching his thumb towards Drury Lane across the street.

Brett looked away and shook his head. "No. I haven't run into her yet."

"You should say hello. It's kind of a natural friendship, isn't it? The coffee shop and the bakery?"

Brett shrugged. "Maybe. Did you want to order something, or did you just stop in to say hello?" He had firmly changed the subject. That was as far as the conversation would go. It was obvious he was choosing to stay away from Hannah. *But why?*

"Ordering. You have my support." He said with a smile. "I'll have one white chocolate mocha with whipped cream."

Brett nodded. "To go right?"

"You know me. I can't sit still to save my life." He grinned.

Luke paid and waited as Brett quietly made his drink. He couldn't remember if he had always been this level of silent or if something had changed. He fidgeted with the magazines Brett had placed by the end of the counter and flipped through a few articles about camping. Before he knew it, he was handed his drink. 'Thanks, Brett. Hope you have a good weekend." He smiled warmly and left.

He felt more confused when he left than when he had arrived. He sipped his coffee as he continued his walk to the gym. He would kill for one of Hannah's cinnamon rolls right now. He would need to make sure he was going to the gym with Hannah in his life. She was a sure way to make him gain ten unwanted pounds. There was no way they would stay undefeated on the ice that way, but damn if he wouldn't trade anything to see that woman's face every day. He couldn't deny that he was in deep. "Shit." He mumbled to no one, but himself

Chapter 9

Hannah

When she ambled out of bed the next morning, Hannah made herself a cup of coffee from her K-cup and turned on a podcast. She wanted to keep her brain busy today while she worked, and a murder mystery was just the thing. She methodically made her way around the house packing everything in sight while she solved mystery after mystery. Well, she didn't solve anything, but she was extremely impressed with the people that did.

Hannah made a pile in the corner of the room with items she would need for the next two days. Her bedding, and pillows, her favorite white blanket, her suitcases filled with clothes, any food she hadn't eaten from the refrigerator, her coffee pot and a mug, any baking items or staples that hadn't fit the first time, toiletries, and all the pictures that hung from her wall that she wanted to hang at the new place sat stacked in a leaning tower against the wall. She hauled the pile down to the Bug load by load and found she had room for a few more things. She grabbed some boxes at random until the car was full to the top. She was sweaty and her arms ached.

Hannah had messaged her parents before bed about loading the truck tonight, and they were coming after work. So, she walked down the block to grab a few items as she waited for them to finish up their workdays. She walked into an outdoor store that she had never considered entering before, and picked out a sleeping bag, some hiking boots, a warm jacket, and a hiking pack. She walked past the snowshoes and skates, the climbing gear, the giant camping section, and kayaking supplies. There would be opportunities everywhere around her in Woodsburrow for new and exciting sports to try. She didn't want to miss out on anything. She hoped she could find some people in the area to tag along with her. Someone needed to show her the ropes.

The excitement that was growing within her about the life that lay ahead was hard to contain. She walked slowly back to her apartment with her bag and watched the people walking past. She smiled at a few, but no one looked up from their cellphones. The ones that were looking forward, seemed to look straight through her. In Woodsburrow, even as a new resident, she received friendly smiles and hellos. There were no familiar faces or warmth that radiated to her here though. The city might be a place full of things to do, but it lacked the warm embracing culture that enveloped Woodsburrow. She was ready to go home.

Her parents parked their vehicle just as she turned the corner and could see her apartment down the sidewalk. Her mom embraced her in a huge hug. "I can't believe this is real." She spoke in choked words. She was fighting back tears and losing.

"It's okay, Mom. You are going to fall in love with Woodsburrow, and my apartment when you come Saturday. The people have just been so wonderful. Everyone is friendly and inviting. Zack should be starting some of the renovations downstairs so you will get to see a bit of the transformation in my shop. It's all so charming. It reminds me of something you would see in the movies. Are you guys going to stop by the farmers' market when you come?"

Hannah's father nodded. "Your mother would like to, and it would be a treat to see you in action."

Hannah smiled. "I can't wait! Bring your appetites because they have the best food trucks plus rotating live musicians. It is the best farmers' market I've ever seen. Thank you, guys, for helping me move. It helps a lot." She hugged her parents tightly. Her mom wouldn't let go.

"That's what we are here for Hannah Bug." Her father said, and he led the way upstairs.

They spent the next forty-five minutes carrying box after box and bag after bag down the long stairway to her father's trailer. Other than the stools from her kitchen that loaded easily, she only had a dresser, which was still very heavy despite emptying it of everything that was normally housed inside, some end tables, her TV stand, TV, and her futon couch. She was completely cleared out in no time. They walked through the apartment one last time and she grabbed a stack of coats in the closet and her gym bag that she had stashed her Julia Roberts collection and her favorite paperbacks in. Her mother ran her vacuum through the apartment while she tried to shove the coats and the gym bag in her already overfull Bug. "We can put that in the trailer, Hannah." Her dad called as he watched her struggle.

"No Dad, it's alright. I've got it." She quickly slammed the door to try to beat the cascade of jackets that would surely rain out when she opened the door next.

Hannah's mom came out the front door with the vacuum not long after. "Are you sure you don't want to sleep with us tonight? You won't have any furniture at that empty place."

Hannah shook her head. "Nope. I want to get settled in. The furniture store I bought from is delivering tomorrow. Set up was included with the delivery. So, I'll have an apartment full of rooms ready to go Friday afternoon. It's just one night. Plus, I'll be doing my baking for the market tomorrow, so I'd rather be there and ready to go, not just starting the drive. It will put me behind." She hugged both her parents. "I'll see you guys Saturday. I love you. Thanks for everything." She got into her Bug and started the long drive to Woodsburrow. She called Luke when she got outside the city limits.

Luke

"Yeah, man!" Luke and Steele high-fived in the locker room. They had been on fire on the ice tonight.

"Crushed it. We will still take the 'ship this year!" Steele said. Luke was thankful Steele was back to his normal self. He had spent a few weeks grieving the big changes in his life but now he seemed to have found his footing again. They took off their gear and walked outside together chatting about the last Yankees' game when

Luke's phone vibrated repeatedly. He pulled it out. It was Hannah. He looked at Steele. "I've got to take this." Steele raised his eyebrows but said nothing.

"Hannah banana, what's up?" He avoided Steele's eyes when he spoke.

"What are you doing?"

"Well, Steele and I are just leaving our hockey game, why?"

"I know you don't know much about me yet, but I'm impatient, and I can be impulsive."

"Oh boy. Did you buy the bowling alley, too? I mean it could use your touches to make it more successful, but jeez girl."

Hannah giggled. "The bowling alley? No! I packed up my apartment early. My parents are still coming on Saturday with the stuff that doesn't fit in my car."

"Hannah your vehicle is too small to be considered a car. That little ladybug is more like a Hot Wheel." He teased into the phone.

"Very funny! My Bug is the most precious thing I've ever owned. I bought her when I was 18, and she is the most loyal thing I've had in my life. Are you going to listen or just be sassy?"

"Sorry, I'm listening. I promise."

"Anyway, would you be willing to help me unload it when I get there?" There was a brief silence while Luke checked his phone for the time.

"When will you be here?"

"In just over an hour."

"Steele and I can both come over and unload with you. We will have you settled in before you can say home. Did you buy furniture yet?"

"Yes. Actually, they are delivering it tomorrow. I couldn't believe how easy that was. They had an excellent selection. I was very impressed."

"They do well for a small-town store. I thought they would have furniture in your style. Nothing too typical for the amazing Hannah. We will see you in an hour. We both need to change, or you might not let us inside."

"Alright, thank you guys. See you then." They disconnected.

He hung up and turned to finally face Steele who was looking at him with an expression that begged for the details. "So, I had promised Hannah I would help her move in on Saturday. She decided she wants to stay here tonight and is headed here to Woodsburrow with a carload of stuff. Would you be willing to haul boxes and whatever else upstairs?"

Steele looked at him. "There is more to this story. Why haven't you mentioned there is something happening?"

"I don't know that something is happening. I barely know her, and you were just involved in a breakup. It seems insensitive to say hey I met a girl that I think I could see differently than the women I've been with in the past."

Steele clapped him on the back. "Let's go move her man. This is a big deal. If you feel like this could be different than it is. We've got to do it right. Do you want to come over to shower? My place is closer. Does she have furniture with her?"

Luke shook his head. "I don't think so."

"I have a blow-up mattress we can bring." "That's good. I'll grab her something to eat too. I need to get something for myself anyway."

They hurried to Steele's place. Luke placed a pickup order at Gearshift, while Steele showered. He went out to his garage to look for the blow-up mattress Steele had said was out there. He found it on the shelf rolled perfectly with an inflator next to it. On the way back, he grabbed the hammer and a handful of nails. Anything extra to make her feel at home, he was willing to do. He wanted her to have the best welcome home she could have. He re-entered the house and heard Steele yell, "Done!" He placed his pile on the counter and headed for the shower. Luke grabbed his bag with the clothes he had on before the game and took the quickest shower of his life. Ten minutes later, they were on their way to pick up their dinner. They wolfed down their dinner and hurried over to the home of the future baker.

Hannah

The last hour of the drive felt like days. Hannah's butt was falling asleep, and she shifted often in her seat to find a more comfortable position. Talking to Luke had made her feel much closer to town than she was. She counted down every one of the last thirty crawling miles. Hannah pulled into her back alley parking spot at 7:30 PM. The men were waiting there for her.

They both had wet hair and clean clothes. She got out of the car and stretched. She shuffled through her purse to make sure she had her key when the scent of soap and men's cologne hit her nose. She turned in its direction and saw Luke's familiar face and strong stride followed up by an unfamiliar man with dark hair and green eyes. He had a friendly smile and held out his hand.

"Hi, Hannah. It's nice to meet you. I'm Steele. I own the hardware store. I've known Luke since we were in diapers. I hope he hasn't been too big of a hassle to you."

"I tend to think he is funny."

Steele smiled. "Good, but don't tell him that. It only feeds the fire. Congratulations on the bakery. I know it isn't open yet, but everyone has been talking about how delicious your goodies are at the market. It takes a strong woman to make a move like this by themselves."

"Okay, chatty Kathy let's get to work," Luke called from behind them as he grabbed boxes from the trunk.

"Just be careful when you open that door." She said as she pointed to the back left. "Those coats are going to fall into your lap, and I place the blame on you if you get dirt into my white Chanel coat."

Luke bowed with exaggerated lowness and swung his arm across his middle. Hannah caught the scent of him, and excitement filled her chest. He was such an intoxicating man, and a smirk fell across her face. "Yes, my lady," Luke said in a low voice and Hannah broke out in a giggle.

The boys made quick work of the unloading, and Hannah couldn't believe how much quicker it was to take everything upstairs than it had been for her to take down. Hannah turned around to them bringing items up the stairs that hadn't been in her car. "What's that?" She asked.

"A few things to get you through until your stuff arrives. We wouldn't want the Queen to be without." Luke winked and flashed his big smile at her and her stomach felt weak. He set down a bag of takeout and a bag with a hammer and some nails on her counter. Steele brought an inflatable mattress into the large bedroom with the easel and began filling it. Luke grabbed the rolled-up sleeping bag, the pile of blankets, and pillows and set them down next to the mattress.

"You guys are so thoughtful. This is seriously the sweetest thing. Thank you. Whose mattress is this?"

"Mine," Steele answered. "Consider it my housewarming gift. I haven't used it in all the years it has been collecting dust in my closet."

"And why the hammer and nails?"

"Because I'm certain you already know where you want some things hung, and making it feel more like home will matter to you," Luke said with a serious tone in his voice. He wasn't joking or teasing her anymore.

He had picked up on her preferences and was trying to be thoughtful. She hadn't asked them for dinner, but they had just known they should feed her. Her cheeks burned at how purely he had seen her. Hannah usually didn't become embarrassed often, but people tended to not see her quite as deeply as he did. "What would you like me to hang and where would you like me to hang it?" He asked while holding the hammer in his hands.

Hannah gathered up the paintings she had brought up and leaned against the kitchen walls and showed him the wall where the long couch would go, the wall in the bathroom, and the wall behind her bed. Hannah stood back at a distance as he patiently moved the paintings along the wall until finally, she had deemed them straight and centered.

"Did you make these?" He asked while he glanced at her.

She nodded. "I frequently painted years ago. I love it, but it has been years since I've made any new pieces. I haven't had much time in the past months to do anything besides work. It's always been difficult for me to balance my time painting and baking anyway, but this last job made it impossible to feel like I even had inspiration to paint. I love it so much though. I like to paint what's around me when the mood hits, and I usually give my piece colors that coincide with the feelings I'm having around what I'm painting. I'm hoping to start making it a hobby I do regularly again."

"It's important not to be all work and no play. I love being a cop, but if I stopped fishing, and hiking, camping, or playing hockey, I'd lose my mind. Those things give you that outlet for the stress you are experiencing in day-to-day life and force you to grow in ways you wouldn't otherwise. Not to mention just being in nature is a way to make yourself feel a part of this big old world. That is my favorite feeling. You shouldn't ever stop something you are this good at. My favorite is this one of the lake." He said studying the canvas with great interest. Hannah smiled a small smile and nodded.

"At my sister's bachelorette party, we went boating on a lake. When the sunset, the lake mimicked the deepest pink and purple hues I had ever seen. It reminded me of cotton candy. I painted it when I arrived home. I was hungover and exhausted, but I didn't want to forget a single hue."

"What about this one?" Luke asked as they lifted the large picture that would sit over the couch. "It's a still life of a couple I made my first wedding cake for. They had an incredible venue and when they had snuck off to take pictures, they walked through the flower garden that was in full bloom and sat down on the wooden benches. Although I wasn't up close enough to see anything but their outlines, I remembered what the bride's face had looked like when she saw the cake and how she looked at her husband when they ordered it. They were truly in love. It was magical to see a couple mesh so beautifully together. I've always wanted that kind of love for myself. I was honored to be a part of it." She said in a faraway voice.

The colors of the flowers were vibrant hues and dominated the canvas. The couple in the middle looked like they had shrunken down and been placed in a magical fairy world. The adoration that shown on their face made it clear that was the only place in the world they wanted to be.

The last one was an abstract full of colors and directions. It was a hard canvas to explain. "This one makes you think and feel a combination of things. The tones seem sad or maybe relaxed kind of like soft jazz. Hannah looked surprised at him. "You must know your art. I can never figure out how to explain that one to people. I made that one at the end of a journey in my life. It's a story for another time." She said with a sigh.

Steele ambled out of her bedroom. "Who would have thought that mattress would have taken longer than everything else combined?" He asked.

Hannah peaked through the doorway. He had made her bed complete with pillows and blankets. "You guys are the absolute best. Oh! I almost forgot. The best thing about helping out a baker is the reward." She brought out a to-go package with two dozen chocolate chip cookies.

"Oh yes! Thank you." They said snatching the sack out of Hannah's hands. They opened the sack together and dug in immediately like a bunch of hungry wolves. "So good." She heard Steele mumbling through a mouthful. Hannah couldn't help but giggle at the sight of them.

"We will leave you to settle in for the night," Luke said as they walked through the door.

Steele descended the stairs. "Bye, Hannah. It was great to meet you. Don't be a stranger!"

Luke turned around to face her. "Goodnight Miss Hannah." He said in a low voice as they made eye contact, and Hannah felt like he was looking deep into her soul. Her breath caught in her chest as she studied him. The air between them felt thick. Her heart pounded in anticipation. His eyes suddenly dropped from her face. Then he turned and walked out the door. A tingle shot down her spine, and she shivered.

Hannah shut the door and walked into the kitchen. She peeked into the takeout bag sitting on the counter. They had gotten her a chicken sandwich with a giant pickle, coleslaw, and some fries. She changed into her pajamas and crawled into bed with her dinner. She was bone tired and her apartment was trashed, but she couldn't have been happier.

She was in disbelief at all the trouble the men had gone through to make sure she had felt at home tonight and on short notice. She thankfully ate her dinner on her own little island. Her blow-up mattress, white fluffy blanket, and greasy delight were all she needed for now. She couldn't help but wonder if Luke had felt the energy that had shot between them tonight. She pushed the thought away. Now was not the time to focus on men. It was time to prove herself as a baker in this town. She would just get some sleep, right here, in her new home. Tomorrow, she had a long day ahead of her.

Luke

Having Steele at his side made Luke more relaxed when he interacted with Hannah tonight. Steele treated Hannah kindly and gave Luke room to have some private interactions with her. Luke loved that she was a painter. He had always been fascinated by paintings. He and his mom liked to go to galleries together. His dad never had an interest in going, and Luke had always loved seeing his Mom examine the scenes. As a child, they would pretend they were in the painting and tell stories about what might be happening there. It was something that not many people knew, but the nostalgia was strong. Hannah lit up the same way talking about them as his mom did. She also had a connection to nature in the same way that he did that was obviously by the pictures she had painted. She just saw the details that were laid out before her differently. He had never met a woman who saw the beauty of the outdoors in the same way he did, and the accuracy of how she had seen the lake in her mind's eye hours later was very impressive.

When it was time to leave, the temptation to pull Hannah into him and kiss her was burning wildly. He felt like a small flame had somehow turned into a forest fire raging within his soul. He would have spent all evening in that apartment with her. It would have given him the same amount of pleasure to talk about her painting and her bakery, as it would to be wrapped around her under that sleeping bag.

"Dude. You've got it bad. Ask her out!" Steele said on the drive back to his house.

"I don't know how to be in a relationship. There is no good in starting something with someone I am that interested in. I'll completely destroy whatever we might be."

Steele looked at him. "Why do you think you are someone not worthy of a steady woman? You use being a police officer as an excuse, but there are police officers all over the world with significant others and families. You aren't unfaithful. I don't believe you have ever cheated on a woman. Why are you so afraid of something more serious? You have seen me with Stacey. Your parents are deeply in love. What is it?"

Luke stared out the window. "I've always just thought I was better off alone, I guess. It's frightening to think about being with the same person for possibly forever."

"Dude, no one is asking you to marry her, and just because you make a plan from two months from now, doesn't mean you have a blood oath for life. Calm down, and just trust yourself to be yourself with her. You need to ask her."

"I just need some time, to be sure."

Steele sighed. "Take all the time you need man. You don't want to jump in before you are ready. Just remember, she is a gorgeous human. Other people are not going to be blind to that. If she doesn't have any idea you are interested, she isn't going to wait for you. You may be watching her with someone else who didn't need to psych themselves up to ask her out."

Luke's shoulders drooped. There was that thought again. *Hannah being undressed by someone else's eyes.* Thinking about it made him feel physically ill and like inflicting pain on the mystery man who didn't even exist. He needed to get it together before someone else got it together first.

Chapter 10

That night, Hannah had the best sleep she had had in weeks. There was a stark difference in the quiet in Woodsburrow from the noise and constant hum of just about everything that had surrounded her in the city. Although it should have rattled her brain having the lack of noise around, she had relaxed more deeply than she had since high school. She had a sense of peace and belonging that flooded her body. She rose early with the sun naturally and headed to the kitchen for some coffee.

She had boxes marked 'kitchen' piled against the far wall that she began to open and shuffle through until she found her coffee maker. She plugged it into the wall, added water, and a K-cup, and found the lone mug that had made the journey in her vehicle. The mug was white and turned colors when filled with a hot liquid. It had a whisk on the side and read, "Watch me whip." She had gotten it last Christmas from her sister Amanda for their white elephant gift exchange. It always brought happiness to her entire day when she started the morning with a sassy mug. Before she set it up to be filled with coffee, Hannah examined it for cracks. She was relieved to find none. She left the coffee maker to do its magic and turned her oven on to preheat.

She had heard Zack come in almost an hour earlier and was dying of excitement to see how far he had gotten the last few days while she had been gone. She knew that too many drop-ins would hinder his progress, but the temptation was heavy with him moving about downstairs. *I won't go down. I won't go down. I'll check after I finish all my work for the day.* Hannah thought to herself. She grabbed her coffee and brought it carefully to the living room floor. She enjoyed her magical bean brew cross legged on the floor while the sun shined in. This was the exact place that her large couch was going to be sitting in later today. She glanced around the room, well if she was able to clean up enough for the delivery to occur anyway, it would be here.

After Hannah had finished her coffee, she started playing a Bruno Mars playlist from her phone and got to work. She emptied the boxes that belonged in the kitchen and folded them down into a pile. She took any boxes with clothes and stacked them in her closet. The jackets were hung in the entryway closet, and she balanced the blow-up mattress against the wall. In the event that something went wrong with the delivery today, she didn't want to be sleeping on the ground, nor did she want to be summoning Steele to reinflate the mattress for her. She found her toiletries and placed them in their rightful places in her master bathroom.

Her travel cooler which contained the random ketchup bottles, butter, and other miscellaneous items that she hadn't finished before the move, had been hidden under the jackets. She carefully placed the items in the refrigerator and parked the cooler in the entry closet. She had a clock her mother had bought for her one Christmas that had a hand-painted sunburst with brilliant yellows, oranges, and reds. She hung it on the nail that had been left in the wall next to the entryway. Hannah looked around, felt satisfied that at least the delivery people would be able to get into the apartment, and went to take a shower.

Hannah showered while singing along at the top of her lungs to "Nothing on You," and then dressed in her baking clothes which consisted of a plain greyish-blue t-shirt and her most comfortable pair of pants. She slipped on her fuzzy slippers because life is about some balance, and she pulled her hair back into a high bun. With a few swipes of make-up, she entered her kitchen, ready to work.

She started her cinnamon roll dough, sourdough loaves, and bagels then switched over to muffins and doughnuts. Although it was still technically summer, she wanted to showcase some of her fall flavors. This would be her chance to reach a large audience of people and hopefully woo them into coming into her bakery for the same flavors when the markets were closed for the year. She started with a pumpkin s'more muffin that mingled the two seasons in one. She made three types of doughnuts, powdered sugar, a new flavor she was calling salted caramel apple cider, and another one that was a chai. She snuck some apple turnovers in the oven that would be perfect for snacking as people wandered around the market. Hannah hoped they would be a big seller. She made some peach cobbler muffins which smelled divine. She couldn't help but eat one of those with a second cup of coffee. After savoring the muffin which had turned out exactly how she had pictured it in her head, she finished her bread loaves and flavored her bagels. She went with the jalapeno cheddar again since it was a big hit and contrasted it with her French toast flavor. The cinnamon rolls were doing their final rise when the chocolate chip cookies she had added to the menu at the last minute at Luke's request, finished baking. She was pleased with the result. Hannah was bringing fall tomorrow. Hannah knew it was good, she just hoped that customers would be willing to start apple flavors and not feel like they were missing out on the blueberry and raspberry ones. She loaded up a tray of cookies and headed downstairs to say hello to Zack.

When she opened the door, Zack looked up from a board he was marking the measurement on and looked back down to place his mark before he set it aside. "You have excellent self-control. I thought I would see you much earlier." He said with a grin.

Hannah smiled at him. "I thought about it many times, but I had some work to do to keep me busy." She handed him the plate. "So, how is it going?" He devoured a cookie before he spoke again.

"Good. I was able to get my hands on all the materials I needed. I have had an excellent start on the front portion. I should have this section done in way less than two weeks. It's the kitchen that will take the rest of the time. Did you get a delivery estimate from the company you ordered from?"

Hannah nodded. "August 31st."

"We should be able to have everything ready to be installed that day. Gary said he would have some time next week to help out with the parts that I need an extra hand with. Would you be opposed to painting a few days with Emily?"

"Absolutely not. I'd love to get my hands dirty a bit and keep you moving forward on the stuff I definitely can't do. That sounds like something I wouldn't mess up."

He nodded and grinned. "That will help with time. Emily has the lights done already as well, I just need to install them, and we are working on the painting process with the table and chairs."

"You guys are so efficient for your first job this size. You should consider doing more jobs like this."

Zack nodded. "We have. We are going to add it to our website. This helps rocket our business. We really appreciate it."

"Don't thank me, you guys are the ones helping me out! I could put a sign out front with your business name on it that says you are the ones doing the construction if that helps. Maybe Emily could print something off with your logo on it?"

"Yeah. I'll ask her to. That would help. I've been peeped at all day like a zoo animal. Not everyone around here has the self-control that you have."

Hannah giggled. "Unfortunately, Zack it doesn't help that you are a good-looking guy. There may be a lot of peeping going on until you finish. Just try to keep your shirt on though or the good church-going women might completely lose their cool."

He grinned. "Noted."

"Well, I'll be gone at the market tomorrow, and then I'm moving stuff in with my parents. My mom will want a little tour, but we will stay out of your way. Just let me know if you want me to see something or need me to make any decisions. Otherwise, I am going to try my hardest not to hinder your progress." They glanced outside as the furniture delivery truck pulled up to the curb. "Gotta go. It's nice work so far Zack. I am very grateful." She said as she walked out front.

An hour later, her apartment had come alive. The blue furniture and rug had been rolled out. Her bed was made, and the spare beds were ready for sheets. She flopped down on the couch and shrieked. "It's perfect!" She was almost done baking for the day and considered going out for the evening. There was a brewery on the other side of downtown that seemed to be the go-to hang-out. Maybe she could meet up with some people and have a night out on the town. She felt like she deserved it. Hannah finished her cinnamon rolls and packed up all her items. Everything sat ready to go for the morning. She was feeling full of girl power and sassiness, so she dressed in a little black dress that hugged her in all the right places and paired it with a pair of red heels. *A week full of wins like this should be celebrated.*

Luke

"Mrs. Nelson, we really should take you into the hospital to get checked out."

Mrs. Nelson had been the local librarian and the kindest lady around when he was a child. This was the third time this month he had picked her up in a location that she wasn't supposed to be with not a clue who she was or why she was there. Her husband had passed away the month before. He wasn't a medical professional and didn't know what was causing the memory lapses, but no matter the cause, he was worried. She didn't have anyone who lived locally who could help watch her and keep her safe. Fifteen minutes ago, she thought Bush was the President and that Glen was waiting at home with her dinner. If Mrs. Nelson got injured, he would feel the weight of the guilt of that. He knew she needed to be evaluated by someone.

"Glen will be terribly upset if I'm not home by ten you know. I think you are making a big fuss about nothing."

It was no use reminding her that Glen had been buried just weeks prior and wouldn't be at home worried tonight. "I am sure I am more worried than I need to be. I would be happy to talk to Glen and let him know that you are safe and that I am the one who held you up tonight."

She patted his arm. "I always liked you, Luke. Your parents did such a great job raising you. I'll go just to appease you, but you need to go talk to Glen."

He nodded as he hooked her arm and took her to his car. "Do you happen to have Carrie's number? She might be able to help me with Glen."

Carrie was her daughter who lived an hour away. If he could get her involved, the Emergency Department could work with Carrie to make sure whatever plan they had moving forward, would keep her safe.

"Of course, dear. My phone is right in my purse there." She had been wandering around with only a little purse slung around her shoulder. He stepped out of earshot to catch Carrie up on the situation and drove her to the Emergency Department.

By the time he was finished talking to Carrie, and the Emergency Room nurses about what had transpired, he went back to the station to write up his report and have a snack. He miraculously finished it without interruptions and headed back out onto Main Street.

It was Friday night so he knew he wouldn't have to go far to keep busy. As he walked out to his patrol car, he saw a sign posted on the light pole. He looked closer and saw a picture of Hannah. The picture was zoomed in and the words insinuated some horrible things about her. He quickly tore it down and looked down the street. The posters had been plastered everywhere. He walked the length of the street in both directions noting where he grabbed each poster from and walked back to his car to set them on his seat. Someone had evil intentions of hurting Hannah. It made him furious. This was not how he expected his community to behave. Everyone seemed excited. They were lucky to have such a good business to add to their downtown. She wasn't selling sex clothing or quick loans. She was just trying to sell people something delicious. He got into his patrol car and drove down towards Gearshift where he had seen the majority of people heading tonight. Maybe he would be able to spot if anyone was acting suspiciously.

The owners of Gearshift had contacted his chief that week to let him know they were concerned that customers weren't respecting the parking laws which was making it impossible for incoming customers to find a reasonable spot to park. On top of that, they were seeing an increasing amount of drunk driving arrests. Luke and the other night shift cop were asked to go out and more closely watch how long vehicles had been parked and write tickets when appropriate. He went through the vehicles mechanically watching for any characters that seemed odd or out of place as his mind drifted to Hannah.

Chapter 11

Hannah

Gearshift Brewery had live music playing on the patio, and the property was packed. Hannah had walked from her apartment, and she snuck inside to order herself food and a drink. Twenty minutes later, she found herself on the patio with the band and a few of the women who were familiar to her. Whit and Bri were eyeing up some of the men as they sat on the far side of the patio. "I think he is the most beautiful man we have seen all summer."

"Definitely," Bri responded to Whit.

Hannah looked over at a man who looked like a beach bum who had just come in from surfing. He had long blonde hair and the perfect tan. His shirt fit tightly, and it was clear that his muscles were very well maintained. "He is cute. Why don't you go talk to him? Ask him to dance." Hannah said.

Whit shook her head.

"Why not? Isn't it more fun if you interact with them too?"

"Perhaps, but I don't have that kind of confidence," Whit said with a sigh.

Hannah watched as the man glanced over at Whit three more times, and Whit did the same. "That's enough," Hannah said grabbing her arm. "Come with me."

She sauntered over to the men. "Hi, boys." She said with her million-dollar smile. The beach bum returned the smile. "My name is Hannah. Have you met my friend Whit?" She asked, moving her body so Whit was positioned between them and giving her a little push forward.

"Hi Whit, Jake." He reached out a hand, and they shook.

Hannah could feel the tiny sparks set off between them as they touched. "Are you from around here?" She asked.

He shook his no. The conversation seemed to erupt from there, and Hannah quietly snuck back to Bri whose mouth hung wide open.

"You are the best wingman I've ever seen."

Hannah shrugged. "Men are easy." She happily finished her chicken wings and fries along with her drink as Bri and Hannah giggled and laughed. "I'm going to get another." She said indicating her drink. "Do you want one?" Bri nodded as she scanned the crowd looking for her own hunk to spend the evening with. "I'll keep my eye out for you, too." Hannah winked and strode off to the bar.

A man in a striped navy suit approached her as she waited for the bartender to notice her. "You might be the most gorgeous woman I've ever laid eyes on. Would you like to dance?" He asked.

She smiled at him although she didn't appreciate the intensity of the pickup line. "Maybe, it depends."

"On what?" He replied.

"If you have anyone with you my friend could dance with as well." She indicated Bri sitting alone at their table.

She would be willing to move past the terrible line if he had someone Bri could enjoy the night with.

"Don't move." He said and disappeared into the crowd. Hannah got her drinks just as he came back with a that looked cute and a bit less cocky trailing behind him. "So, yes?" He asked.

She nodded. They followed her over to the corner that Bri was sitting in. The man he had brought beside him with sandy-styled hair immediately stuck out his hands to invite her to dance. Bri was stunned at her luck and accepted giddily following him out to the dance floor.

Hannah was pleased that her new friends both appeared to be having a great time. They both shot her thank-you glances. Hannah turned to the man in the suit, took his hands, and joined him in a dance. Hannah was surprised that she enjoyed herself. The man, whose name was Jesse, was nice. She didn't feel any kind of strong attraction, but she was comfortable spending time with him, and they seemed to have good conversation. They exchanged numbers, and Hannah excused herself. Bri and Whit were not going to be leaving the men they had attached to anytime soon, and Hannah was tired. She had no intentions of participating in any afterparty activities with Jesse, and she was ready to go home to her beautiful new apartment. She had a long day ahead of her, so she grabbed her purse and headed towards the door.

Another man stopped her and asked her to dance, and she politely declined. He was an attractive blonde, but she had made up her mind that she wasn't looking for a man tonight. She was feeling checked out. It would take more than a comment about her looks and a dance to convince

Hannah that a man was worth her time at this point. She strode out the door.

A man in uniform was out front writing some tickets. He glanced over as she descended the steps. "Hannah?" He asked.

"Luke?"

He looked her over head to toe and abruptly caught himself. He turned away as his cheeks burned, and he immediately became tongue-tied. "You, umm, wow that dress looks amazing on you." He nervously stuck a hand in his pocket and shifted his stance.

"Thank you." She smiled and smoothed her dress. She was in such shock at the sight of him that she hadn't noticed any of his nervous movements. She suddenly felt self-conscious about the sexy dress she had been wearing.

"Date night?" He asked.

She shook her head. "No date. Just celebrating my wins this week."

"You must have gotten your furniture today."

She grinned. "It looks so good."

He smiled back at her. "I didn't see your loosely defined 'car' parked around here." He said as he looked himself around for it.

"I didn't drive. I knew I was planning on drinking. It isn't a far walk."

He looked shocked. "You walked here in those shoes? Let me drive you home."

"You look busy. I'll be fine I promise."

"Hannah," he said more firmly, "please let me drive you. I have something I need to show you anyway."

Hannah could hear the serious tone in his voice, and although she thought he was worrying too much. She agreed.

Luke finished writing his ticket and held the door for her to get into his car. He shuffled around his stack of papers in the front, finally came up with a handful that he had been looking for and handed them to her. "I found these while I was patrolling tonight. I took them all down, but they were up all over the downtown." She took the stack from him and examined them.

There was a picture of her that took up ¾ of the paper in her bra and underwear stepping out of the lake dripping wet. She hadn't thought anyone was at the lake on the land side when she was there, and fear swept over her face. *Someone had been watching her and hiding while they did it.* Under the picture, it read: *Do not support Hannah Jones. We don't want someone representing the businesses in this town acting like this.* Fear was written all over her face.

"You didn't know anyone was there, did you?" Luke asked softly.

She shook her head. They sat quietly for a few minutes until the blackness that had been taking over Hannah's vision started to dissipate.

"Why would someone try to make my image rotten? So, I fail? They are insinuating that I have loose morals. I've never behaved lewdly. I was just swimming in the lake like every other person has been doing this summer. How does that make me bad?"

"It doesn't." Luke answered. "And you don't have to justify going for a swim."

"I've always liked to swim," Hannah said, her voice sounding far away. Her body began to shiver, and Luke reached over to turn the heat on. "In high school, I was a state champion. It was a big deal at the time."

Luke nodded and placed his hands over the top of hers. "I'll drive you home and get you inside. Everything is going to be okay."

As they drove, Hannah sat in silence.

"Have you talked to anyone here who sounded unhappy about you opening your business?" Luke said glancing from the road to her eyes.

Hannah shook her head. "No. I mean I haven't met everyone, but no. I know cooperation was in talks with Merri when I bought the place, and she opted to sell to me, but I have a hard time believing that they would get that hung up on some small-town location."

Luke sat silently. Hannah glanced over at him and saw worry flash across his face. He said nothing.

When they got to Hannah's apartment, he insisted on doing exactly what he had said he would, and he walked her all the way up to her door. "Do you want to see my couches? You came all the way here."

He grinned. "Normally I wouldn't give a crap about a couch or I might think you were coming on to me to get me inside, but knowing you, Hannah, you probably bought the boldest, most unique set you could get your hands on. Just like you. Show me." Hannah smiled as her heart pounded loudly and led him inside. "You wasted no time, did you?" He said looking around the room that had been unpacked, and the items ready for tomorrow's market sitting neatly, piled high on the counter space. Hannah turned on the lights.

The blue couches gleamed in all their glory. Luke laughed. "They look great Hannah. They suit you, and this place perfectly. It's like this apartment was made for you. It even matches your flower painting." He shook his head with a smile while he took it all in. "We are very lucky to have you here. Don't let whoever this fool is make you think any differently." He added seriously.

She shook her head. "It takes more than that to knock Hannah Jones off her game." Hannah smiled brightly with confidence.

"I'll see you tomorrow. Sleep well. Remember to lock the door behind me." Luke shut the door and walked down the steps.

Luke

When Luke saw Hannah appear before him, he thought she was a vision, and he was delirious from the lateness of the night. She looked gorgeous in that little black dress. Once he had convinced his brain that she was real, the next thought in his head, was who she was here with. *She had to be on a date with someone already. Steele had been right.* His heart sank. *Had he been too slow?* But she had denied being out with anyone which gave him renewed hope. He immediately remembered the posters, and with how she looked tonight, he couldn't let her walk home. Men would be looking at her like she was prey, and her alone on the streets made her a sitting duck. "I have something I need to show you." Despite hating himself for having to ruin her sunny disposition tonight, he needed to tell her now so she could protect herself against whatever this was.

The way her face fell and the fear that filled her eyes broke his heart. Hannah hadn't had a clue that someone had been at the beach watching her. That was concerning. Someone was following her around without being noticed. Luke would need to pass that along so his force could help. She had been taking an innocent swim in the lake. The same innocent swim that every other person who had visited the lake that day had done. Then, she had been posted all over town like some kind of bimbo. Now she felt shame, for doing something that brought her enjoyment and wasn't intended to be offensive to anyone.

He was thankful to see her brighten up at the thought of showing off her new couches when he brought her home. Luke had wanted her to be vigilant, but he didn't want her to live this important time of her life in constant fear. Her bubbliness was one of his favorite things about her, and it made her unique.

When he got back into his patrol car, his personal phone rang. *Who was calling this late?* He grabbed his phone. "Hello?"

"Lukey my love, what's up?"

"I'm just working Molly."

"I'm fine thanks for asking. So, I wanted to call because I'm coming up tomorrow. I'm going to the farmers' market with Becky. I know you work so I won't have much time to see you, but I need a quick trip. Can we get dinner maybe before your night shift? When are you on days again?"

"How do you have this much energy right now? It's one in the morning. Are you driving?"

"Travis and I had a fight. Logan is still at camp, so it's just me. I needed some air." Silence on the line.

He knew she had been crying. "Let's do dinner, yes. The Cozy Kitchen this time. I've been spending too much time at Gearshift." He felt the anger once again rise in her chest now directed at Travis. His aunt deserved much better than this. He took a deep breath, so he didn't sound testy over the phone.

"Did you tell her yet?"

"Who?"

"Don't play stupid Lukey, you know I know."

He let out a giant sigh. "Not yet, but I'm working on it. Don't tell her who you are if you stop by tomorrow. Please. Let me get there on my own time."

"I'm so excited for you Luke. It's going to be amazing to see you with a girl! Of course, I am stopping there. I need to support her venture!"

"Just act normal when you are there. I'll let you know when I'm ready for her to meet my crazy aunt."

She laughed into the phone. "Love you, Lukey. See you tomorrow."

"Drive safe. I'm sorry you are having such a hard time. You don't deserve it. I love you. Good night." He clicked off the phone. Dispatch was calling him out on a new call. He glanced at the clock. Six more hours to go before he could hit the sheets. Time to get back to work.

Chapter 12

Hannah

Hannah was relieved the next day to have a much shorter drive to the market than she had in previous weeks. She set up her stand and greeted her friends around her. She walked the rows, seeking out the section of farm stands. Grant Farms seemed to be the largest one among the options, and she remembered the name from her stop at the grocery store. Hannah introduced herself to a woman named Caroline and asked her about getting some farm fresh fruits delivered to the bakery seasonally. Caroline had a strong business sense and loved the idea. "Unfortunately, we don't have a commercial selection of apples. I do grow enough pumpkins and squash though. I have peaches in season now along with the early pumpkins that could be ready."

"Would you mind dropping it off sometime later this week? I think I'll take what you have this week and then again on September 1st. I'll have my commercial-size refrigerator and freezer at that point."

"Absolutely. Nice doing business with you, Hannah. I wish you the greatest success. A woman with confidence like yours is a powerful thing. I love to see strong women moving into the community." She smiled warmly.

Hannah strode back over to her stand as she spoke with customers trying to get the first peak at her offerings today. She had already officially taken orders for some upcoming birthday cakes, and a wedding that was taking place in early winter. A man at one of the nearby artisan cheese stands had snuck through the crowds and poked his head through the forming line to ask if he could take her on a date. He had a cute baby face, and Hannah was impressed that he had gotten up the courage to ask in this busy environment. So, she said yes, and they exchanged numbers. A fun night out with some good company would break up the week

She was dressed in a green and black checkered flannel button-up with jeans and low cowboy boots. Her whole being was radiating the coming fall, and she wore it proudly. She silently hoped her customers would be happy to welcome some autumn flavors into their lives today and took one last look at her stand before she walked behind it. She spotted her parents walking through the rows, not a minute early or a second late. Hannah chuckled and beamed. It warmed her heart to see them here, and she loved that they had arrived exactly when she had expected them.

A lone musician's voice and an acoustic guitar floated through the air. She closed her eyes a minute and let the music flow through her. She always looked forward to the musicians. She hoped her parents would enjoy their time here today and appreciate all the little things that made this place so special. She wanted her mom to leave today with the sense that her daughter was in the right place, chasing her dreams, while feeling both comfort and pride. She watched her parents disappear into the crowd as a line formed almost immediately at her stand. People spoke excitedly about her flavors and whispered among themselves while they waited.

A beautiful woman with sleek red hair first in line approached her. "I'm a sucker for apple goodies. I'm so excited you have some today! I'll take a turnover and a caramel apple cider doughnut." Hannah smiled relieved that fall seemed to be an accepted flavor right off the bat today. *Thank goodness.* She thought with a sigh.

A few customers had seen the fliers that had been hung around town before Luke had taken them down and whispered to each other. Hannah heard a few of the comments and speculation that floated among them. She was embarrassed to have had her customers see them, but everyone was too polite to say anything directly to her about it. It made Hannah feel frustrated. She was trying to form a lifelong place in this community and develop friendships. Someone was intentionally jeopardizing that.

She had wanted to open Drury Lane with people looking at her from a new perspective, seeing her as a respectable baker and not judging her by her looks. This was supposed to be a fresh start. Even so, whoever had hung the fliers seemed to want to ruin her business, and it was having the opposite effect. Hannah didn't want whoever the culprit was to think they were bothering her in the slightest, so she shined her Hannah personality brightly. Orders continued coming in for future events at a rapid pace. At this rate, she would be busy despite not yet having an open storefront.

Her parents finally made their way to the front of her seemingly never-ending line. Her mother had bags of candles, wine, pottery pieces, small décor signs, and a bag of fresh fruits and vegetables. "What a great market! I picked up a few housewarming things for your new place and stuff for ours. You have had a steady line here all day!"

Hannah nodded. "I'm sold out of my sourdough line. That is always very popular. My fall flavors are going fast, too."

"We are so proud of you, Hannah Banana. It's so great to see you looking happy while talking about your baking again. You looked so uptight at the Goose butt place. Now you look like my little girl who loved to bring me miniature chocolate cakes out of that play oven and beamed every time I finished it." Hannah's dad said.

Hannah smiled. "I feel that way too. It brings me back to the reasons why I started in the first place."

Her parents ordered each variety of muffins and went off to the food truck congregation. "Can we buy you some lunch? I'm sure you haven't snuck away with all the customers you have had."

"That sounds great. Anything with BBQ would be perfect. I've been smelling it all day. My mouth is watering just talking about it." Her parents waved goodbye and headed off.

Hannah was sold out of all her goods with thirty minutes to spare and had four notebook sheets full of future orders. This had been easily the busiest market she had been a part of all year. The word was that the next two would continue this way. After that, the market closed until the following year. She didn't realize how sad the thought would make her feel. She wasn't planning on such a large portion of her business and joy to come from a farmers' market, but the sense of community and wonder that surrounded her and the new faces she got to meet in bulk were intoxicating.

As she packed up, she realized that Luke had not been there that day. She felt a pang of sadness. She looked forward to seeing him even if it was only for a few minutes. He was funny and exciting. and it was nice to see a familiar face. He could make the most mundane conversation interesting and wild. Not to mention the surge he always gave to her senses made her crave him more and more. Even though she loved his company, he wasn't obligated to come visit her stand every time she was here. She shoved the feeling of loneliness aside and loaded her car. She walked through the short distance to meet her family down by the guitarist and devoured her BBQ chicken while they chatted. She listened. She was too tired and hungry to talk, and she loved listening to the cadence of her parent's conversations. It wasn't long before everyone was packed up around her, and the vendors had begun to leave. "Well, should we take a look at this building?" Her mother asked. "What is it you are calling it?"

"Drury Lane. I'm ready to go if you are." They got up and walked the now nearly empty fairground to their vehicles and headed to Hannah's place.

Hannah gave her parents a tour of her building. Her mom loved the vines draped over the old brick exterior. "It looks like it's right out of a storybook." She examined the street surrounding them. "The whole downtown is quaint. There is so much to see!" Hannah smiled. She knew her mom would love it. Her mom noticed a flower bed that had been vacant this year. "You could plant some really pretty annuals there next year." Hannah was not much of a gardener, but her mom was, and she would love a reason to have her come down and spend time with her.

"I'd love your help with that, Mom." She said and her mom beamed. Hannah brought her parents to the store and introduced them to Zack and Emily. Emily had brought in the tables and chairs and Zack had installed the new lights. "You guys! You did such an amazing job. Emily, it's just like the picture I had in my head. I can't believe how much you have gotten done already!"

Hannah embraced Emily. Hannah and Emily explained the vision of how the rest of the store would look to her parents. They nodded along.

"Hannah, this building is a great find. It's sturdy and has a very classic brick and beam look." Her dad said as he examined the walls and floor.

"I can just see your customers lining up. It's an amazing place, and I see so much of you in it." Her mom had pride in her eyes, and Hannah felt than same pride well in her chest. They could see the bakery as the gem that it was. Hannah and her parents said goodbye to Zack and Emily and headed outside.

"You picked an excellent location, Hannah. Your vision is strong. I am very proud of you. You have a head for this." Her father said.

"Thanks, Dad. Are you guys ready to see my apartment now?"

"Yes. Let's grab a few things and head up." With hands full of boxes and bags, they walked up the stairs. Hannah let her parents in, and they set down the heavy loads.

"Hannah this view is incredible!" Her mother said walking over to her living room window. She led them around her apartment. "You weren't kidding with how large this is! There is a ton of room. It makes your last apartment feel like a closet. This is bigger than a small house!" Hannah agreed.

They headed downstairs to finish moving her stuff out of the trailer, and Luke walked across the road. He was dressed in uniform today. "You didn't think I forgot, did you?" He said as he walked towards the trailer.

"You are working today." *That's why you weren't at the market.* "You don't have to help. It's fine that you are busy."

"I overslept after working the night shift last night. I had planned on sneaking in for my cookies at the end of the market. Yes, I do. I said I would help, and my word is extremely important to me. If a man has no integrity, he has nothing."

"Very well said." Her dad said coming over. "Drew." He said as he stuck his hand out.

"Luke. I'm Hannah's friend."

"I love that she is making friends with the men in blue. We appreciate everything you do. It's not easy being in law enforcement these days."

"I am lucky to have a supportive town. I wouldn't want to work anywhere else, that's for sure."

Her mom had been eyeing Luke up and down, and Hannah swore she saw inappropriate thoughts flash through her eyes and then disappear. "I'm Hannah's mother, Katherine." She said sweetly.

"It's a pleasure to meet you. You look so much like your daughter." He said and flashed her a smile.

Hannah stood behind her parents and rolled her eyes at Luke. He turned on his charm a bit brighter and snuck a wink at Hannah. "I had promised Hannah I would help move the rest of her stuff in. It's a great apartment she has, but furniture up these stairs is a bit tricky."

"We appreciate that." Her mother said. "Thank you, Luke."

Luke grabbed a box and the four all finished carrying everything that couldn't be counted as furniture upstairs. Then they moved on to her dresser and stools. After they were safely upstairs, only the futon remained. Hannah pulled and Luke pushed the mattress until they got it in the front door. "Which room do you want this in?" He asked without stopping hoping not to lose momentum on the floppy oversized thing.

"Either one of the spare bedrooms works. We can set it up against the wall."

Luke chose the larger of the two rooms and they went down to get the frame. Her dad had managed to disassemble it into three parts and although each of the three parts was incredibly heavy, they got it in the building. Her dad and Luke sat down on the floor to put it back together.

Hannah put on a pot of tea for her and her mother while she sat in the living room unloading the items, she had bought for her at the farmers' market. In the guest room, the topic of conversation had changed from the futon to football. Hannah giggled as they debated the best quarterback of all time. "Your father could use some sports talk. Your sisters' husbands aren't into sports. I think John might be into soccer, but he doesn't watch soccer." Her mom took out the hand-poured candles she had found in all of Hannah's favorite fall scents. She had a fall wreath that had been made of straw. She had found a bottle of Hannah's favorite wine as well as her own. She bought a handmade tea bag holder for Hannah's collection of tea flavors. She found some hand soaps and lotions. The collection poured out over the living room floor.

"Mom you didn't have to get all this."

"I know I didn't, but the people at the market were so lovely, and I wanted to support your new town. I want you to feel my love and presence even though you will be farther away now."

"Oh Mom, I'm not that far away! I always feel your love. I wouldn't be the woman I am without you."

Her mom's eyes welled with tears. "It's so hard to have your baby leave. You will know the feeling someday." Hannah hugged her Mom until her crying stopped and went to grab their cups of tea. Hannah listened to her mom's stories as they sipped. Her mom told her about her group of kids that had been attending her Friday night programs. She talked about BINGO night and who had started attending again after the big fight and who had not. She talked about this week's bowling scores. She told it with such animation that despite not knowing who any of the stories were about, she loved to listen to the tempo of her voice. Hannah relaxed into her couch.

Hannah's dad and Luke stepped out of the backroom. They were in an obvious goodbye dance in which Luke had probably mentioned a few times that he "better be going," and each time he spoke it, he moved a step closer to the door, but the conversation continued. "Dad," she said getting his attention. "Maybe we should let Luke go. He is on duty remember."

"Oh of course, of course." He stuck out his hand, and they did a rough handshake. "Thanks for all the help. Watch out for my daughter now."

"I will of course. You all have a good afternoon now." Luke said as he smiled at Hannah and Katherine and disappeared out the front door.

"I like him. Good people around these parts." Her dad muttered. Hannah smiled. They might be more smitten with Luke than they were with her town. Her parents stayed a few more hours helping unpack, hang items, and hooking up her TV and speaker. Once they were satisfied, she was all safe, they said their goodbyes.

"I'll let you know when opening day is official. My hope is Labor Day weekend. You could come and stay for the weekend if you guys wanted, and then the baby will be here soon. I'll be back for that. Hopefully, I can stay at your house."

Her mom smiled with tears misting her eyes. "Of course, you can stay with us. My baby is all grown up. I can't believe it." They all hugged.

"Drive home safe guys! I love you! Thanks for all the help. See you soon!" She waved as her parents pulled away.

She looked around at her apartment, and at once, the silence of being alone caught in her chest. Hannah wasn't used to that feeling. She loved her freedom and independence. She had never slept over at a boyfriend's house. She hadn't even considered moving in with Mark before their marriage that was never to be even though he was insistent that they do a trial period. Her favorite sports included swimming, and she enjoyed walking. Those were solo activities that required no rules or other participants. She loved spending her days in the company of others, but in her free time, she loved having no constraints.

She thought about her parents driving home talking about their day and all the people they had spoken to, the things they had done, and whether or not their little girl was ready for the big life of a small business owner. It had to be something amazing having a person to share all those pieces of your day with. She had never craved a connection like that. Back in the city, she could just drive to her parents if she wanted company with intimate conversation. Here, once the bakery closed, she was all alone. She sighed.

Almost as if on cue, her phone rang. She saw Abby's face on the screen. "I'm engaged!" She screamed into the phone. Hannah smiled. She had seen this coming. She felt a twinge in her heart to know she couldn't be there to celebrate with Abby like they had when Mark had proposed to her. They had drunk wine and watched romantic movies all night long while they spoke excitedly about a wedding that would never happen. Abby had been a good friend over the years and the loneliness only grew stronger.

"I'm so happy for you, Abby! He is such a good guy. You deserve this!" The conversation went on for the next hour while Abby shared every detail from the proposal and her ideas for the wedding. When they finally hung up the phone, Hannah swore she could hear the silence echo off the walls. She decided to busy herself.

She spent the few hours until dinner unloading boxes and cleaning dishes from the market. She jammed to a pop-rock playlist and had the apartment sparkling and everything put into its rightful place in three hours. She was so grateful for everyone who had helped her move. It had turned a job that may have taken her weeks, into a snap. It saved her so much time that would have been wasted and now could be spent on her new business.

She had a candle burning from her mom. Her books were sitting on a small shelf in the living room. She had placed her fuzzy blanket and slippers on her blue couch. She had her bed made exactly like she preferred it to be and her lamp from Whiskey Leather sat next on the bedside table. She grabbed one of the stools from the kitchen and drug it into her bedroom and placed it by the window.

She didn't know if painting would just come back to her, or even if she would have any vision of what to create, but Woodsburrow was a beautiful place that would hopefully be filled with precious memories for her. That was the perfect combination for lighting a spark. She sat still in the quiet allowing her brain to shut off the busy portion that was always planning, thinking, and wanting, and switched on the deeper area where her ideas and visions came from.

It wasn't like solving a math problem and finding the answer to one hundred and fifty divided by seven. It came from a messier place. When you opened the drawer, ideas would fly at your face. You would need to let one catch your eye and grab it to see if it unlocked the door to more. Then you needed to look around to see if the rest of the details were hidden somewhere in the second glance and hope they came into focus. She relaxed and felt herself being transported to that other world. She picked up a brush and started to paint the watercolor across her canvas.

She was so lost in her faraway domain, that she was startled when the light that shone on her canvas altered in brightness. The sun was going down, and she had been there for hours. She looked at her creation. "Wow." She whispered. She hadn't made anything with this amount of intricate colors and details before. Hannah couldn't believe she still had that gift even though it had been dusty and hidden away on a shelf. It felt good to work her creative brain. That had been something she had forgotten she craved. Her stomach growled. Satisfied with her session, she wandered off into the kitchen.

Hannah opened the fridge. She was tired and just wanted to eat. Her patience for cooking was not there tonight. She opened the pantry and pulled out some linguine noodles. She found a jar of vegan alfredo sauce that was her favorite because she loved alfredo, and it was nice to have something that she knew would be quick and easy and guaranteed to taste good.

She pulled out the frozen shrimp and tossed them in a pan with lemon juice, lemon pepper, onions, and mushrooms. She had broccoli in her fridge that would start to be less likely to be eaten if she let it sit another day. She stuck that on a roasting pan with oil, garlic, salt, and pepper and popped it in the oven. She showered and changed into her giraffe pajamas while dinner cooked.

In twenty minutes, she had a delicious meal, that she enjoyed in her clean house. She set the food down at the wooden table and went to get a glass of wine to go with it. The Blackberry Merlot that her mom had bought her today went perfectly with the white sauce. By the time she was done eating, the moon and stars were shining brightly in her living room. She slipped into her cool fresh sheets, belly full and mind at ease, and she sighed. Hannah drifted to sleep with all thoughts of loneliness a distant memory.

Luke

When Luke had gone to bed the night before, he set his alarm for 10:00 AM. The second part of his shift had been just as busy as the first half and he was dead tired. He had showered before laying down, and when he did a belly flop naked onto his bed, the darkness immediately lulled him to sleep. He didn't move once throughout the night.

As he awoke the next day, instant panic hit his chest. *What time was it?* He grabbed his phone and checked the time, 3:00 PM. He groaned. He had overslept, and he had dinner with his aunt before his shift tonight. He had told Hannah that he would see her in the morning and had completely bailed on her entirely. He didn't know if she had noticed or cared either way, but it wasn't a good start to building a foundation of trust. *How could he make it up to her?* He struggled to fill in the rest of the fuzzy details as he gradually restarted his brain. *It was Saturday!* He had said he wanted to help carry the rest of her stuff into her apartment. He had to leave now if he didn't want to let anyone else down.

Luke jumped out of bed and threw his uniform on. He wouldn't have time to come back and change before work. He texted his aunt with a time they could have dinner and added: "I hope you didn't embarrass me today. I'm running over to help her move her stuff in." His phone immediately vibrated with a response. "I kept my promise. Go get her! See you at five." He let out an exhale. Luke knew it took Molly every little bit of control to not welcome Hannah to the family prematurely. She was dying to have another woman in the family and see him in love. He smiled and shook his head. Molly was a romantic and a sap, but even so, she was one of his favorite people. He hustled to his car and drove down to the bakery.

He saw the trailer parked and still packed full and did an air pump. He didn't miss anything. *Now could he bring himself to interact with her parents and not look like a fool?* He smoothed the wrinkles in his uniform and strolled forward when he saw Hannah approach the vehicle as her parents stood close by. "I promised I would help." He had told her, and her parents had been immediately taken to him. He thought her dad was pretty interesting and reminded himself of his father.

They had gotten caught up in conversation, and he hoped that had won him brownie points with Hannah instead of making her think that he didn't care about being around her. She had noticed he wasn't at the market this morning, which meant she had been looking for him. The thought made the electric connection that had been building between them flare up. The more he spent time with Hannah, the more he was certain he had to have her in his life.

After a heated debate about the Yankee's chance at the World Series, Luke had stolen a glance at the clock, *shoot.* He needed to leave to meet Molly before work. He had started to carefully make his way to the door. This had taken longer than he had hoped, and he had flown out the door without remembering to tell Hannah goodbye. He wasn't sure he was helping his chances or hurting them.

***

Molly was there waiting for him at the Cozy Kitchen when he flew in through the door a few minutes late and prodded him for every detail. "Her apple desserts were to die for. I've had some excellent turnovers in the city, and hers absolutely crushed those." Luke chuckled. "I'll be back to try every apple item she makes."

"Things are not going so well at home, huh?" Luke could tell she was steering the conversation on him to keep it away from whatever problems she was having in hers.

She shook her head. "Counseling has been a joke. He isn't taking any of it seriously. I think there are some big changes in my future. In the meantime, I'm just trying to get to graduation for my baby."

"And then?" Luke asked.

Molly shrugged. "The future is unwritten."

Chapter 13

Hannah

Hannah had been in a crazy transition the last few weeks, but despite the behind-the-scenes work she would be doing to open the bakery over the next two, life seemed boring in comparison, and she was grateful for that. She had arranged a deal with Charlene that she would bake six pies daily until further notice. She had promised to drop them off until her shop opened, and then the first server of the day would begin picking them up on the way into the diner to start their shift. On Monday, Hannah went to drop off chocolate and blueberry pies and spent much longer than she expected chatting with Dawn. When she left, she called the man from the cheese stand whose name was Brandon, and they set up a date for Tuesday night.

He took her to a small petting zoo in a nearby town. It was a clever location that wasn't a typical date, and he was a nice guy. They did have much to talk about and although she might describe him as sweet, or a cutie, there was no chemistry there for her. He was a perfectly okay guy. Hannah could tell that he was having a great time, and she just couldn't muster up the energy to pretend that she was as well. She wouldn't be seeing him a second time. She was relieved when the date was over.

When she arrived home, the streets were dark, and all was quiet. Although the stillness seemed to engulf the entire street, Hannah had the feeling that someone was watching her from someplace hidden. Hannah stilled and looked right and left. She listened quietly as she stood motionless. Although she didn't see anyone, she swore she could hear someone breathing. "Hello?" She called hesitantly. The breathing seemed to have gotten quieter and fear rippled through her veins. She quickly unlocked her door and went inside, making sure she locked it behind her.

On Thursday, she went out to eat with the laid-back businessman from the brewery. He took her to an expensive French restaurant down the river that ran through the town and went south. The location was stunning. The building was quaint. It had a cream color exterior with a bright red door. The plant life they had surrounded the building with made you feel like you had stepped into a hidden garden. They had done an excellent job with the restaurant, and the food was divine. She had ordered multiple appetizers because she just couldn't choose. Each one was delicious, and the leftovers would be plentiful. The conversation flowed with Cal, and although the attraction wasn't strong, he was interesting, and Hannah had a nice time. Hannah was grateful he didn't try to kiss her. They both agreed to go out again next week.

Caroline Grant had brought a load of blackberries and peaches to the bakery. Hannah was more than happy to make her menu around them for the week. "There won't be much more this year. I'll probably have one load of apples and pumpkins I can drop off, other than that, you will have to wait until spring."

"I'll be eagerly waiting! Working with fresh fruits has made a real difference in the flavor of the final piece. Thank you!" She handed Caroline a bag of raspberry muffins she had played around with that week along with a check. It had taken her so many tries to get them just right, that they wouldn't be making it on her market menu that weekend. They were however, the perfect thank you.

"Thank you, Hannah. I have a farm full of hungry men who will appreciate this. See you later!" She disappeared into the street with a big smile.

The farmers' market that weekend was just as busy as everyone had hyped it up to be. In anticipation, she had baked even more than her last week's haul which had been her largest sales so far. Because she had gotten her delivery of peaches and blackberries from the Grant's, she had blackberry muffins, peach scones, peach bourbon Bundt cake, peach almond mini tarts, blackberry hand pies, and her regular selection of doughnuts, cinnamon rolls, and sourdough items. It had taken her the entire day on Friday and into some of the night, but to see it laid out on display, made it all worth it.

Her first customer of the day was Luke. She was thrilled to see him, she realized as her heart jumped like she had received a special surprise. There hadn't been a reason for them to see each other since moving day, and Hannah found she missed his zest in her daily life. He bought a cinnamon roll and a Bundt cake for his mom. He lingered just a bit longer than normal while they talked about nothing in particular. Her heart pounded so loudly as they interacted that she feared she wouldn't be able to hear everything he was saying to her. The line started to become long, so he said goodbye and disappeared into the crowd clutching his cake.

Hannah found herself missing him almost immediately after he walked away. It left her befuddled. She had never craved the company of a man like this before. It had her distracted, and he stayed on her mind the remainder of the day.

The rest of the market flew by. She constantly had customers. She was frequently asked when she was opening her storefront. She told them she would be publishing it in the paper when she knew for sure but expected to be opening Labor Day weekend pending the arrival of the rest of her kitchen.

It was noon before she knew it, and she was left with six doughnuts and two mini tarts. She was satisfied that it had been a phenomenal day. Hannah began taking her setup down and loading it into her Bug. On the driver's seat sat a little brown sack. She looked around, but the sack had been sitting there for more than a few minutes. She wouldn't find anyone walking away. Hannah grabbed it and looked inside.

There was an order of cheese curds and cheeseburger with the works. Someone had left her lunch. It was still warm as if it had been timed for the end of the market. She smiled. Whoever had left it, had been extremely observant. She had been missing lunch on the days of the market due to how busy she was. She got to smell the delicious food trucks, but never made it over to order before they left. She sat down and ate her lunch with a big smile plastered on her face. *Takedown would just have to wait.*

Hannah had started sneaking off to the lake before sunset multiple times a week. Now when she went, however, she made sure to wear her one piece and have towels with an oversized sweatshirt for after. Even if someone wanted to be sick and flip a situation into something it wasn't, they would have a hard time explaining how they thought a perfectly innocent swim with a woman who was more covered up than most, was inappropriate. On the nights she swam, she always felt inspired to paint when she returned home. She had finished a piece of Evergreen River, another of the best night skies she had ever seen while she sat on the beach. She was currently working on a forest-inspired one to give to Amanda when the baby arrived.

She had given up on chasing down Brett at the coffee shop for now. She didn't know why she hadn't heard from him, but it felt intentional. Luke hadn't been able to find out anything specific either. Hannah had heard someone call his name at the grocery store, and she had looked up and seen him turning to the voice. She had said his name to try to catch him and introduce herself, but he glanced over his shoulder, spotted her, and quickly walked away. It was odd behavior, and she wondered if he had seen the fliers and been more bothered by them than most people were.

Hannah wasn't going to spend any more of her energy on it though, at least not right now. If he wasn't interested in speaking with her, it wasn't worth any more effort. The pie orders were going well, and she had made her first bridal shower cake as a self-employed baker. It required the most amount of creativity she had used in the kitchen in quite a while, but it turned out magnificently, and the bride was crying with happiness when she delivered it. It was extremely satisfying to see all her time translate into a grateful customer. She couldn't wait to do more.

When she wasn't pie baking, Hannah had spent her time creating an online footprint for her business. It took time to design her Drury Lane logo online and curate the beautiful backgrounds and posts that were necessary to draw the attention of potential new customers. She made her website live and ensured she had an accessible Facebook, Instagram, and TikTok business account. She also made sure that when people Google searched her, they would receive accurate information from Drury Lane on the main page.

It all took much more time than she anticipated, and although she wanted her customers to be able to find her and her hours when they looked, she didn't plan on being a daily poster. She didn't spend her life online and didn't plan to start living that way now unless she needed the business boost after opening. She hoped to draw crowds who loved her food and had heard about her from their neighbors and friends. After the huge business from the farmers' market and the pre-order book that sat in her lap, she had made plenty of money to get through until early next year. She knew that the fall months brought leaf peepers, and there was nothing better than a warm pastry while you rode or hiked around enjoying the cool fall weather and magnificent colors. She expected a steady flow of tourists until the trees were bare. Then, there would be holiday baking to do. Hannah hoped that all that would be enough buzz that she wouldn't have to waste her time creating content.

Luke

Luke had spent the whole week absorbed with thoughts of Hannah. He tried to keep himself busy, but there wasn't much to do on his days off besides fish. He had attempted to go a few times and had found himself engrossed in a fantasy about Hannah in his bed. Needless to say, he had ended up leaving early and heading into town for a bite to eat. He had dropped in to talk to Zack about the renovations during the week as he had intentionally walked past Drury Lane hoping to see Hannah's face.

Zack had impressive skills as a woodworker. They chatted about his different techniques and what he would be working on next. Although Luke was handy, he would have considered himself more of a tinkerer than a craftsman. Growing up on a farm, you needed to know how to fix most things with what you had. He knew his way around a toolbox, but he had never tried to create something from scratch with such ornate detailing, and an end result that was beautiful instead of just functional. Hannah had spotted talent with the eye of a tiger and had done well hiring them on.

A hurricane couldn't keep Luke from attending the farmers' market that weekend. So, Saturday morning, Luke made sure to set his alarm ensuring he was one of the first people at the market. He knew he needed to show Hannah consistency at the very least if he still didn't muster up the courage to tell her how he felt. She had looked for him the week before, so he knew there was a chance she felt the same. Luckily, when he arrived, there wasn't anyone else lined up at her stand yet. He had time alone with Hannah.

They chatted about her week. She had told him about the website she had built, and how it wasn't her favorite part of the business so far. He also was not interested in the social media scene, but he made a mental note to take a look at it. She had mentioned attending the petting zoo in the area, and even though she didn't say why she was there, the thought of her being on dates with others crept into his mind. He didn't have the right to be jealous about what a woman who had no obligations to him, was spending their time doing. It muddied his mind so severely that he ended up leaving with an entire Bundt cake. He did a mental head slap. He had given Hannah the excuse it was for his mother. He needed to do a better job pre-deciding what he wanted to order so he worked on autopilot instead of ordering random items.

Luke headed to the police station to drop off the Bundt cake. He had been meaning to thank Tori for switching to nights in the coming fall. He was finding it increasingly difficult to function on such skewed sleep schedules. He felt lucky that to have a coworker whose life worked better with those hours. He put the cake in the breakroom and turned to find Tori.

"Hey! What are you doing here? Aren't you sick of this place yet?" She called as she spotted him while walking back to her desk with some coffee that could never be described with the word "fresh."

He sniffed the air. The smell of coffee burnt as thick as mud filled the air. "I brought something that will improve that cup. Do you want me to make you a new pot?" He asked with his nose wrinkled.

"No. I'm in a bad mood, and I'd like to stay crabby for a bit if you don't mind. You bringing me gifts is not helping with that." She snapped.

"Bad day?" Luke asked.

She nodded and sighed. "James and I had a fight while I walked out the door this morning. He has had a heavier load with the kid's summer activities this year. It's been a lot. Raising kids and balancing a career not to mention a marriage isn't easy."

"I can't imagine," Luke answered quietly.

Tori was an amazing woman. He loved working beside her. She had been married for ten years and she and her husband adored each other. It was hard to see them fighting like that. Tori sighed.

"Is there any way I can help? I'm not a kid expert, but I could take them to the park a night if you need a night out together."

She smiled. "That would be nice. We haven't found a reliable babysitter, and some one-on-one time would be infinitely helpful. He has already sent me three apologies, but I'm holding out for a better one."

Luke hugged her shoulder. "Let me know when you want to cash in on that help. In the meantime, get some Bundt cake to go with that nasty cup of coffee."

Luke left the station after serving Tori a giant slice of cake and tossing that awful pot of coffee. He had made a fresh pot after she left the breakroom. He spent his afternoon lazing on the couch while he scrolled through the different social media sites that Hannah had made. It was clear in what she had told him that she didn't have the same excitement concerning them that she had towards her painting and baking, but they were good. Her website was eye-catching and well-organized. It was clear and easy to navigate.

Her Instagram page included a few well-taken photographs and looked professional. He was excited for her to have her opening day. She deserved to feel the support of their community, and he hoped he could do whatever needed to be done to keep any false twisted information about her from circling around the rumor mill. He would have to stay more involved in the gossip than he was used to. The thought gave him a crawling feeling, but it would be worth it to see Hannah with pride on her face.

When night fell, Luke picked up Steele to head out to Bonfire night. It was an event that their buddies threw every year as a sort of unofficial class reunion. Usually, twenty people would attend, and they would catch up on the year. They had chosen a location on the state forest property that had a fire pit the very first year during the summer after graduation because they could drink there, but they continued because of the quiet. Luke always enjoyed being out in the woods without the sound of vehicles or the light of the town against the night sky. Most of the guys that attended had gotten married or even were fathers. They had all settled down from the wild and crazy boys there were as children, but it was fun to gather and talk about the good old days.

Luke and Steele pitched their tent, and an extra for anyone who might need it and went over to get the fire started. They had done the setup every year, and Luke preferred it that way. Steele was always the responsible one, and in thinking ahead, they usually avoided sticky situations from evolving. As they started the fire and set out the beer and snacks, they chatted.

"So, how is it going with Hannah?" Steele asked.

"Well, I haven't told her how I feel yet, but every time I see her, I sound like less of an idiot."

Steele shook his head chuckling. "You know you are overthinking this. When was the last date you were on?"

Luke considered this for a beat. "I had a couple dates with that blonde in May. She was so annoying though. I should be asking you that question Mr. Single and Ready to Mingle."

"This conversation isn't about me. I went on a date a few weeks ago. It turns out, I'm just not ready for that yet. What about before that?" Steele prompted.

"You are not getting out of that comment that easy. We will be talking about that date. Before that was Sadie last fall. We were together for a month before she got upset that I didn't want to go to a wedding with her because I didn't think we were ready. All of it has just turned me off to real dating. It's taking me longer this time to really think that it's worth pursuing the attraction." They looked up as people were starting to join them.

"Ask her," Steele said and walked off to greet the groups that were approaching them with a smile. Luke sighed. Could he get it together before someone else made the first move?

<u>Chapter 14</u>

Hannah

Hannah and Emily had decided to paint the walls on Sunday afternoon. They had more fun than they should have for how sore their bodies would be when they finished. Zack was in the back working on the kitchen since the front was finished, well finished except for the painting. "How did you and Zack meet?" Hannah asked.

"Well, Zack and I have been together since either of us was old enough to be interested in the opposite sex, so however old that was. I have never second-guessed wanting him at my side. Everything is better with him there."

She smiled. *So, Zack and Emily were high school sweethearts.* Hannah thought. That explained how they had such impressive teamwork. They were from Brookville which was south and followed the river. It was a similar-sized town to Woodsburrow.

Emily had always loved art and had studied in community college for a year until she dropped out. "I just wanted to be able to pursue that according to my intuition and not be told what to do from the institution. My mom was furious I didn't finish, but it felt like a waste of money."

"I absolutely get that. My family thought it was ridiculous that I was in a baking program instead of getting a real degree. I didn't have any formal training before then, so I finished the program, but I learned so much more from the different people I worked with through the years. That was the most valuable resource. It's hard when you choose a non-traditional career route."

Emily nodded. "Zack went to work in construction after we graduated. There was a company in town that was just packed with renovation jobs, and the pay was good. Eventually, I had branched out into creating items that were a functional art form, and I was having Zack build me different tables and such to paint or carve. We sold enough that he was able to quit his job. Now we have time to travel and enjoy the outdoors, plus we love what we do when we work. Not to mention we enjoy being able to do it together."

Hannah smiled. "You guys look so in love for being together all those years. You look like a bunch of kids who just started dating."

Emily laughed. "Well, the longer we are together, the more deeply we connect with each other. The chemistry just never fades for us. I am thankful for that."

"I'd love to find that someday. I get so bored with partners easily. I end up getting squirmy and needing my own space. I need to find someone with a lot more zest for life and excitement, and someone I want to share both the special and dull moments with."

"You will find someone. Keep being you. The right one will gravitate to your light."

Hannah and Emily were all full of paint, and the room was finished. "Wow," Hannah said looking around. "Can you believe how good it looks? It's exactly like I pictured it. Do you think you could find me a giant chalkboard for up there? I could write my menu on it."

Emily nodded. "Easy peasy!"

"I can't thank you guys enough." Hannah's eyes filled with tears. "It's out of a dream. I'm going to have my own place! It's amazing."

Zack wandered out of the back. "We will be ready to go by next weekend. Everything is going as planned, and your delivery is confirmed for coming this week?" She nodded. "Make it official then. Even if something comes up, we have some wiggle room."

"I'm taking you guys out to eat on Friday to celebrate."

"That sounds great, Hannah. I'm so excited for you." Emily said.

"I think we are going to call it a night," Zack said. "We will see you in the morning."

***

Hannah placed an ad in the paper announcing her opening on Labor Day weekend. It was set to run in Friday's edition. She called her mom to officially invite her up. Of course, she had already planned on spending the weekend with her. She was almost more excited than Hannah was. They would be arriving Saturday morning and staying through Sunday. Her sisters planned on coming up as well to see the store. It made her feel proud that they cared enough to attend. The support of her family made her hold her head a little bit higher as she counted down the days to the weekend.

She started to prepare the storefront. She drew out her menu with prices and spent extra time creating her image of the oversized bakery hat and muffins. She got the paper towels, bags, boxes, tongs, and all the other little things that made the front come to life. On the storefront window that oversaw the seating, she drew a giant mural. She made an eye-catching drawing of a scene with pumpkins that ran along twisted vines. Sunflowers towered over the sides in full bloom. She made baskets of burgundy mums and giant maple and birch trees with their leaves in vibrant colors. She gave each one of the objects faces and personalities. Vines became arms and legs. Petals became hair. She felt satisfied that the whimsical image would catch anyone's eye. She kept the message simple. "Opening soon!" With Sunday's date written below it, and the hours she would be open the week following.

As she was working on the window, a woman approached her. She was in her early 60's with white hair and a smile that could make anyone feel welcome. "Hi there! My name's Marg. I was wondering if you had any job openings available." It turned out, Marg, had retired early from a cooperate job and moved to Woodsburrow to be around her kids and grandkids. She was loving life outside of the cooperate nonsense, but she wanted something part-time that would keep her busy and would bring her around new people. "I miss some of that."

"I hadn't considered it, but I think it's perfect. I could have you here during the market, and it would give me some time to have some partial days off and fill some orders without having my attention divided. You are hired."

Marg spent the next few hours helping Hannah tidy up as they got to know each other better. Marg had spunk. She had been a climber in her youth and still climbed now, but at a level that was less life-impairing if something should go wrong. She loved to ski and whitewater raft. She had fascinating stories, and Hannah loved her immediately. Marg had been married but divorced in her early 40's. She hadn't remarried and was one of the most beautiful and radiant 60-somethings that Hannah had ever met. She was excited to have Marg a part of her team.

She went out mini golfing with Cal that evening. Although last week, she had enjoyed his company fine, this week, it was clear he was interested in progressing their relationship towards something more physical. Her mind kept drifting to Luke's jokes and his laughter and those lips. She didn't feel as relaxed as she felt when he was around. Hannah recoiled when he tried to advance on her. No spark existed with Cal. It gave her the creepy crawlies to have him touch her. Who had she been kidding? If the man beside her wasn't Luke, then she wanted no one at all. Maybe it was time to give dating a rest.

***

The next day was the delivery of her appliances and items for the kitchen. She woke, early and went down to unlock the front door of the shop. She wasn't sure when Zack was due to arrive, and the delivery time was scheduled for essentially any time today. She felt like a kid on Christmas. She squealed as they brought in and installed her sinks and giant refrigerator, ovens, and stainless-steel countertops. She signed for the delivery, and Zack politely encouraged her to leave until he was done installing the items that hadn't been a part of the installation deal. She listened to his advice and made herself scarce the rest of the day.

By 7:00pm though, everything was complete. The store was ready, and she was ready to start using it. It was audacious and wild that she was a small business owner in her own little town and baking and spreading love again. She paid Emily and Zack, and they went out to celebrate. The bar was packed, but they were able to order drinks and got some mini tacos, French fries, and burgers anyway. She was going to miss seeing her friends daily. The last market was this weekend, so they wouldn't be seeing each other there either until next year. They had been hired for another big job after someone saw how grand Hannah's store had looked from the street. Whiskey Leather had a busy and bright future ahead of them, and Hannah couldn't have been prouder.

Hannah drank more than she usually did. The alcohol was making her feel giggly and free. She was so happy that this day had finally come, and her friends were having great success as well. A few men had approached her to buy her drinks and ask for her number. She accepted the drinks, and shared a few dances, but didn't waste her time giving them her number. Hannah felt bored with the men she had met lately. The excitement from her bakery kept her more engaged than their boring pick-up lines. Eventually, it was time for Emily and Zack to leave. "Do you want us to give you a ride home?" Emily asked.

Hannah shook her head. "I just have to walk around the corner. I'll be fine! You guys get home safe. Call me sometime soon!" They waved goodbye, and Hannah stayed at the bar. She wanted to have one more drink before she went home.

She felt a shadow drift over her on her left side. "Hannah the magnificent, how are you this evening?" Luke had also been drinking and his voice had a looser tone than it normally possessed. Hannah's smile brightened and her heart fluttered. Her body felt like it was covered in goosebumps with his body so close to hers she could feel the heat radiating off it. "I think you are the most popular woman in this bar tonight." He smiled and Hannah felt his eyes looking deeply into hers.

Her cheeks flushed pink. "You are drunk, Luke." She said as shivers shot through her.

"Maybe. But even drunk I can tell you don't want to spend time with any of these clowns. I saw your friends leave. Do you have a ride home?"

Hannah shook her head. "No, I'm walking."

"Walking? When the entire bar population has been watching you and desperately devising a plan on how to be the one who takes you home tonight? No. I'll get my coat and take you." He closed their tabs and went to collect his coat. Hannah hadn't even had time to react, and she felt flattered by his protectiveness.

The women who were sitting at the bar had been eyeing Luke up as well, and a few approached him as he walked over to his jacket. They placed their hands on his arm and angled their bodies close. Luke smiled politely, removed their hands, and made space between them as he put his coat on and tried to move his strides towards Hannah. His eyes immediately went to Hannah's and confidently held her gaze. He excused himself from the woman. He said goodbye to his corner of buddies and returned to Hannah.

"Well, I'm not the only popular one in the bar tonight." She replied with a grin. "Don't let my safety make you miss out on a good time." She added as she raised her eyebrows at him.

He looked at her intently as he searched for the words. "I'm exactly where I want to be tonight." He said simply, hooked her hand around his elbow, and led her out the front door.

Luke

Luke couldn't believe his luck when Hannah entered the bar. Thursday night before Labor Day was traditionally a night the locals went out to celebrate the end of summer tourism. Autumn had become more and more popular over the years, but traditions were engraved deeply into the roots of Woodsburrow. It was also the last weekend that Luke would be on nights, and he was excited. With all those reasons to celebrate, Luke had gone out solo. Steele's family did a campout in his parent's backyard for Labor Day weekend and everyone attended. Christopher was in town along with Emma and Mike, so he wouldn't be seeing his right-hand man. Clay and Matt were already there when he entered and waved him over.

"Happy See-yah night!" Clay greeted him as he gave him a hand-hug handshake.

"It's been a doozy of a summer this year," Luke said shaking his head.

"I've heard a ridiculous amount of chatter on the scanner this last two weeks," Matt added.

"Every shift has just been packed with something to do. I go back to days though soon, and I am ready. Night shift is wild. Tori is such a badass for loving it. I'm ready to get some fishing in and not sleep like a bat."

Clay laughed. "I'm thankful I went into teaching. The whole summer off is a win." The conversation changed to baseball, and more friendly faces entered the bar.

Luke loved to be surrounded by people he knew. The noise level in the bar continued to grow as the drinks flowed freely and the night went on.

Luke wasn't there long before Hannah walked into the bar. Despite the sheer overstuffed volume in the bar, she stuck out like a sore thumb. Luke could have spotted her a mile away. She had a huge smile on her face and looked radiant. Luke thought he might lose his mind. He watched her saunter in obviously elated with life. This weekend was a big weekend for her. It was the biggest market of the year and opening weekend at Drury Lane, all on top of the holiday.

He loved how relaxed she seemed despite the amount of stress she was obviously under. She was full of confidence and positivity, and it was sexy. He watched from across the room as he sipped his beer. He could see all the heads turn and look at her as she mingled throughout the bar. Men looked at her like she was a piece of red meat. He could almost see the drool running down their faces. Many approached to buy her a drink and each time his fists remained clenched until they left her side. He drank his beer quickly trying to drown his feelings. He turned back to see Hannah saying goodbye to her friends, and she was left alone. He could see the men who had been watching her prepping themselves to approach her. He had liquid courage flowing through his veins, and he had enough. He left his group and strode over.

The buzz of the alcohol helped him steady his thoughts as he convinced Hannah to let him walk her home. His thoughts brought him to Steele's words and how he believed that he could do this. Maybe that was it. He needed to talk to Hannah like she was a friend. So, he let the floodgates go and talked about anything that came to mind. When they had finished the walk to Hannah's apartment, his thoughts drifted away from friendship to much darker things. He smelled vanilla on her skin and watched her beautiful lips as they parted to speak to him. He wanted her right here and now. It took every ounce of control in his body to tell her good night. He left her apartment and decided to take the long walk home to cool off.

Hannah

Hannah knew there was more to be said between the two of them. The chemistry was strong, and the tension could be sliced by a butter knife. She had never felt such an intense connection with a man before, and the amount of excited her body was becoming for something as simple as a touch of his elbow was making her thoughts blurry. As they walked though, they didn't speak of chemistry or a possible romance, Luke talked about hockey and camping, of the tallest peaks he wanted to climb, and the best trails he had run on. Hannah asked questions about the area, the trails, and the views. Luke returned with questions about the bakery and her interests and favorite music. He swore he would be there for opening day and made her promise to make his favorites, her cinnamon rolls and chocolate chip cookies.

It was like spending time with a best friend. A friend that also made you feel like you wanted to tear their clothes off. Hannah had never experienced that with a man she was interested in. It was clear he had the adventurous spirit she had been craving in a partner. When he walked her to her front door, he whispered into her ear. "Goodnight, Hannah. Sweet dreams." Then he turned, shoved both his hands deeply into his pockets, and walked back the way they had come. Hannah was left wondering if she had imagined the entire thing and went inside.

She didn't know why she felt so interested in a man who at this point had said nothing about being interested romantically in her. He hadn't tried to kiss or touch her inappropriately. He didn't call or text her in an effort to make conversation. He politely visited her farmers' market stand, helped her move some boxes, and got her home safely a few times. She needed to stay focused on the present. *Luke was just a nice guy and a very valuable friend.* She reminded herself. But as she slept that night, she dreamed of being under the sheets with Luke exploring much more than just friendship.

Chapter 15

Luke

Luke slept until noon the next day. He made some scrambled eggs and bacon and ate the bowlful in his boxers on his couch. He had planned on doing nothing today, and it was glorious. He was still in his boxers when the mail arrived. He grabbed the paper from the mailbox attached to his porch and brought it back in to the couch he had spent the entire morning on. When he got to the personal opinion section, he wanted to strangle Matt. *How could he print something like this in the paper?* It crossed the line and insinuated more than was appropriate. He was hot and threw the paper down on the ground. Luke was ready to give Matt a piece of his mind. He paced around the house for the next hour. Whatever he was going to do next was not going to be done naked. He jumped in the shower and scrubbed until his skin was raw.

Luke dressed and called Matt. He picked up on the second ring. "Hey man, what's up? Wicked turnout last night, huh?"

"How dare you print something that devastating to a small business owner of our community!" He immediately yelled into the phone. "I'm embarrassed that you chose to represent our community, and the paper in that manner. There is nothing okay about that. I highly suggest that you consult your lawyer because depending on how my superiors see it, you may need it." He hung up the phone. Now he would need to figure out how to tell Hannah.

Hannah

Woodsburrow was packed with tourists in town for Labor Day. Every neighboring campground was at capacity. Hotels had no vacancies. Boats covered Lost Lake and Evergreen River. The downtown shops had a constant flow of customers.

Hannah baked the entire Friday for the farmers' market and started prepping for opening day on Sunday. It was hard to watch all the business she was missing pass by outside, but it would be foolish to skip the market tomorrow just because she was impatient to open. She would make more in the four hours there than she would all day open in her shop. She was breaking in her kitchen though, and she was able to bake twice as fast as she had over the last two months. It was magnificent.

She had pies upon pies prepped to bake on Sunday that went into the freezer. She made doughnut dough that would need to be popped into the fryer. She made four types of sourdough bagels, English muffins, and whole wheat sourdough bread boules along with the white boules. Hannah whipped up cookie dough that would be ready to bake and made plain cinnamon rolls along with ones with walnuts and raisins. She rolled out sugar cookies and made them shaped like maple leaves and frosted them after cooling with maple frosting in vivid reds and oranges. She made peach and apple kringles. She finished her blackberry scones with beautiful shining icing.

At the end of the day, Hannah felt like a real baker again, and her kitchen looked like a real bakery's kitchen. She cleaned up her mess before she ambled up to her apartment to soak in her tub and put on some lounging clothes. The day had been long, the baking had been endless, her legs and feet ached, but she had been both efficient and consistent. It was everything she had been dreaming it would be.

When she lowered her body into her giant soaking tub filled with bubbles and vanilla scent, she signed. She sat until the aching subsided changed into her pajamas and went into the kitchen to make herself dinner. Hannah was exhausted. She had whipped up a pizza crust when she had made her bread dough earlier. She rolled it out and placed it on her pizza stone. Hannah topped it with sauce, and freshly grated mozzarella, and sprinkled pepperoni slices all over it. While that cooked, she spun together a Caesar salad. She ate her salad at the table while her pizza baked. She had poured herself a glass of the other wine bottle her mother had bought and was sipping it quietly. Thinking of her mother reminded her of her candle, so she strolled over and lit it. She looked over at the pizza's timer, ten minutes left yet. Hannah decided to do a walkthrough of the house and ensure all was ready for her parent's arrival.

She had made both spare rooms with the bedding sets that had arrived in the mail. She had ample fresh towels and had gone for groceries the day before. She quickly ran the vacuum and tidied her room up. She was shutting the vacuum off and nodding to herself in a satisfied manner, as the timer went off. Hannah pulled the pizza out of the oven and heard a knock on the door.

Hannah peeked out the peephole and saw Luke in his plain clothes standing outside her door. His hands were in his pocket as he nervously shifted his weight. Hannah opened the door. "Luke? What are you doing here?"

He looked at her. "From that reaction, I can tell you haven't read the paper. Can I come in? Is that pizza?" He asked smelling the air.

Hannah smiled. "Of course. Come in. No, I haven't had time to read the paper. I've been working all day. I can't say that I am in the habit of reading it even if I'm not busy though. What's up?"

He sat down, shuffled through the pages to the one he was looking for, and slid it over to her. "Here." He said pointing. He appeared to be pointing to an opinion section.

Someone had anonymously written up a column about Hannah and her new bakery. They talked about how she had been fired from many jobs back in the city for being incompetent. It spoke about her working at a dancer's club for money because she hadn't been able to cut it as a baker. It called her food from the market mediocre, and it urged people to rethink visiting her opening this weekend.

Hannah sat frozen unable to speak. "Who would do this? I've never done anything malicious to anyone in my whole life. Why would the paper print this? This isn't like a restaurant review. It's defamation of my name and my business."

Luke agreed. He reached for her hand and held it. His hand was warm, and his fingers enveloped her like he was trying to give her the strength she felt like she didn't have.

Tears started to pour down her face uncontrollably. "Everything has been going so well." She sobbed. "Everyone seems to like my food at the market. I have special orders lined up through the rest of the year. My shop is ready to go. Who would say that I worked as a stripper? I volunteered at a homeless shelter frequently in the city. I haven't been in trouble for anything in my entire life. I never got fired from a job before. Unless you count putting in my two weeks' notice and being told not to return. All of this is lies."

Luke spoke softly. "I know it is. Hannah if someone is trying to ruin your business, we can catch them. When they step a toe out of line, we will get them." He pulled her into his chest and rubbed her shoulder.

They sat there not talking and not moving as the minutes passed. Hannah listened to his heart beating and felt the calm that seemed to radiate off of Luke and flow through her body until her crying slowed. "Do you want to stay for pizza?" She asked.

He grinned. "I thought you would never ask. I'm starving."

Hannah giggled but Luke's stomach gave a loud grumble. "Let me get you a slice before you wither away." She teased and brought the pizza over to them at the table. They ate for a while as Hannah thought. *Who around her could be this angry with her?* The article was made to look like a restaurant review, but an angry one. It wasn't appropriate to comment on any of those things, especially if it wasn't true. She hadn't seen or heard anyone lurking about since that feeling of being watched the other night. "Luke, I don't have any clue who could have written that.

I know I had that note weeks ago, but we don't even know those two things are connected. I haven't had any negative encounters with people. I went on a few casual dates, but those people never even knew I was the baker in town." Luke watched her as she spoke. She thought his eyes had gotten wider when she mentioned going out on dates, but if they had, he had returned them to a neutral size before she could decide if that comment had bothered him.

"I've made a point to be around too, and I haven't seen anyone." So that was it then. He was around trying to catch the bad guy and be a hero, not because he was sexually attracted to her. Hannah pushed a strand of her blonde hair behind her ear. "We are just going to have to keep our eyes peeled. You are likely to see lots of new and old faces in the next few days. Keep an eye out for anything odd."

Hannah nodded. "I will."

They had eaten the entire pizza when Luke decided it was time for him to go. "I'll see you tomorrow at the market." He told her and reached out and tucked the strand she had touched earlier behind her ear. She looked up startled by the touch, and they stared at each other intently. Finally, Luke shoved his hands deeply into his pockets again. "Good night." He said and he left and disappeared down the street.

***

Hannah was distracted the next day at the market. Her parents were due to arrive along with possibly her sisters. *Someone was trying to make her look incompetent and even worse, like a bimbo, and what on Earth was going on with her and Luke?* She worried that the article would scare off her business, but luckily, most of her business today would be tourists, and even more luckily, an article like that in a small town didn't ruin your business, it increased your sales. She had a hard time keeping up with the customers and the noise level of the market was much louder than it usually was. Music from a soft rock band jammed from the speakers, but even that was muffled in the sound of the crowd. She briefly said hello to her parents and went back to filling orders. She hadn't even gotten close to making it until the market closed and had sold every single item that she had baked for the day.

Hannah cleaned up her space at 11:00. She couldn't believe it. She wandered off to meet up with her parents who were sitting by the food trucks listening to the band. Couples had begun dancing and clapping broke out after almost every song. She ordered some spicy tacos with a Doritos hard shell and sat with her parents. "Is anyone else coming?" she asked her mom loudly over the music.

She shook her head no. "Piper is sick, and Amanda isn't allowed to travel per her doctor. They both sent cards though."

Hannah smiled. She had wanted to show off her new business venture to her sisters who had mocked her when she started baking professionally, but they both had important lives. Piper needed her mommy, and she wanted Amanda to have an easy delivery after the fertility issues they had struggled with for so long. She understood. They sat and listened to the band and Hannah ate her tacos. Before long, a man slipped onto the bench beside her. She glanced over.

Luke was eating BBQ ribs and acting like he belonged right where he sat. "Umm, hi?" Hannah said.

He looked at her with BBQ on his chin and smirked. "Hey. I went to order my usual, and you weren't there so I figured you had to be here with the food."

"And so, you thought you would join me?"

"Yes." He said wiping his chin and continuing to eat his ribs.

Hannah smiled and went back to her tacos and the strawberry shake she had decided she needed. Her dad greeted Luke, and they chatted like best chums. Hannah laughed, shook her head, and decided that Luke being Luke was one of his best qualities. It felt comfortable to have him here.

Before long, they had been invited to join Luke's parents at a supper club called Crazy Eights, and her dad excitedly accepted. After Luke left, and the three went to Lost Lake for some time in the sun. Hannah and her mom people-watched and laughed at some of the crazy decisions being made that day, her favorite was the family with the queen-sized blow-up mattress being pulled behind the Pontoon.

They went back to her apartment, and Hannah unloaded the remnants of the day. She threw the dishes into her commercial dishwasher and went upstairs to join her parents. They had placed their bags into the spare bedroom with the futon. They were now comfortably settled on the couch and had taken over the TV. National Geographic was on, and they were debating the narrator's knowledge of the subject he was speaking about. Her parents were sitting on the couch leaning into one another like they always did. Her mom laughed as her dad did an impression of a British man, which was terrible. Hannah's heart felt light. They had come twice now to show their support, and to Hannah, there was nothing more valuable that they could give her. She changed into a blue jumpsuit with a ruffled V-neck for dinner and settled onto the other couch.

It felt good to just lounge that afternoon. Hannah laughed through the funnier impersonations her father did like the monk and rolled her eyes at the not-so-great ones like the islander. Hannah needed this downtime with her family at her side after the week she had had. It was nice to have the walls filled with laughter, and the expectations be nothing but what it was. Her parents were ready to leave for Crazy Eights early. Her dad had never been a minute late for anything in his entire life. They pulled into the parking lot and were walking to the front door when Luke pulled in with his parents.

Drew and Katherine were soon introduced to Bob and Becky. They were the sweetest people Hannah had ever met. Becky had the most beautiful smile plastered on her face. She was a stunning woman and would turn the heads of watchers of any age. Her husband Bob was tall broad-shouldered and soft-spoken. He had dark hair and stood firm and steady. He tended to hold his wife's hand, and Becky frequently shot smiles that were just for him. They sat down to dinner, and Hannah learned that Luke's parents had been farmers their entire life. They had a very successful beef farm that they had converted to buffalo which did even better, landing them retired. They liked to take cruises and camp in the RV. Bob had a dog named

Bryant who was a hound dog and mostly enjoyed sleeping. No questions came up about who Hannah was, why Luke was spending time with her, or why they were all around this table together. Hannah didn't know the answer to most of the questions herself, but she was happy that they didn't enter into this conversation.

She enjoyed spending her evening time with the Wrights and so did her parents. Hannah ordered gnocchi with a ricotta filling and vodka sauce. She couldn't believe the quality of the food from this supper club. It was a gem. Afterward, she wanted one of her desserts.

"A chocolate chip cookie would be perfect right now," Luke spoke to her so only she could hear. She looked over at him surprised. He smirked. "You were thinking it too, weren't you? You aren't very good at hiding the emotions and thoughts on your face."

"Number one, I wasn't trying to hide them. Number two, I know, and number three yes, I was thinking one of my desserts would round this meal off perfectly." She said with a smile.

"It's true." He said and winked.

Luke

After watching Hannah break down from the article in the paper, Luke felt a primal instinct to protect her. He wanted in. He wanted to watch her in her glory and in her pain. When he saw her eating with her parents at the market with that beautiful laugh that lit up her entire face, he knew her day had been a success. *She deserved it.* He prayed she would have just as much luck with the official opening on Sunday. He prayed with all that he had that the community would show her support. He ordered some food and sat down next to her.

The relief he felt with her body relaxed next to him was undeniable. He began to feel at home there, and her dad was just as enjoyable to talk to as he had been the last time they had talked. The conversation turned to local fishing spots and restaurants and without thinking, he invited them to dinner. His mom had been clueless about his attraction to Hannah, but after this, it would be crystal clear what his intentions were. *How was she going to be able to maintain her cool?* He didn't know, but he swore the woman in his family was going to give him a heart attack someday.

After lunch with the Jones', he called his mom. "Hey, Mom."

"Lukey." She said. "What's up?"

"Are you and Dad busy tonight?"

"No, I don't think so, why?"

"I just invited Hannah and her family to dinner with us." The phone was silent. "Mom?" He asked.

"Luke, is there something you want to tell us?" She asked.

"Well, not yet there isn't, but I wouldn't be surprised if there is something to say in the coming weeks." The high-pitched sound of his mom squealing into the phone made his ears ring, and he moved it away from his ear. "Mom, you are going to ruin things before we even start anything if you can't keep your cool." He muttered.

"I can't wait to meet them! What time did you tell them?" She said excitedly.

Chapter 16

The next day Hannah rose at her typical baker's time, early. She pulled out the items she had started on days before and had doughs rise, warmed up the oven and oil fryer, and mixed fresh batches of what she hadn't started yet. She couldn't believe how excited she was this day had finally come. Drury Lane was opening in mere hours. She hoped that the article hadn't scared off the people who lived in this town. She hated constantly worrying that someone was trying to ruin her business before she had a chance to get started. She had never been so happy as she had been in this time she had been living here, and with every fiber of her being she wanted to be baking here and living in this town for years to come.

Hannah had soft jazz streaming through the speakers of the store. The lights were on a dim setting as she walked to and from the kitchen in the back to the displays in the front. Her excitement grew as the clock ticked on. She hummed to herself as she carefully placed item by item. Her display came alive with three types of cookies, peach pies, fresh doughnuts, sourdough loaves, cinnamon rolls, apple fritters, blueberry, apple cinnamon, and peach muffins. She had peach turnovers, and apple ones had their entire row. She whipped up some more items so she could bake later in the day if it was needed.

With five minutes to spare, she dusted herself off and went to the front of the store. The sunrise was big and bold through the front windows with vibrant purples and reds. She closed her eyes and made one final wish that today was a good day. She took a deep breath and opened her eyes. She could hear soul pouring out of the speakers, and the room around here smelled like something out of a dream. Satisfied, she knew she couldn't have done anything more. At 8:00 AM, she unlocked the doors.

Her first customer arrived at 8:15. It was an elderly woman, who was in her early 80's. A man who was probably in his 50's strode around the Cadillac and helped her to her feet. He walked her in with his arm wrapped around her. She had her purse slung around his shoulder. Hannah greeted the woman with a friendly good morning. She smiled widely and returned the welcome. The man excused himself and asked to use the restroom, and Hannah directed him to the back of the store. Hannah and the woman proceeded to chat about the items in the display case. The woman said "I've always had a sweet tooth. My doctor says it's not good for my health, but I think he's wrong. I was married for thirty years and had a good marriage but being with Charlie makes me feel youthful again. Everyone needs to get themselves a Charlie. There's nothing sweeter than a handsome young man in your bed." Hannah smiled holding back laughter.

This woman had found the secret to her youth and longevity and had found it in a man who was 30 years her junior. "Never underestimate the power of good romance." She grinned like the cat who ate the canary and ordered two of everything in the case. As she began to fill a takeout box, Charlie appeared purse still flung proudly over his shoulder.

"Did you order, Evelyn?"

"Yes, dear. I think we will just try two of everything."

Charlie smiled a knowing smile. "That sounds great." He handed Evelyn her purse, and Evelyn paid.

"It was nice meeting you guys!" Hannah called as they walked out the door. She hoped she would see them again. Something about that woman's cheeky smile and the glow on her wrinkled cheeks brought Hannah a lot of hope. If this woman could find love in such an unlikely place, there certainly was hope for everyone else. Charlie had seemed more than content to be her side piece. Hannah chuckled and filled the display back up again.

At 8:30, her parents came down the steps and checked out the store. "Oh, Hannah! It's perfect!" Her mom declared with her arms in the air.

"You did a fine job kiddo." Her dad added with pride.

Her mom bought a few doughnuts, and her dad got a cinnamon roll. "We are going out shopping downtown while you are open this morning. Do you need anything while we are out? What time do you close?"

"Two today, and not that I can think of."

"Your dad is going fishing this evening with Luke and Bob, so it's just the two of us for dinner. I'll cook something up for us."

"Thanks, Mom. Have fun Dad. See you guys later!" They went out the front and continued down to the elusive coffee shop.

By nine, people had started coming in droves and didn't stop. Doughnuts flew off the shelf in dozens, and cookies went in packs as well. Her pies sold like hot cakes, and muffins in packs of six. People were buying in bulk for their weekend events, and Hannah was thrilled. Whit and Bri had arrived and were impressed. "Hannah! You have transformed this place! It's fantastic!" Bri said.

"I can't believe you baked all these today. It smells heavenly. I swear it's something out of my dreams!" Whit added. Hannah was thankful to have their support. She enjoyed their company, and it was nice to be around women her age. "We will take a dozen cookies. Some of each flavor." Hannah was happy to load the still-warm cookies into a box and handed it over to Whit. They opened the box and inhaled.

"Oh my God. Who needs a man when you have cookies?" Bri said. They all laughed, but Hannah wasn't sure that even a fresh cookie every day could compare to the touch of a man. The two paid and wished her luck. It was eleven when Luke ambled in and her breath caught in her throat. Somehow, he had picked a small lull, and Hannah felt pure happiness at seeing him in her shop.

"Hannah Jones. Your bakery has had lines of people on the streets all day. How is it going?" His face was full of pride.

She nodded with a smile on her face. "Really well. I am going to need to bake the overflow items I made just in case in the back. I couldn't be happier."

He hesitated and studied her for a few minutes, and Hannah's heart quickened with what he might say next. He swallowed softly and smiled. His eyes went to her display case. He scrutinized every item. Hannah's heart pounded in her chest with him standing this close to her. He was dragging his feet, and she knew it, but whatever he was avoiding saying, he didn't say it. Instead, he ordered one cinnamon roll and one chocolate chip cookie. He shrugged. "Classics. If I had one of your cinnamon rolls and one chocolate chip cookie for the rest of my life, it would be a life well lived." He looked her deeply in the eyes.

"I guess that means I'll see you tomorrow, then?" She asked quietly.

"I wouldn't miss it." He answered. He turned and walked out the door without looking back.

Hannah snuck into the back to run some dishes through her dishwasher and put a few dozen cookies into the oven along with some loaves of bread that were ready to go in. She started items for tomorrow and busied herself in the kitchen until the bell at the front entrance dung. She brought her freshly finished cookies with her to the front. She could see the people coming in from the streets in a new mob. "Fresh cookies! I'll take those." The first woman in line exclaimed. Hannah was more than happy to bag them for her and moved on to help the next customer. It was two o'clock before she knew it, and she locked the door and let out a "Whoop!"

She went through the swinging doors to the front and cleaned up the surfaces. She bagged up the few muffins that hadn't sold and scribbled a reduced price on them for the next day. She spent the next hour in the kitchen prepping for tomorrow, cleaning, and putting away dishes. When she was done, the kitchen sparkled, and she had greatly reduced the time she would need to spend here in the morning. She left the kitchen and headed up to her apartment.

Her mom was not back yet, so she showered and put on her baggy black sweatpants and her dark pink sweatshirt. She slipped on her fluffy slippers and sat down on the couch with her white blanket and a book. Her mom strolled in at four, groceries in hand and some bags from Driftwood and the clothing boutique. "I'm making my curry!" She announced as she sat her bags down in the kitchen.

"Yum! That sounds perfect." She was feeling like all things comfort, and there was nothing more soothing than her mom's curry.

Opening day was out of the way, it had gone well. She hadn't been ruined by whoever was out to destroy her, at least not today. A few people had mentioned how rude the article was and how they had contacted Matt at the paper and had shared their disgust at him printing something so atrocious. It had been mortifying to discuss with people who were new faces to her, but it was relieving to hear that people were not buying whatever image this person was trying to portray. Now she wanted to curl up on this couch and hang out with her mom for the rest of the day. The interactions with customers had gone well, but the day had been draining. "How did your first day go?"

"Really well. I was steady for almost all day and people were buying for their Labor Day parties, so I went through nearly everything I had and then some."

"I am so proud of you for being brave enough to follow your dream like this. I've never wanted to do anything wild or out of the box, and sometimes I think my life might be too boring and predictable."

"But aren't you happy?" She asked her mother.

She nodded in response. "I am. I love your father and the life we have lived together thus far. I love my community and being a part of my children's and grandchildren's lives. Those things all bring me joy. I just don't have that extra gear that you have to chase after dreams. "

"You have that sparkle and audaciousness that no one else has. Remember when you were nine and insisted on wearing your fairy princess outfit to school? You wanted to have the whole get-up on., the wings, the crown, the sparkly slippers, and the tutu. I tried reasoning with you for an hour. There was no reason to wear a costume to school in April, but you insisted. Your little face was so determined. I gave in and let you wear it, but I was afraid you would be teased all day long and you would come home in tears with a note from your teachers."

Hannah grinned. "The teachers loved it. I was the fairy princess helper all day, and the other kids thought I was the coolest kid in school."

"You always were one of the most loved kids after that. You always wanted everyone included in your birthday parties. Multiple boys asked you out to dances every year, and never once did you alter who you were to please anyone."

"I won't ever change myself for someone else either. I am who I am. If that doesn't work with someone, then I am in the wrong place."

"I am sorry I gave you such a hard time about Mark. He is so much like your brother-in-law that I thought he was perfect for you. When you first brought him home, he treated you like you were the only woman in the entire world. He practically worshipped you. You seemed to like that attention and support, but I can see now what you mean about not bringing more of his own personality to the relationship. You deserve a partner, not a fan club. You need someone to help you chase your dreams and lead you down new and exciting roads. Someone you enjoy spending time with and want to bring to family events because you are proud of them. Someone adventurous and wild enough to match your energy, but soft enough to honor your emotions. Mark didn't possess those qualities, and no matter the effort I put in, it wouldn't have felt right to you."

"Thank you, Mom. I'm sorry it took me so long to realize he wasn't the one. Everyone was so attached to him at that point. That felt like the worst part of the breakup, letting everyone down. After the engagement, every imperfection he had just surfaced and glared in my face so strongly I couldn't ignore it any longer. Any positives that I had seen in him, I couldn't see anymore, no matter how hard I tried. I dreaded our time together. I never wanted to plan the wedding. It just felt wrong. I knew it wasn't right."

Her mom nodded. "I thought it was strange that you didn't want to talk about the wedding. I thought it was just you being you though, and maybe some nerves. When your father proposed, I couldn't stop looking at my engagement ring. I loved the way it gleamed in the light. The heaviness and foreignness I felt on my finger made me constantly fiddle with it to see if it was really there. It was like a dream. It was a more intense bond than I had ever felt before that, and I felt a newfound reason to be at his side. I was so proud to be his fiancé. We started planning the wedding almost immediately."

"I never felt any of that," Hannah added.

Her mom nodded. "I am sorry I gave you a hard time about the Golden Goose, too. I had no idea you had dreams for any of this. I thought the Goose was what you had always wanted."

"I did strive to work there, but once I started, I realized it was a terrible place to be. I almost immediately started dreaming up my place. That was when I moved into that studio with the cheaper rent. Pierre was a toxic boss. He was so controlling over everything from the baking process to customer interactions. The days were long. The customers were rude. This place has been so different. Everyone has been so grateful. I've had many repeat customers already. None of them have complained that the color is wrong, or the size is off a centimeter. The customers at the Golden Goose liked to complain just to remind you that they were better than you, to make you feel like some kind of servant. They were terrible humans. They treated the staff that ran their households even worse. I wondered for a while if I even wanted to be a baker at all."

Her mom shook her head. "That's terrible. I wish you would have shared some of that with me."

"I thought not talking about it would make it easier to stomach as I worked through my obligation and saved my money. I completely shut that life off when I left the doors for the night."

She nodded. "It's probably for the best. The Goose has had some less-than-perfect mentions in the paper lately. It wouldn't have been worth staying at some place you hated for the prestige of it all."

"That's strange. I don't know when the last time was that they had bad press. Pierre would do anything he needed to avoid it. I'm glad I am not a part of that. I'm much happier here."

"I can see that you have exactly what you need around you." Hannah felt like she was speaking about more than just Drury Lane. "Has Luke told you how he feels?" She asked.

"Luke? What do you mean?" Hannah replied.

"Yes, the man who seems to appear in thin air every time we visit and acts like it's as natural as breathing to be by your side."

Hannah's cheeks burned with embarrassment. "He hasn't said anything to me about anything more than friendly banter. We haven't been dating or anything." Her mother smiled.

"And how do you feel?"

"Like he is the first man I've met that seems exciting. He is entertaining and adventurous. He is helpful and supportive and seems to know I need him near even when I don't ask. I can't stop thinking about him, but I don't know that he wants anything from me other than friendship."

"Maybe he is telling you more than you think." Her mom added.

Hannah shrugged. She hoped Luke could sense the unlabeled something that floated between them. The bond seemed to pull them back together often and strongly. She pushed the thought away. He had yet to announce any feelings towards her, and she doubted he would today or even tomorrow. It was best not to focus on thoughts that were outside of her control.

While her mom finished making the curry, they continued their conversation in the kitchen. Hannah loved the warming smells of curry. It was the baked good of dinners. She ate hungrily and helped herself to a second bowl. When they finished their food, her mom showed her the wares and outfits she had bought while she was out. She appeared to like Hannah's new town, and that warmed Hannah's heart. An hour later, her father came back from fishing with an ice cream pail of fileted fish. Apparently, it had gone quite well. Her dad enjoyed his time spent with Luke and Bob. They had planned to go fishing again on their next visit. He ate a bowl of curry and joined the women in the living room to relax. By nine, Hannah couldn't keep her eyes open any longer. She excused herself and went to bed.

Her parents left the next day around lunchtime. Her heart ached again when they said goodbye and she watched them walk to their car. She was thankful that the customers were there to keep her busy. Hannah's second day had been busy like the first with people picking up goodies on their way out of town. She sold more savory items that were well suited to eating at brunch than the day before. Marg came in for a few hours before closing to get her feet wet at the register while Hannah was able to clean up in the back. She prepared her items for baking the next morning and was able to leave a little after two. Luke had come in for his cinnamon roll and chocolate chip cookie in uniform earlier than yesterday and had said little.

Hannah left after closing and went directly to spend the remainder of the afternoon at the beach which was now cleared of all the commotion the holiday weekend had brought. She swam laps and settled on the sand with her book as the sun dried her back. She lay contentedly for hours. When the sun was setting, and it began to get harder to see, she went back to her apartment. She again felt the sense of eyes on her and a strange sound of metal clanking made her jump as she unlocked her door and hurried inside. *Was she imagining this fear or was someone out there?* Hannah put on some music to drown her thoughts and tried to settle in for some painting time followed by a bowl of her mother's leftover curry.

***

The next few weeks flew by with every day feeling the same. She went full-on fall flavors, and everything sold like hotcakes. The town loved having a bakery with fresh homemade goods, and Hannah adored her customers. She had enjoyed baking with the fresh produce from Caroline and had already placed her orders to continue in the spring. She was starting to know first names, and preferences of the regulars she was developing. Her baking became more refined as she knew what flavors were loved and where she could try new items and new toppings.

Luke never missed a day she was open for his cinnamon roll and chocolate chip cookie, but the interaction was always brief, and he seemed distracted. He hadn't looked at her the same way that he had opening weekend and although he was friendly and funny, his words were limited, and the conversation wasn't inviting. She started to feel like she had severely misread the signs he had given her. Hannah felt confused, and instead of racking her brain trying to figure the man out, she threw her entire self into her work.

Luke

Luke had been so relieved that his parents had been able to get through dinner acting like normal people. He also had been right about Hannah's dad reminding him of his own. They seemed to have an instant connection. Before he knew it, they had plans to go fishing together. Hannah would be working the shop the next day, and he knew her parents would just being hanging out, so it seemed like the right invitation to make.

They had planned to take his dad's boat out on Evergreen River. Luke made sure to sneak down to the bakery to see Hannah Jones in action on her first day. He couldn't believe the lines that were forming in the store, and out of every five people who bought something from her, one went over the Woods and Brew. He was glad Brett was getting some business as well. Maybe he could relax a bit and let go of some of his anxiety.

He thought that was the day he was going to tell her while he stood in her shop. The chemistry and heat between the two of them burned brightly, and she watched him expectantly. But he had been distracted by the incoming of new customers which snapped him out of the daze, and the courage disappeared. It was starting to make him feel like less of a man. He had taken women home from the bar more than once over the years, and he had never hesitated to ask a woman out before. *What was it about Hannah that made him act like a juvenile?*

After that day, he had vowed to try again every day she was open until he spit the words out. At night, he dreamed of having Hannah beneath him in his sheets, and every morning he loyally showed up and ordered his cinnamon roll and cookie. The fear of sharing the truth increased with every interaction. His mind raced every time he looked into her eyes clouding his thoughts. He could see the disappointment in her eyes when he left with his brown paper bag. He could feel his chance of something incredible slipping away. Why couldn't he just tell her?

Chapter 17

When Drury Lane had been open for two weeks exactly, her sister's water broke. Hannah closed the shop for the next two days. She drove back to the city to stay with her parents bearing gifts of her painting, clothing, a blanket, and soft towels for her new little nephew. He was born that evening, and when she held him, she was smitten. Tears filled her eyes. Her sisters were mothers, and she was so proud to have a role in these precious little babies' lives. She baked and made dinners for her sister's freezer and cleaned the house for her discharge. She spent time with her little spitfire niece which was some of the best parts of her visit. She took Piper to the World of Fish Aquarium and out for ice cream. Piper's expression at the sight of the fish swimming was the most precise face she had ever seen. She loved that baby girl intensely.

When her sister and Gage finally discharged, she met them at their house with fresh lasagna and a giant oversized brownie pan, which she had frozen three more pans for her sister. She had baked dozens of lactation cookies which sat both on her counter and in her freezer. Her sister was in tears from the hormones of birth, and extremely grateful. "I'm proud to be your sister." She told Hannah. "You have always been so different than Jenny and I," Amanda said. "I always looked up to your freedom and generosity. I was never the outgoing spark of happiness that you always were. You always seem to know how to love people around you. You just know to be generous and make them feel joy and welcome. You are never afraid to take chances or say exactly what you think. I am honored to have you in my life, and Gage's."

Hannah's eyes filled with tears, and she embraced her sister in a giant bear hug. "I never would have been able to have the braveness to be myself without Jenny and you looking out for me. You always gave me that safety blanket to chase my dreams and live boldly. I always knew I had your love. I love you."

Hannah wished she could have stayed longer to bask in her nephew's newborn cuddles and scent, but she had to get home. Two days of the Drury Lane closed as a new business was not ideal, but it was important to take this time with her family. Unfortunately, she couldn't spare any more days. She drove her Bug home in the thick fog while she tried to distract herself from the thought of leaving her sweet nephew. She was not used to not being around for things like this like she had in the past.

When Piper was born, she was able to spend weeks cooking for her sister and letting her nap. She did not know what it was like to be a mother, but it looked exhausting. It was sometimes hard for her to find things to bond with her sisters over, but the birth of a newborn was a special time when everyone knew how to come together over. This time around would be different. She would need to get used to the alterations the distance would cause. She changed her thoughts to the menu for the morning, but when she got to cinnamon rolls, her thoughts fled to Luke.

It had been two days since she had seen him, and she missed his company. He hadn't said much at all when he had been to see her lately, and she wondered if he had found someone. She hadn't had the chance to even know if he felt how she did. Maybe he hadn't ever been interested in her at all.

The drive to Woodsburrow seemed to take twice as long as normal. By the time she pulled into her parking spot, the newborn bliss had faded, and Hannah was feeling sour. She pocketed her keys, grabbed her overnight bag, and slammed the door to her car. She walked up the stairs. Her thoughts transported her back to her parent's home in the city. She got to the top of the stairs and was shocked to see a figure standing in the dark leaning against her apartment door. Her heart began to race, and she jumped.

Luke

Luke had been waiting for hours in the cold for Hannah to arrive. He had been shocked when he arrived at Drury Lane a few days earlier, and the bakery was closed. Her sign said she had the birth of a new baby to attend to and that she would be open again tomorrow. All of that meant, she would be here tonight. Not seeing her for days had made him senseless. He had been moody at work and had paced around his house like a caged animal. He wanted to see her face and hear her beautiful voice.

He had gone to Gearshift that evening simply to drink, and there were enough rumors about Hannah to fill a dumpster. He tried to drown the noise with shots and moved closer to the TV with a beer. Unfortunately, the talk seemed to follow him. There was talk about what had happened in the city and what she must have done to piss someone off the way she did. Someone had mentioned seeing her on dates with two different men this summer, and the rage grew in his chest. After someone commented on their doubts that someone with her looks had any business skills, Luke glared at the man like a rabid dog, chugged the rest of his beer, and left. He couldn't listen to this absolute horseshit, and it was clear to him he needed to man up. The magnetic pull to be with this woman had not weakened in any of the months they had been together, and the more he learned about her, the more he wanted more. The rumors that circled her made him want to protect her like a human shield. He couldn't deny that it felt like a natural instinct.

Luke walked to her apartment door and settled in. He wasn't leaving until she came home, and he broke through this barrier he had formed between them. The buzz of the alcohol in his brain and the dark of the night lulled him to sleep. He awoke abruptly to the sound of her walking on the stairs shaking the ground beneath him. When she entered his vision, he began speaking and didn't stop until he had let everything out.

Hannah

"You know, I've never had trouble talking to women like this before in my life."

"Luke?" He looked like he had been standing here awhile. The shadow of him was dark, but his voice was unmistakable. He began to come into focus as Hannah approached, and although he smelled musty like he had been in a bar, his speech was crystal clear.

"Hannah, I'm so sorry if I scared you. I got here, and you weren't here, but I couldn't leave. I decided I would stand here until you showed up, however long that was. I can't let myself behave like a coward anymore. I finally mustered up the courage tonight, and I wasn't leaving this spot until I'd said exactly what I've been wanting to say. I've been here for hours. I forgot that you had been gone, but I still wasn't going to leave. I didn't want to lose my nerve."

Hannah walked forward, unlocked her door, and set her bag on the inside. She walked back outside and gently grabbed Luke's arm and guided him inside. "Come inside. We can talk in here. Sit down, Luke." He followed her inside but wouldn't sit. She closed the door behind him.

"Let me get this out, Hannah, please."

Hannah sat down and watched him intently. "I'm listening, Luke."

He continued. "I've never met a woman like you before. I tend to enjoy the company of women for a few dates, occasionally a night or so, but it never works out longer than that for one reason or another. I've never been with a woman that I want to make time for every day of my life. I want to play hockey with the guys. I want to go on fishing trips and deep country camping trips. I don't want to have to ask permission or forgiveness for pursuing my interests. I have never met a woman that made me feel like they could keep up with a lifestyle like that."

"Not only that, but I'm a cop. That job isn't easy, and it comes with odd hours added stress, and worry for the ones that care about me. Fear often causes controlling behavior. It's been the death of many of my relationships.

I can't change the wildness inside me, and it makes it hard to settle down. The thought of being with only one person for an indeterminant amount of time scares the shit out of me. But with you, I want you along for the good and the bad. When you are by my side, I want to parade you around everywhere. Hannah, I don't have a clue how to do this, so I don't royally mess it up. Steele has dated Stacey. He knows what he is doing. I don't have any experience at all. And then you just come along lighting up every room you enter."

"Everyone always says their woman is the most beautiful woman in the world, but you look like you belong on the cover of a magazine. You are fearless and confident. You would jump off the high rise on a dare and nail it like you've done it every day of your life, then climb up and do it a second time for fun. Everything about you drives me wild. It's like you have the spirit of a wild horse, and it makes me feel like maybe I don't have to be someone different to have you be mine. Every time we aren't together, I spend time thinking about how I can get just a glimpse at you. When I watch you burst out laughing, and it's not because of me, it makes me jealous that that laugh isn't mine. I crave you like a heroin addict. I asked your parents to dinner because I wanted them to like me and my family. Maybe if they liked me, you would too. I come into the bakery every day for a cookie and a cinnamon roll just to be around you. I feel like some seventh-grade boy with my first crush. I'm not sure if I should pull your hair or kiss you. I've tried to convince myself that it's not as big of a deal as I am making it, but I don't have any interest in looking or being with any woman on the planet. The last woman who came onto me, made me feel annoyed. Just your baking alone is enough to make any man go down on one knee. I need us to be together."

He ended standing directly in front of Hannah looking pleadingly into her eyes. Hannah's heart raced as she sat perfectly still on the couch. She had waited for weeks and weeks to hear him say those words, and *he was telling her he didn't know how to be what she wanted?* She couldn't even believe how ridiculous that sounded. *Mr. Hotshot Cop that paraded around with the most confidence she had ever seen in a man? The man who made her feel like he was looking into her soul when he looked into her eyes? That man felt like he didn't know what to do?* "Luke, what don't you know?"

He looked at her a look of defeat on his face. "What kind of man you need me to be, so I get a real chance at this."

She gave him a confused look. "First of all, in a good relationship, you get to be yourself. I don't want you to be someone other than you. I think you are funny, confident, and charming. That fact that you have a restless soul is all the more enticing to me. I love how you always know I need you, even when I don't ask, and that last part is a plus because I'm not good at asking. You've supported my biggest dream while I got Drury Lane opened up. That tells me volumes about how you would support me in the future. Now if you are asking what my type is, the last man I almost dated wanted so badly to please me, that he had become devoid of personality himself. He never wanted to disagree or argue so I made every decision. I hated that. I love adventure and risks. I love trying new things. I am messy and passionate. I love people and baking. I love to create art and sing poorly at the top of my lungs. I am never going to be anyone but me, ever. So, what I need in a partner is someone who is going to see all these parts of me, remember that I think roses are clique, and that mac and cheese is always better with gouda, and know that when I decide to do something that I will do it, and you can either watch me or help me, but don't try to hold me back. I need someone exciting and adventurous because I get bored easily with passionless everyday mundane living. I need someone who has just as much desire and fuel for life as I do because that's the only kind of human that can keep up with me." Hannah said grinning at Luke.

Luke looked at her for the longest time as he studied her. "Where did you come from?" Hannah had had enough of the stalling, the waiting, the uncertainty, and now the talking. Luke had given her the green light. He wanted her too. Hannah felt like her heart was exploding inside her chest. She strode over to him and grabbed his face. She pulled it down to hers while she rose on the tips of her toes and kissed him like she had waited a lifetime to kiss those delicious lips.

He gave a jolt of surprise and immediately pulled her closer to him. The energy between them felt strong enough to create a hurricane. He backed her up against the wall and kissed her. Each kiss was strong and possessive. He covered every inch of her neck starting from her right ear and ending with her left. His hand slipped under her shirt and grasped her breasts. Hannah moaned from the pleasure rising in her chest. "Hannah. You smell like vanilla and taste like one of your sweet rolls. It's intoxicating."

Hannah grabbed his belt and pulled him closer. Luke lifted her feet from the floor, and Hannah wrapped her leg around him.

Luke swayed down the hall with Hannah draped around him. His arms were like a vice grip around her. It seemed he was afraid she would run off like a frightened fawn if he put her on the ground. He found the master on the right and threw her down on the bed. He stroked his fingers down the crest of her hips slowly slid her shirt up over her head and threw it aside on the floor. He ran his hands over her body his fingers teasing her bra line and grasping her breasts. Hannah rolled her head back and pulled him into her once again. He returned to her face and began kissing her. She loosened his belt and slid her hand down grasping the hard erection that was pressed tightly against his jeans. He groaned and returned his body up against hers.

He reached behind her unclasped her bra and yanked it from her chest leaving her exposed. He pressed her mouth against her nipple and rolled it in his mouth, his tongue rolling in circles. Hannah cried. "Luke."

He removed her hand from his pants and held them down above her head as he traced a line of kisses from her mouth to below her navel. She could feel the excitement and heat that lay beneath her jeans. He slowly unbuttoned them slid them down her hips and peeled them from her body until they were able to easily drop to the floor. He ran his hands in the hem of her underwear and sent zings into her belly. Then, he plunged his hand down under the thin layer of modesty that she had left.

"Mmmm, Hannah." He said as he felt the wetness that he had stirred from her. He plunged his fingers into her body, and she moaned with pleasure.

Luke was greedy and every moan or cry that escaped Hannah's lips only made him want more. He returned to his trail and continued kissing until his lips were above his fingers and she could feel his exhales brush against her. He placed his mouth on her and continued until he felt her grip the sheets and scream his name. He brought his face up with the grin of a child who had eaten the last piece of chocolate cake.

"My turn," Hannah announced as she flipped him onto the mattress and tore off his shirt. She dragged her fingers down his hard chest and rippled abs. She nibbled his ear lobe and moved to his belt line placing kisses against it like was an imaginary boundary. She shuffled his pants down until he was exposed.

His hands continued grasping her breasts and following the outline of her shape pulling her hips into him. Throwing her pants on the ground, she returned to him and steadily stroked his large erection while she placed it inside her mouth. He began to move his hips faster and faster. "Fuck, Hannah." He declared as his ecstasy peaked, and his body melted into the bed. Hannah curled up beside him, and he grabbed her and pulled her as close to him as she could. "Hannah Jones, you have completely turned my world upside down." He whispered as she both drifted off to sleep.

Luke

When that big ball of anxiety had burst, and Hannah had walked over to him tonight, every bit of control he had been exercising was shredded to pieces. Luke brought her into the bedroom with the desire to taste every square inch of her body.

Luke was no stranger to women or sex, but something was different with Hannah tonight. He felt a strong desire to explore every inch of her and memorize all that he saw, but he wasn't in a hurry to rush through. He wanted to do this differently, so Hannah knew he wanted her for so much more than her beauty. He needed to show her he wanted her friendship and valued everything about her presence beside him.

Luke listened in the dark to Hannah's slow easy breaths. She lay in the crock of his arm and the smell of her flooded his senses. He couldn't believe he had spent all of his time the past few months missing out on this. This wild woman with a tender heart felt like an extension of himself that he had been missing. She seemed to glow with unending joy and beauty. He felt like he held a china doll in his arms, and he prayed with every thread of his soul that he wouldn't mess this up. As his thoughts returned to her even breaths, he drifted out to sleep like a traveler who had finally returned home to rest

Chapter 18

Luke

When Luke's alarm went off the next morning, he was filled with regret that he had to go in on the dayshift. He would have given anything to stay in that warm bed tangled in the sheets with Hannah's beautiful resting face, her warm naked body, and the desire to repeat last night, with a little twist to the ending. He started at her until he knew he couldn't afford to spend any more time there, or his captain would chew him a new one. He grabbed the fluffy blanket off the stool and covered her up so she wouldn't wake before she needed to. He knew that Hannah was an early riser, but with the excitement that filled her last week, she needed every bit of rest she could get.

He arrived at work with not a second to spare and was given a raised eyebrow look by the other dayshift officer who was all ready to go for the shift. He grinned slyly back and grabbed his stack of paperwork he had not yet finished. From that moment on, it felt like he was behind. He spent most of his shift behind a desk and everything he attempted to complete took longer than normal because of his thoughts shifting back to Hannah. He wondered exactly where that conversation had left them, not to mention their time after the conversation was over. *What kind of together were they?* The thought of sharing her with any other man was too much for his brain to bare, and he knew they would need to define that line.

Hannah

Hannah awoke in the morning to her alarm. She was alone, and the bed was cold. She reached over, but the bed was cold. The sheets had been pulled up neatly, and there was no evidence Luke had been there at all. Luke had left, and it felt like the night was just a dream. She couldn't believe the fireworks that had gone off between them in the bedroom. She craved and needed more, but had she done too much too soon? She usually didn't worry about sex, but something was different about the connection between them, and she found herself self-conscious of her bold confidence and her decision to seduce him. He had left without saying goodbye. She didn't have a note or a message. Maybe he had been drunk and came over as a good ending to his night out. He probably thought she was a floozy. He wouldn't have been the first person to downgrade the type of person she was based on her looks.

There was something about Luke though that was so much different than the men she had dated before. He had taken so much time to be around for her before he had even made a move at all. He had told her exactly how he had been feeling and didn't hold back. Hannah loved that he was adventurous. The thought of backcountry camping sounded amazing. *If he wanted to go off on a fishing trip, so what? What kind of woman got upset that he had interests outside of her? That was just childish and pettiness.* She certainly didn't expect him to want to go swimming with her every time that she wanted to or drop everything to go on a shopping spree. It had driven her crazy in the past when boyfriends had done exactly that. She wanted a balance between genuine interest and time spent apart. It was undeniable that the man was gorgeous and fantastic in bed. Their chemistry and the ability to read each other's needs had been something she had never experienced before. She believed that they could be good for each other. She hoped he felt it, too.

She spent the morning in her kitchen with her music on as Buckcherry and Matchbox Twenty blared from the speakers. She flew through her baking and said a silent thank you to the Hannah in the past who had prepped enough so today wasn't totally impossible to be ready on open on time. The menu wouldn't be as large as it usually was, but the pies were plentiful and so were the doughnuts. She had cinnamon rolls and iced banana nut muffins. The cookie dough went into the oven as she unlocked the front door for the day, but not before she changed the music to Frank Sinatra. She didn't know how her customer base would respond to Buckcherry at 8:00 in the morning.

The day was steady. Customers were excited she was back in town and many were in to hear about the baby and see pictures. Her final sales at the end of the day were fine. After crunching the numbers, she did her obligatory one-hour prep in the back for the next day. She wanted to feel more prepared than she had today. She planned to wake up earlier tomorrow, so she could return her menu to its normal variety. Hannah yawned. She really needed to get more sleep than she had gotten the night before. She was grateful she arranged with Charlene to have the opening server pick up their pies to start the day. That extra few minutes was vital to be in her own kitchen, especially on days that Marg wasn't there.

Tomorrow was a Marg day, and Hannah was glad. Despite just having a few days off, Hannah wanted time to reacclimate herself and maybe take a nap. She also wanted to spend some time updating her website and social media. She wasn't sure what the slowdown had been about today, but she thought it was important to bump up her social media in times like these. Hannah had fall specials that she would be running, and she wanted the famous leaf peepers to make their way into her shop this weekend. A few beautiful pictures and some quirky dialog might be just the thing to make that happen.

She made her way up to her apartment, showered, and put her mom's leftover white chicken chili on the stovetop while she lounged in her satin teal pajamas that felt silky smooth on her skin. Her phone vibrated as she grabbed her laptop and sat down on her couch with her white blanket. She saw a message from Abby. "Girl! Did you see your page? Who has a bug up their butt?" *What was she talking about?*

She pulled up her Facebook account, and she saw exactly what she was talking about, and it wasn't just that site. Instagram and her website had the same pattern. When she went through her social media sites page by page, she noticed a trend. Someone was posting fake negative reviews on every single page. It was anywhere from one to five postings per site. She knew they were not authentic because the details didn't match reality. They didn't even match an altered version of reality. They talked about cake orders and pink frostings on cupcakes. They complained about the woman at the counter like she was some kind of teenager. Some complained about irregular opening times and bad drop-offs. She had done very few cake caterings to date, and none of the situations had been similar to what this person was claiming.

She had yet to see an item inside her bakery with pink frosting, and she was always open at the same time. The quality of her ingredients was questioned along with her prices in the same paragraphs. *Someone was still adamant about ruining her business.*

Hannah panicked as flashes of Drury Lane for sale flashed in her mind. *Where would she go?* As much as she missed her family, she had no desire to leave Woodsburrow. And what about Luke? She had just started exploring those waters, and she wasn't ready to quit. That was, however, if he was still interested. She flagged all the comments that she could citing them as false reviews. She made enough posts on each that the specials and photos would drive an influx of customers again this weekend. She hoped the browsers would be distracted by the star ratings and would focus on all the real comments from the businesses around town. She was thankful that The Cozy Kitchen had been tagging her with her pie deliveries. She hoped it would be enough to convince new customers to make the trip to visit Drury Lane and not a neighboring city. There was nothing else she could do tonight. It was the risk you took with putting anything online in today's world. She would just have to remain focused. She planned on monitoring every few days to make sure all was still well.

She encouraged her customers to start leaving reviews to help grow her business. She prayed it would be enough.

She put her computer down, unable to think about the possible negative outcomes to her business loaming in front of her and devoured her white chicken chili. A chill had set into her bones from the fear of losing her business. She was grateful for the warmth that spread through her body right down to her toes. The taste of her mother's cooking was both her favorite and exactly what she needed tonight.

When Hannah was finished, her mind buzzed with the events of the last 24 hours. There was no way she could sleep now. She sent Abby a message thanking her for the warning. "Somebody seems to want Drury Lane to go down. I don't have a clue who. Love you girl." Abby sent back a message filled with hearts. It was hard on nights like this to be so far away from her support people. Just to have her mom or Abby here on her couch to vent with would make all the difference. A text from Luke would help. She looked down at her phone again. No new messages. *Where was Luke?* He had disappeared long before the crack of dawn, and she still had heard nothing from him.

He had made it clear he felt clueless about taking on a role in her life, but the deafening silence made her feel used and exposed. She was used to men fawning over her and working hard to catch her attention. Luke didn't seem to care about that at all. She had had casual sex before and knew the drill, but when she did, it was something she had chosen. She had not intended her encounter with Luke to be a one and done night. Hannah wasn't one to be dumped or ghosted, and she certainly didn't like this deafening silence at all. She didn't understand what had happened last night to make him so distant today. He usually always had the uncanny ability to know when she needed him. *Why wasn't he here now?* Those reviews could be devastating to her business and whoever was writing them, knew that.

She sat down at her easel and began to paint, the rest of the world slowly slipped away. She felt herself pulled into the colors as she clung to the vision her brain tried to make her hands put on paper. When her mind was completely stilled, and she inspected the canvas, Luke's face stared back at her. She captured his smile right after he told a joke and knew it was good. His eyes shifted to catch everyone's reaction and the glint of enjoyment flashed in his expression in seeing his audience's faces. Even how he held his head was in his likeness. She felt his presence, the safety net and happiness his energy brought to her world, just with seeing his image in front of her.

"Woman, is there nothing that you can't do?" She heard from behind her.

She whipped her head around. "Do you always have to have a dramatic entrance?" She teased as she saw Luke still in uniform leaning against her doorframe with his hands crossed across his chest.

He grinned. "Yes. It comes with my character. How did you do this so well? You weren't even looking at a picture of me." He approached the canvas and examined it.

Hannah shrugged. "I never use pictures for my paintings. I don't use them while decorating cakes either. It muddies the imagine I have in my mind. When did you leave this morning? You didn't come in for your cinnamon roll today."

"I had to go home and shower before work and grab my uniform. The entire day I was drowning in paperwork and chasing my tail. I thought I was going to get out on time, but I got called emergently before my shift was up. The guy taking over wasn't in yet, so it became my problem. It was a terrible way to end a long day." He said. "I didn't know where we left things last night, but I felt like I had a better chance on having it cleared up if I showed up in person. That worked well yesterday." He smirked at her.

"Well, where do you want that to leave us?" Hannah asked trying not to look too eager.

She had been fooled once or twice by a man that had told her he was interested in dating, whose interest magically had waned after they had ended up between the sheets. She wasn't going to be standing here looking like a fool if he had changed his mind. "I am exactly where I was last night. I want to try this thing with you and me. I don't know that I am qualified to real monogamous dating. I want to know what expectations you have from me, so I don't mess it up from pure ignorance."

"Well," Hannah began, "we should go on dates."

Luke nodded. "Dates I can do. Dinners, movies?"

"I am into almost anything but bear in mind I've been bored with men in the past."

"Keep it spicey. Noted." He said nodding. "What else?"

"There is certainly no need to ask my permission when you do things. I am not your mother nor am I your keeper, but it's common curtesy to let me know that you are doing them. For example, if you always have hockey on Thursday nights, great. If you are leaving on a ski trip for four days with a man named Fabio, wonderful. But I appreciate the heads up, so I know number one not to expect you and two not to send out a search party because you have been missing for three days."

Luke nodded. "That wouldn't be good for my image."

Hannah smiled. "And if you are thinking something, its best to just say it. Whether I've pissed you off, you have an alternative opinion, or you are thinking about me, and we aren't together, you can't go wrong with speaking your mind."

"Now talking, that I can do. Well, usually, when I'm around you it seems to depend on what I am trying to say."

Hannah giggled. "Are we finally going to really try this?" she asked.

He wrapped her up in his arms and squeezed. "We are." She turned her body into his and pulled him down for a kiss. Her heart raced and anticipation grew in her chest. He pulled away and removed his hands from her and forced them into his pockets.

"I'm going to leave now. I really want to do this right. I think the waiting is better for both of us." Her face dropped as disappointment flooded her body. "I really want this to be a lasting thing, Hannah. So, it's important to me that I do things properly. You are different than the women I've been with in the past, and I want to make that clear. So, when can I pick you up to take you out? Are you free tomorrow?"

"Actually, Marg runs the counter for me tomorrow after I get everything set up."

He grinned. "Perfect. What time can you be ready?"
"Hmm, ten I guess."

"I'll be here at 10:00." He pulled her in and playfully nibbled on her ear. She giggled. "Good night, beautiful." He whispered, and he slipped out the door.

Life with this man certainly would not be boring. Hannah thought with a smile.

Luke

In typical summer shift fashion, Luke was sent out on a call just before his shift ended. So, a shift that should have allowed him to leave on time, turned into overtime. He became restless and hungry. He wanted to eat a dozen of Hannah's chocolate chip cookies as he spoke to each of the persons involved in a domestic dispute. After the husband and wife had been sent to separate locations, he hurried through his paperwork and sped to Hannah's apartment. When he climbed the stairs and knocked on the apartment door, he heard only silence. He opened the door and tentatively stepped inside. "Hello? Hannah?" He called. Nothing.

As he listened longer, the sound of brush strokes broke the eerie silence that filled the apartment. He moved quietly towards the noise and saw Hannah engrossed in a painting like she had been transported to another world. He had called her name when he opened the door, and she hadn't heard him. Even now as he stood in the doorway, she didn't sense his presence behind him. He examined the picture she had been working on. It was him, almost exactly. It wasn't just his eye color, hairstyle, and facial shape she had mastered perfectly; it was his facial expression and mannerisms as well. It was like looking in a mirror. He let out an audible "Wow." And added, "Is there nothing you can't do woman?" She had turned quickly, obviously startled by the noise, and gave him the most beautiful far-away smile he had ever seen.

***

When Luke drove home, he knew that despite his exhaustion from his night with Hannah followed by the extra-long shift, his night was not yet over. Hannah had shown him some of the reviews she had gotten on her social media accounts. He could hear the fear in her voice. She knew that bad press could lead to Drury Lane's downfall. He felt rage at whoever had felt the need to assert their power from the other side of a keyboard. He knew when he got home, he would comb through every single review to see if he could find any type of pattern.

He still hadn't had dinner, and he had promised Hannah some dates full of magic, starting tomorrow. He had never been on dates more exciting than dinner before, and Hannah needed to be impressed. He could tell when he had shown up tonight that Hannah had felt uncertain by his presence. The lack of communication following the massive fireworks display, they had created last night probably wasn't his best first move. She had made it clear she wasn't expecting him to hoover over her or vice versa, but she did want to be kept in the loop. She didn't want to feel like a cheap hook-up, and Luke knew she wouldn't put up with him treating her like she was one. He needed to get it together and impress this woman, and it started with the date tomorrow that he had yet to plan and had less than twelve hours to plan it in.

<h1 style="text-align:center">Chapter 19</h1>

It was a crisp Autumn day. The sun was shining brightly, and the leaves shone magnificently in the sunbeams. Despite this, it was freezing outside. Hannah had put on her jeans, her tall hiking boots, a thick navy sweater, a black vest, mittens, and a matching navy hat with the biggest white fluffy pompom on the top. She didn't know what Luke had in mind, but he had told her to dress for the outdoors, so she was prepared. When she climbed into his truck, two coffees sat in the middle counsel. He had stopped to get her a pumpkin spice latte and a black coffee for himself.

They drove out into the country for what seemed like miles. The leaves danced in the gentle breeze, and the sunlight that passed through the leaves made the world around her ignite. Hannah's sipped her delicious brew and held it tightly in her hand letting its warmth thaw her already chilly fingers. Luke held her hand while he drove and despite her frequent asking where they were going, he continued answering "You'll see," with a giant smirk on his face. After driving until Hannah was sure she couldn't find her way back to town even if she tried with a compass, the thick trees had started to become infrequently, and the fields spilled out over the landscape around them. The fields of corn and soybeans gave way to a break in the pattern to something completely new. As they approached, Hannah got a better view of what the massive plants were. "Sunflowers! Oh my gosh Luke they are magnificent! I've never seen anything like it."

Luke parked the truck in the empty parking lot. "It's not just any patch of sunflowers either. This is Rob's sunflower patch. He started planting it the year he lost his wife to cancer. It has changed over the years from a tribute to her to a competition which she would have loved almost more than the flowers themselves."

Hannah looked at him confused. "How can sunflowers be a competition?"

"The sunflowers patch contains a maze. It's supposed to be two miles long though I don't know that anyone has measured it, and I believe that measurement is wildly inaccurate. It seems to become longer every year, but it's best not to complain. Whoever finishes it in the fastest time that year gets his largest pig and more importantly, bragging rights. Last year was the first year I was beaten. That high school quarterback won by fifteen minutes. I don't intend to lose again. Grab your coffee and follow me."

Hannah smiled. This was another side of Luke she hadn't seen before. He had tenacity and determination with his strong competitive drive. Not to mention it was incredibly sexy. "I love this, but what happens if we get lost?"

Luke waved that off. "It rarely happens, and if we have our phones, Rob can find us on the tractor."

Hannah giggled. *Of course, he would.*

They spent the rest of that afternoon following the map that Hannah was positive that was the worst map she had ever seen in her life. They were howling with laughter as they ran into dead ends and never-ending circles. It was the most fun she had had in ages, and the cheer he let out when they ran out of the exit made her laugh even harder. He checked his watch.

"That's twenty minutes faster than last year. You could read that map better than I ever have."

"I don't know that I could read it at all! I'm pretty sure the right and left were flipped. I mostly made the directions up. What do we do with our time? How do they know how fast we finished?" She asked.

Luke wandered over to the only tree by the parking lot. A notebook hung off the side of the tree in a plastic bag with a pen. He slipped the book out and wrote their names and time down. Hannah giggled again. "It's very official." She said through her laughter.

He grinned. "Very, suiting for this type of event. Don't you think?"

"Absolutely." She answered. "Perfectly fitting."

Luke

"The reigning champ is back!" Luke said to Steele with a high five as they left the rink.

He laughed. "I can't believe you still had the fastest time this year even though you took Hannah with you," Steele said in disbelief. "I made Chris go with me this year, and we still didn't get close to your time. I don't understand what you do in there and how you can navigate with that useless map."

"It's all in the magic. Hannah turned out to be a huge asset in the map reading portion." Luke said with a grin.

He had noticed how relaxed he had become since letting Hannah into his life. He had been holding his worry heavily for too long, and as a man who didn't worry about anything, he didn't know how people could hold the weight of that every day. "Does it feel as impossible as you thought it would be? Being with Hannah I mean." Steele asked with a grin.

Luke shook his head. "I know. I was being dramatic. Having Hannah just makes everything better. I'm taking her ax throwing tomorrow night. She is going to love it."

Hannah

Hannah trudged forward as negative reviews continued coming in on her accounts that were so grossly incorrect, that she knew they were fake. In all the reviews she had read, only one that she had seen appeared to be real. Someone had been served the wrong flavor doughnut when they had ordered on a busy Sunday. Hannah immediately responded that she would be more than happy to give them a dozen on the house to make up for a mistake that she hoped wouldn't happen again. She had learned in customer service that it was best to be apologetic and overgenerous if you wanted your customers to continue their loyalty to you.

The Harvest Festival was only a few weeks away, and she had been asked by the organizers to service a Drury Lane booth for the weekend. Hannah was tickled to be invited by name. Events were a huge deal to the community of Woodsburrow. Despite all the stress the fake reviews and demeaning article had caused, it at least felt like Woodsburrow was proud to have her as one of her own. It wasn't the same type of recognition that would have been celebrated at the Golden Goose, but to Hannah, this was better. She had written out her menu crumpled it up tossed it in the trash, and wrote out a new menu, only to do the same thing. It had taken her five attempts to feel satisfied with the list that sat in front of her. She would be serving apple pies, pumpkin pies, apple cider doughnuts, pumpkin bars, pumpkin scones, gingersnap cookies, and caramel corn. The food stand was wanting to make soup in a bread bowl, and they had asked her to bake the bread and her sourdough boule would be perfect for the job. The flavors of fall were her favorite and all of it made her mouth water.

***

It was a Friday morning when Dawn came in to pick up pies for the Cozy Kitchen. "You know," she said. "I didn't think much of it, but people have been talking lots about that article in the paper and the bad reviews that have been posted on Facebook. I haven't read them myself, but there is a lot of speculation going on because of how comical they sound. From the way I've heard people talk, it sounds like whoever is writing them is off their rocker."

Hannah felt a small sigh of relief leave her lips and she smiled at Dawn. If the word on the streets of Woodsburrow was that some crazy person was leaving reviews for Drury Lane, then Hannah didn't have to worry about her business decreasing. Woodsburrow would continue to strongly show their support.

"Thank you for not thinking that stuff was true, Dawn."

"I've spent enough time talking to you to know that you care about the items you sell and the bakery. I've never once seen you cold or looking down upon anyone. You are one of the friendliest people I've ever met."

"Dawn, that means the world to me." Hannah felt like she should hug Dawn. This woman had no idea how much such a little observation she had wanted to share meant to Hannah. She slipped her a slice of pumpkin and chocolate cheesecake from the special of the day into her bags.

"I appreciate you, and I love that my pies are being served at the diner. It makes me proud."

"Thank you for this," Dawn said as she held up the bag with the cheesecake and smiled. "But listen, what I wanted to say is a few weeks ago a man came in talking about Drury Lane. He was mumbling on about rats in the kitchen, and the owner having a history of drugs. He started to get a bit out of hand, so we had to remove him. Luckily, the police didn't need to get called, but we almost needed to. He didn't seem like he knew what was going on so at the time I just chalked it up to him not being right in the head, but after hearing all this other stuff, I am worried he might be targeting only you."

I've thought the same thing, Hannah said to herself. "Could you see what the man looked like?" She asked.

"It was hard to get a good look at him. He had let his hair grow long and shaggy, and he looked like he needed a shave. He wore a silly-looking hat despite being inside, and he was shorter than most folks. Honestly, he looked like he was wearing a disguise, but a ridiculously awful one."

Based on that description, there was no one Hannah could place. "Thank you for telling me. Let me know if you see him again."

Dawn nodded. "I will. Bye, Hannah. Be safe."

"Have a good day at the diner!" Hannah called as she left.

It made Hannah worried that someone had been personally going around town and talking poorly about her, but she hadn't seen anyone fitting that description around Drury Lane. It was certainly suspicious that this man was talking about her shop. That could mean it was the same person who had been dragging her name through the dirt, but it could just be a coincidence. If the man had been on drugs, he could have been rambling about just about anything. She made a mental note to catch Luke up to speed on what she had found out. He could at least decide if it was relevant information or not.

That evening, Luke took her to ax throwing. Hannah had no idea that throwing axes was a sport, or that you could attend it as a date. They had to drive thirty minutes to get to the closest location. Hannah and Luke played until their arms couldn't throw anymore, and they headed back to her apartment. "You could come up for some dessert." She teased as he parked to drop her off at the door. She had a sensual tone to her voice as she brushed her fingers across his cheek and made him groan.

At the sound, she climbed over the seat her body on top of him. He became immediately restless as he pulled her face into himself and kissed her passionately. He dropped his hands slowly to her waist and moved her body to guide her into his erection. "God Hannah. You are like heroin I swear."

"Give me one solid reason why you can't come upstairs." She whispered into his ear as her breath touched his cheek with every word.

"I want you to know I'm into you for more than your body, and I am certainly not just trying to get naked in your bed."

"I know that. Come upstairs, Luke." He looked at her like she was testing him.

"I don't play games. I want you in my bed. I want you to take me ax throwing and then come upstairs and give me the happy ending I've been craving all night. I don't need you to prove to me that you can withstand our chemistry. Being with you is like having a best friend, and it's the most awesome feeling I've ever felt. I've seen your dedication to me since the moment we met. After that night in my room, all I can think about is how much I want the whole package."

He opened his driver's side door, lifted her out onto the street, and stepped out after her. Luke grabbed Hannah and gently kissed her. Hannah kissed back with more force. She was impatient and fidgety. Luke moved her body and pressed it into the side of his truck using a firmer passion than hers, and he grinded himself into her. She pulled him even further into her. They finally managed to untangle themselves and Hannah ran up the stairs dragging Luke after her.

When they unlocked her front door, Hannah immediately began taking all Luke's layers of clothing off.

She removed his jacket and t-shirt and was working on his belt when he reached under her breast line and ran his fingers along them. He moved his reach lower and gently slipped off her shirt over her head. He proceeded to pull her breasts out of her bra and applied firm pressure to her nipples. He reached around and dropped it onto the mound they had created. He picked her up around his waist and carried her into her bedroom.

They removed their jeans, and excitement fluttered in Hannah's chest. She was impatient and wanting as she pulled him to her. He slipped on a condom swiftly and placed himself inside her. She cried out as he thrust himself into her until the sounds of them orgasming together filled the room. Luke rolled off to her side, cautiously examining her. Hannah smiled at him and hopped out of the bed. She came back with mini cream pies. Luke laughed. "My thoughts exactly. Bring those here!" They ate until the richness filled their stomachs.

Hannah looked at Luke and gave him a grin. He barely had time to react before Hannah straddled him and laid him down on the bed. "Round two." She insisted, and he was more than happy to oblige.

Luke

Having sex with Hannah was unlike any other sexual experience Luke had in his life. She made the time in the bedroom fun and exciting. He wasn't worried if she was having a good time or if he would be impressive enough. She was loud and made it obvious she was enjoying herself. Luke loved that he didn't need to guess what was going on in her brain. He preferred that greatly to the mind games women had played with him in the past. She was just as adventurous in the bedroom as she was in her day-to-day life, and that drove Luke wild.

Hannah looked relaxed and comfortable as she lay naked beside him, and the grin she had every time they finished, just had you wanting more. If she wanted something, she wasn't afraid to take charge and get it for herself. Round two had been filled with positions he had only dreamt about. The need to have her was strong and seemingly insatiable. Before they had even finished, he already wanted more.

***

After dealing with the worst parts of Woodsburrow all day, it provided him balance to be showered in Hannah's unending positivity. The way she greeted him at the end of a long day, and laughed his jokes made him feel like this was where he belonged. Hannah was who she was. She didn't play games, and she was confident both in herself and in Luke. Instead of the fear he had harbored towards women in the past, he never felt like he was trapped with her. He felt proud and looked forward to their next time together. He loved taking her out in public and hanging out with her. Their conversations were never lacking and always easy. It made him feel like he was a more whole version of himself. Hannah loved being around people just like he did, and they shined as a couple in public.

Hannah was always willing to try anything new and reached outside of her comfort zone with ease. She had been asking lots of questions about his outdoor activities. He planned to take her hiking and give her a close-up view of all that fall had to offer in Woodsburrow. Fall was passing by quickly as the trees dropped their radiant leaves in preparation for the coming winter, and he hoped that he would find time in his work schedule to make that happen. Hannah was an amazing human being and deserved only the best life every single day. Luke wanted to be the one to give that to her.

Chapter 20

Hannah

Hannah had convinced Luke to run her stand with her at the Harvest Festival, and he had arrived dutifully at 9:00. He loaded up her baked goods and treated them like bombs that might spontaneously combust at any moment. He helped with set up and the laughter and banter between them made them look like an old married couple instead of the new lovers they were. Both of them were excellent with people and every customer that came was greeted like they were friends and family. Hannah recognized many of her regulars and was thrilled to see so many people stopping by to not only buy doughnuts to eat while they enjoyed themselves at the festival, but pies to take home. However, it became evident as the day went on that everyone wanted a peek at them together in such a public setting. The town was not used to seeing Luke with a woman in that manner, and she felt eyes on them from all directions.

When it was time to close down for the day, Luke and Hannah walked through the fairgrounds that were now lit up with the soft glow of jack-o-lanterns, orange Christmas lights, and soft music. They held hands and walked the paths weaving down the rows.

"Tell me more about your family," Hannah said. "I thought your parents were so sweet. Your mom is lovely, and your dad looks at her like she is the brightest star in the sky. He seems like the soft-spoken type. My dad seemed to love his time with your dad."

Luke smiled. "They are pretty cool. I got lucky. I've always been very close with them. I don't have any siblings. Steele was always the closest thing to a brother that I had. My parents have been together forever. They both grew up here. My extended family is small too. I think that's why we seem to feel so ingrained in the community. They feel just as close as family to me, and my parents raised me that way as well. We always attended and volunteered at every event. It's a part of my history."

"Did you always want to stay here in Woodsburrow?"

"I knew early on that when I became an adult, I wouldn't want to live anywhere else. I needed a career that I could pursue in my backyard. I love to lead and be part of a team. It led me to becoming a cop."

Hannah nodded. "I can see that. It gives you that sense of protecting your own. You said your extended family is small. Do they live around here?"

Luke nodded. "My grandmother on my dad's side lives in an apartment complex in the independent living building. My mom's parents are here too. She has a younger sister named Molly. I grew up with Molly more like an older sister or a cousin than an aunt. She isn't much older than me. She got pregnant in high school with Noah. Travis, her husband, was the high school quarterback at the time. My parents helped with Noah as Travis went off to play college football, and Molly went to the local community college for human resources. Somewhere in between there, they got pregnant with Logan, and then they got married. It was a hard adjustment when they moved to the city because having them around was just the everyday norm. I am still really close with Molly and the boys."

"I'd love to meet her sometime," Hannah said.

"Well, you have actually." "I have?" "Molly and Travis have been having some problems lately. She won't talk about it too much, but Logan has one year left of high school and Noah is in college now. She has been spending a lot of time visiting here either with Logan or by herself. She has gone to your farmers' market stand and into your shop. She loves all things apples. She has red hair and green eyes and looks similar to my mom."

Hannah thought back to the hundreds of people she had seen in the last few months. *A red-haired woman who ordered apple things.* Hannah remembered the first day she had brought fall flavors to the market. A pretty woman had been very friendly and had ordered every apple item she had. She thought she had seen her a few times in the store on weekends too ordering an odd mix of apple items, one of each no matter if it was a cake or a pastry. Hannah nodded. "I think I know who she is. She is always very friendly like she wants to strike up a conversation, and orders one of whatever Apple item I have on the menu. Why hasn't she said hi and told me who she is?"

"I made her swear she wouldn't. She knew how much I liked you and told me if I didn't tell you soon, she would."

Hannah giggled. "I like her."

Luke smiled. "I'll make sure you get to meet each other officially. That's it for my family. What about yours?"

"My parents raised us in the suburbs. My two older sisters both attended college and married their husbands who they met while at college. I have a niece Piper and a nephew Gage. I am the only one who chose a different path. I attended a baking program and got as much experience as I could from as many people as possible." She shrugged. "I don't have anything too exciting hidden in there. I had no idea I would end up in Woodsburrow. I looked for a place to open my shop around the city but there wasn't anything. It was serendipity that I ended up here. I couldn't be happier about it though. I love that about life though, you know? You just have to be willing to take risks because you never know where life might be leading you."

Luke squeezed her hand. "I agree. I never would have predicted meeting you this year or feeling the way I do. I honestly didn't think I was capable." Hannah smiled.

Hannah snuck over to the bathrooms and Luke waited for her return. Today had been a magnificent day and she reflected upon the perfectness of it all. Luke had been by her side all day. The community seemed to be supporting her no matter the horrible comments that made their way online. She felt contentment in a way she hadn't felt before. She left the bathroom and headed back to rejoin Luke.

A woman stood at his side, and Hannah waited to watch their interaction before walking back to rejoin him. She could hear their voices. "I haven't seen you around in a while Luke."

"I haven't been around." He replied.

The woman leaned into him. "You know you are always welcome to come by." Hannah could hear the desperation in her voice mixed with the flirtatious tone.

"I won't be needing to stop by any time soon," Luke answered.

"If you change your mind, you know where to find me." The woman said and turned and walked away.

Hannah approached Luke. "What was that?"

Luke jumped. "Nothing happened, Hannah."

"It's not what happened. It's that instead of turning her away you moved her to the backburner. Did you not see how desperately she was trying to impress you? I will not be shuffled with other women Luke. No one is forcing you to be here. If you want to be with someone else, just go. I should have known all that babble about not knowing how to do serious relationships was just because you are a womanizer." Hannah didn't stop to let him speak and immediately stormed away from him.

"Hannah!" He called. "Come back here!"

Hannah refused to turn around and power walked all the way to her Bug and drove straight home. She was not going to play games with this man or any other no matter what her heart had to say.

Luke

Luke had not seen their first fight coming. Things had been going perfectly, but with the passion that they held between them, and the strong personalities that they both had, disagreements were bound to happen. Luke knew that even the most compatible couples would fight at some point in time. Living in harmony constantly was only possible in fairytales. Yet he didn't think he would have a chance of reconciling with her tonight.

The woman who had approached him had been someone he had taken home from the bar years prior. He hadn't seen her in months, and he didn't have any idea that she was still single. Hannah was right though, she was desperate, and from an outsider's view, who knows what that interaction might have looked like. Hannah had left Luke standing alone and returned to a woman standing very close to him touching his arm. It didn't look good for him. He should have told her he was taken and looked to introduce Hannah, but he thought that hurting her feelings would be rude. In trying to spare the woman from looking like a total fool, he had made Hannah feel like she was only one of the many lovers in his life. This couldn't have been further from the truth. He needed to show her that she was the only one he wanted. Not to mention, letting whatever this was fester, could create a degradation in their relationship that he had feared would ruin everything he wanted.

He decided he was going to have to do something dramatic and chose an overnight trip to the mountains. If that required him to put in vacation time to make it a priority, he would do that. His parents had never gone to bed mad, and although Hannah would never speak to him tonight even if he insisted, he would fix it as soon as possible. He put the pieces of the plan in motion and waited for Hannah to cool off to a level low enough that she might actually listen to his apology.

Chapter 21

Hannah

The next day, Hannah ran her booth solo and had nonstop business the entire morning. Luke hadn't called, and he hadn't shown up to help like they had planned. Hannah couldn't believe he was just letting her walk away this easy, and if he cared this little, it was for the best that she did what she did. When she finished for the day, she took the dirty dishes back to the bakery to run through the dishwasher and decided to get prepped for the next day. She loaded the dishwasher angrily and clanged around her kitchen making it functional for the next day. She locked up Drury Lane and headed upstairs. Luke was standing outside her door.

"What do you want?" She snapped at him as she fumbled with the lock. "Can't you just call like a normal person? Do you always have to just show up here every time you have something to say?"

Luke grabbed her key out of her hand calmly and without a word unlocked the door to her apartment. They walked in together. Hannah was fuming and kept her distance from him. "Hannah, I am sorry. I wasn't trying to keep that woman on standby. I just didn't want to hurt Ericka's feelings, which I realize in retrospect that choice completely didn't factor your feelings into the mix. You are so bold and confident that I didn't stop to think that you could be hurt by that. I do not have feelings for any other woman. I've barely spent any time thinking about anything other than you and I. I'm sorry. I was wrong."

"That sounds rehearsed," Hannah said as she stood with her arms crossed.

"Well, I'll admit I was up all night worried sick that I had made that mistake I had been terrified about making. I might have practiced in front of my bedroom wall a few times."

Hannah softened as she studied Luke. He had large circles under his eyes and his frown lines looked more pronounced. His facial hair had grown out in a five o'clock shadow. He looked older in a way, and it was clear he was feeling worried.

"Can I take you someplace? You have the bakery closed on Tuesday, right?"

"Yes."

"I'll pick you up tomorrow around four after you close for the day. Pack an overnight back of outdoor clothes and your hiking boots. Please don't walk out on us. Let me try to fix this."

Hannah paused a moment. He had apologized and his crime was in not being assertive enough. *Was that worth throwing away everything that they had begun to build?* She didn't think it was right that she should punish him forever for a small error in judgment. "Don't be late," Hannah smirked at him.

He grabbed her and gently kissed her lips. "Good night, Miss Hannah."

The next day was October first, and Drury Lane was filled with all things spooky. Hannah had decorated the inside with witches, goblins, and trolls. Leaves had already covered the entranceway, and she added some hanging ghosts to accompany them. Hannah was wearing a Hocus Pocus shirt with a giant witch hat and long dangling earrings that looked like broomsticks. She had made her maple iced maple-shaped cookies which had become a best seller. Red velvet cupcakes sat in the display case that were topped with little ghosts. She had made witch finger cookies for pizazz. She had eyeball cake pops and mini zombie poke cakes. Fall baking brought out Hannah's creativity and put her right into her element. She could stretch the boundaries a bit without being off-putting. She had decorated the store until she ran out of decorations and adorned the front window with a spooky scene. It had been an excellent day.

As she cleaned up in the kitchen, she couldn't believe how much her life had changed in three short months. In June, she was living in a studio apartment engaged to a man who was driving her nuts. She was working a job that sucked out bits of her soul daily. She had managed to find pieces of happiness to make her life manageable, but that wasn't how she planned on living out her days. After fighting for that change, she so desperately needed, she now had a fiery passion with the man she was with, and she hoped they would continue to grow what they had begun. She loved Drury Lane, and the customers who had been with her since the beginning and despite her constant worry about when the next false libel would be spread, they had loyally stuck by her side. She loved her apartment and the view out of her windows. She loved that she had been exploring her love of painting again and was proud of the pieces she had begun to create. She loved this town with their regular festivals, and welcoming attitude. *How life had so sweetly changed.*

Luke

After what he considered to be a successful apology to Hannah, he called Steele on the way to his truck. "Steele, can I come over? Are you busy?"

"Not busy, just getting home from the store. Is everything ok?"

"Yeah, everything is fine. We can talk when I get there." He hung up the phone and drove the short jaunt to Steele's.

Steele was in his flower bed weeding. Luke shook his head. "How is it that you were born an old man?"

He asked with a smirk. "It's important to keep your curb appeal up," Steele replied calmly and finished weeding as Luke approached him. "What's up?" He asked.

"I need you to teach me to cook something." Steele studied at him closely.

"Dang." He said. "She has gotten to you hard. I've been telling you that you need to learn to cook for years and you have blown me off every time. I'm making Jambalaya tonight. Come on in and we can do it together."

Steele was a patient teacher. He went through the steps of choosing fresh produce. He showed him the proper way to slice and dice, so the pieces weren't an overwhelming size. He copied the recipe for him as they waited for the dish to cook. "Wow," Luke said later. "This is delicious."

"You should learn to make a few more dishes. They are so much better than getting takeout daily." Steele teased.

"I might. This is perfect for what I need now. Thanks for being my brother." He said with a grin.

"I'll turn you into a proper man yet." Steele joked back. He was ready.

Hannah

Knowing Luke, when he said dress warmly, what he meant was make sure you can withstand subzero temperatures for long periods of time. Hannah packed a backpack with spare clothes and layered herself in whatever she owned. She brought her long hiking boots and grabbed her coat. She was ready and waiting when he showed up at four. Her bags overflowed like it was a vomiting creature. Luke looked at her and laughed. "You said dress warmly and didn't give me anything else to go on."

"I did." He said holding his hands up in defeat. He grabbed her bag and her hand and led her down the stairs to his truck.

They followed the highway north for about thirty minutes until a small mountain range came into view on the horizon. "I didn't know there were mountains here!" Hannah gasped.

"They are small ones, but a mountain of any kind should be respected as a mountain."

Hannah nodded. "I agree. Wow! They are magnificent." They were in their prime glory as the sun was descending in the sky and the light shimmered off the remaining leaves making them appear to glow. Luke pulled onto a side road as he followed the sign for Cliffside Inn. The place was beautiful and had a swimming pool with a hot tub outside that overlooked the mountain. Luke helped Hannah with her bags, and they headed inside.

When they entered their room, they threw down their bags and walked around to explore. There was a fireplace that burned real logs along with a jacuzzi tub, and a small kitchen was attached. The view out their window directly overlooked the mountain and she could see the pools in the back. She turned to look at Luke with a huge grin on her face. "This is incredible. How did I not know this place existed?"

Luke shrugged. "Not many people do. It hasn't wildly taken off in the tourist crowd like other places mostly it's an escape for the locals." He pulled out his cooler which contained the makings of their dinner. "Now relax, my lady, while I prepare you dinner." Hannah giggled.

Hannah had begun to sweat so she stripped out of some of her layers and sat on the couch while Luke did commentary of himself chopping vegetables and searing meat. When he was done, Hannah had a sore side from laughing, and the jambalaya smelled amazing. Hannah devoured her bowl hungrily since she hadn't remembered to eat lunch that day. She ate a second bowl while she sipped her Pinot Grigio. "Luke this is impressive!"

"My list of recipes I can cook is short and simple, but I'm hoping to add more to my resume. Especially if I have a beautiful woman reassuring me that it's delicious." He smirked a slightly cocky, slightly goofy smile.

"Okay, smart guy." Hannah joked back.

After Hannah had drank her third glass of wine, she decided to get into the hot tub. Luke had just gotten done showing her on his field map exactly what route they would be hiking in the morning, and Hannah couldn't wait to see it in action. She wasn't much into the planning of adventures, she usually jumped into such things with spontaneity although she could see the importance in the safety aspect of making a plan.

Wordlessly, she got up from the table and turned on the water in the tub. As it filled, she stood facing the windows and she began to remove her clothing. One item at a time, she tossed to the side and without turning to look at Luke, sunk into the hot tub. The temperature was perfect, and her body felt so relaxed from the good food, plentiful wine, and hot water. She felt the water level fluctuate as Luke slid into next to her and pulled her on top of him. Hannah had been thinking about kissing those lips all night. Passionately, she leaned into him, and quickly with roughness, they made love.

Afterwards, he pulled her close to him and they silently sat looking at the mountains, their hands entangled together. There was some type of wholeness and freedom this man gave her. She felt like a superhero woman who could be thrown off the top of a building and be scooped up and saved by the protagonist and brought back to his lair to be tenderly loved. It was exciting and reassuring all at the same time. It reminded her of the love her parents shared but with Hannah's flair thrown in. It was nothing like the life she had ever lived with Mark. In fact, since ending their engagement, she hadn't thought of him once other than breaking the news to her parents and sisters.

She didn't find herself comparing Luke to Mark. It was as if she had stepped forward into an entirely new chapter of her life and left him on the page he needed to stay on. Luke had never questioned her ability to be a business owner. Even with the reviews that he had seen coming in, he never doubted her. There was something special about that.

"I love you, Hannah." He said. His voice was quieter than she had ever heard it before, and it quivered with the words.

"I love you, Luke." She snuggled into him closer. Happiness and heat rushed through her.

"I've never said that to a woman before," Luke admitted.

"Never?" Hannah asked curiously.

He shook his head. "Never. I've never even been close. It's terrifying to say to someone for the first time."

Hannah nodded. "Absolutely and even harder if you have never had that conversation before." She pulled his face down to her and kissed him. He picked her up and carried her to the bed as the jacuzzi tub sat forgotten behind them.

When Hannah awoke the next day, the sun was fully blaring down on them, and Hannah's body felt relaxed and warm. She didn't want to move. The fire flickered and the room smelled of fresh coffee. She reached over back for Luke. The bed was empty. "Luke?" She called.

He popped his head up from the couch. "Are you up Hannah? Come sit with me. Bring that heavy blanket. I'll grab you a coffee."

Hannah wrapped herself in the big olive comforter, walked over to the couch, and slumped down. The heat of the fire brushed her face as she laid her head on the side of the couch. Luke returned with her coffee placed it behind her head and set his refilled mug on the opposite side of the couch. They sat and drank as he massaged her freezing feet. Hannah excitedly shared the menu items she had planned for October, and Luke beamed watching her. Hannah could see he enjoyed watching her talk about Drury Lane. It felt good to let everything out about the day, good or bad. When they finished their mugs, he got up to make them scrambled eggs with toast.

Hannah ate hungrily, barely stopping to evaluate the flavor of the eggs. When she was done, she got up to shower off the sweat on her body from the night as Luke began to tidy up the room. She dressed in her hiking gear, and they headed out the door. The hike was an all-day affair and Hannah had never done one like it before. She was excited to try something new and challenging. Luke was confident she would have no problems keeping up and was excited for her to see the parts that made hiking truly unique.

He seemed to go into a zone, explaining the different trees and animals, or where they were in approximation to other locations. Hannah listened and had to often remind him to slow down. A few times she had told him she wanted to stop to get a better look at the view when really, all she wanted was to catch her breath. Luke was so entranced by his own stories, that he didn't notice. Hannah had never seen him get swept up in his commentary like that before and knew that the woods were to him what the water was to her. The thought made her smile to herself. When they reached the top, Hannah's gasp escaped her. "Amazing." She whispered. She completely understood at that moment what made a grueling hike like this something that one would attempt again.

Luke smiled to himself and agreed. "It really is."

Chapter 22

Hannah

The rest of October was full of baking for long hours at Drury Lane. Hannah had a few orders for baked goods at a few Halloween parties, and it was some of the most fun items she had created. Despite her longer days and earlier mornings, Hannah made sure to carve out time for Luke. They were easing into a more comfortable everyday existence. Hannah accompanied him to Gearshift and sometimes watched him on the rink. Luke looked proud to have her at his side.

On Halloween night, Hannah entered Gearshift tucked into Luke's arm dressed as Marilyn Monroe. The entire bar turned to look at her in her floor-length red sequence dress with a slit that reached her thigh with red heels. She had on the iconic red lipstick and Marilyn's blonde hairstyle wig. She loved being in character and it hadn't taken any amount of convincing to get Luke to dress as Joe DiMaggio.

"Oh my gosh, Hannah! I've never seen anyone do a better Marilyn!" Whit squeaked as she joined her at a table.

"I love that you went with a different dress than the typical white. It's perfect." Bri added.

"You guys look amazing too!"

Bri was dressed as a pirate, Whit had opted for an Egyptian Queen. They both did look amazing. "I can't believe you got Luke to do a couple's costume with you! Usually, he chooses something completely outrageous. One year, he dressed as a box. I can't remember what his punch line was."

Hannah shrugged. "I brought up dressing as Marilyn and he practically made the suggestion himself." "I can see why," Bri said as they all glanced over at look who was staring at Hannah from across the bar. Hannah looked back at him and smiled. He returned the smile and gave her one last long look before he returned to his conversation.

*****

November focused on the town's Thanksgiving Feast which was celebrated the Saturday after Thanksgiving. One of the local barn-style wedding venues donated their space and every local business supplied something for the event. Hannah had been invited to make the buns, pecan, and pumpkin pies, and another dessert of her choice. Each year the proceeds were donated to the battered woman's shelter which was the only one of its kind in the area. They were always at capacity, and the fundraiser kept the lights on at the shelter. Hannah was excited to be able to help out at a charity event for such an amazing cause. Her friend Shawna would have never been able to do the things she was doing in a safe space today without those types of resources. Every woman in an unsafe situation deserves a way out and a fresh start.

She was making regular pumpkin pie and pumpkin cheesecake, and she had chosen salted caramel apple crumble cake as her extra dessert. She had thought about making something with cranberries, but she was attending the dinner with Luke, his parents, grandparents, Molly, and her children. She hadn't seen Molly lately and after Thanksgiving was done, she wouldn't be featuring apple desserts for a while, and she couldn't wait to watch the delight on Molly's face while she savored the dessert. She wanted Luke's beloved aunt to like her.

The week of Thanksgiving would be her busiest yet. She could already tell Christmas would be the same way. The orders were stacked high for pies and buns for Thanksgiving dinners all over town. She was worried she wouldn't get them all done and get the baking done for the store every day as well. She had enlisted Marg's help for a few extra days that week and had simplified her menu for the time being.

Her family was getting together for a Thanksgiving evening supper, and Luke was attending with her this year. She would get Thursday night and Friday to celebrate her holiday. Then she would need to get straight back to business because along with the Thanksgiving Feast she was attending and bringing items to, it was small business Saturday. All the local businesses were open earlier and holding sidewalk sales, and Hannah would have to ensure she had made enough of her most popular items for the hoard of shoppers they were anticipating. She loved the holidays and was thankful for the surplus of business, but she was exhausted. She would be closed two days next week to reset from the overfull week.

***

On Wednesday morning, Hannah was running through the list of orders in her head along with the mile-long to-do list that seemed to be only increasing in size. Frank Sinatra and Dean Martin blared through her speakers. She reviewed her pie count for the fourth time today, and a customer walked through the front door. Before she could put her pencil down and turn her attention to them, the customer spoke.

"I think I'm finally allowed to speak to you now." She looked up to find the woman with the red hair standing in front of her counter.

"Molly!" Hannah said.

"So, he did finally break the ice enough to talk about me. He has always struggled with building meaningful relationships with new people, and I never understood it. I think he is terrified of failure. I was worried he wouldn't take the chance of failure with you." Hannah smiled.

She immediately loved Molly's ability to be blunt and at the same time be cheering for her nephew's success. Hannah would do the same for anyone she loved. "I would agree. He likes to be the best at everything he does. I have only seen him lose once at Yahtzee, and he sulked for an hour." Molly threw her head back in laughter. "Are you home for Thanksgiving already?"

Molly nodded. "The boys are both off for the week, so they are here with me as well."

"What about Travis?"

She waved the question off. "He is traveling this week. He works for the NFL in the broadcasting division, so he is never around for Thanksgiving."

Hannah thought Molly looked relieved at this, so Hannah changed the subject. "We are reaching the end of my apple season. I am not sure what I will feed you after Saturday."

Molly smiled. "You remembered."

"Of course. I bake to spread joy, and I do a better job at that when I know everyone's favorite things. I've made my mom tiramisu for every bad day and every time I've been in trouble since I was ten." Molly laughed so hard that she reached for her side.

Molly was a radiant young woman to be a mom of young men, and she looked even younger when she laughed. Hannah could sense a hint of sadness in her aura though but couldn't place the cause, although she suspected Travis may have something to do with it. "I am a sucker for strawberries and all things gingerbread as well."

"Very few people do not cite chocolate as a top five favorite," Hannah remarked.

Molly shrugged. "I've always suspected I was different. My sister has told me no less a few times." She said with a smile.

It was clear that Molly possessed the same free and confident spirit that lived within Hannah's soul. She knew that along with being close to Luke, she was close to his mother as well. Hannah relied on her sisters to be her foundation and Molly, she suspected, probably did the same with Becky and Luke. They were alike in so many ways, and Hannah was thrilled at the idea of having someone with a kindred spirit entering her life. Hannah nodded in response. "My sisters are pretty sure I'm adopted. Although my mom denies it every time they bring it up." She teased back.

"Different is more exciting anyway, and what is life without a little excitement?"

"I agree." Hannah loved Molly immediately and could see a lifelong friendship building. She enjoyed Luke's parents as well and was so happy to have people around her so far from home that felt like family.

"Well, I'd better pay and get going. I'm sure you are crazy busy this week and don't have too much time to be visiting with Luke's aunt."

"I always have time for Luke's family." Hannah smiled warmly.

"Still, I feel like I'm hoarding you." She ordered her apple turnovers and apple cinnamon crumble muffin and strode out the door. She seemed to glide as she moved, and she held her head with poise and confidence.

Hannah had been struck by her complete support of her business from the start. She wanted to be one of Hannah's cheerleaders, even before Luke had decided to man up and talk to her and had remained a regular customer despite not being a resident of Woodsburrow. Hannah admired the way she generously supported the people she loved and did it without hesitation. She was excited to spend more time with Molly this weekend. She was not usually around people with similar dispositions as herself, but with Luke having almost identical qualities to own, was it any surprise that his favorite aunt was likened to him?

Luke

"Now that she is coming to Thanksgiving, can I tell her? It's killing me not to say anything when I go into her shop." Molly begged on the phone.

"Yes, you can tell her now. I've told her about you, so hopefully, she doesn't think you are a totally crazy person." He teased back.

"I'm so proud of you, Luke. Hannah is a beautiful human and seeing you with her has sparked a maturation in you that I have never seen before. She is making you into a better man." Molly said. He smiled. He knew she was right. He cared about something bigger than himself and wanted to be the man he thought Hannah deserved. He hadn't changed himself, he was still Luke, but he had more intention in his daily choices. He wanted to share his family with her and develop a deeper bond with hers. He loved her sense of adventure. She had already asked him about ice climbing and winter camping. *How could he ever possibly find a better match for himself?* He was certain there wasn't one.

Although he already knew her parents, Luke was terrified to attend Hannah's Thanksgiving. Her sisters didn't know him, and from Hannah's description, they seemed a bit hard to please, not to mention his experience with children was limited. He didn't dislike them; he just possessed no knowledge of what you did with children. The only children he had grown up around were Noah and Logan and they had been more like siblings at the time. He didn't know how to interact with children as an adult. He had taken Tori's kids to the park as he had offered, and no one was hurt in the process. Actually, those little guys were fun.

Luke went through six outfits while he attempted to dress for the day. Half of his shirts were way too wrinkled to wear to an event like this. He settled on a suit that was too dressy to be worn as is. He swapped out the suit jacket for a sweater and styled his hair that had become a mess after his frantic dressing disaster. He studied himself in the mirror before leaving the house. He was really doing this. Luke was meeting "the family" for the holidays, and he already knew he wanted Hannah to be a part of his Christmas. He prayed her family wouldn't think he was a childish jokester who was too immature to be with their Hannah. He wanted them to see him as family because he was already contemplating the idea of Hannah becoming a part of his.

Hannah

When Luke finally arrived in a dressed-down suit, Hannah was done baking all her orders, but she still had some deliveries to make on their way out of town. Hannah had never seen Luke so done up. He was dashing, and she was proud to be at his side. She knew her sisters would love his charm, and Mark would be long forgotten from their family table. Hannah had dressed in a long plush maroon dress with a V-neckline. "You look amazing," Luke said with a grin.

"You aren't too bad yourself." Hannah smiled back. He was the same Luke she saw almost every day in plain pants and a t-shirt, but her pulse quickened the same when he appeared in uniform. He looked strong and official, and they stared at each other with longing eyes. The longing never seemed to diminish between them. They had a supercharged connection. It was as if she had found a male version of herself, and he felt the same. The desire to both be with and entangled in each other never dulled.

"We have to go now if you want to deliver your pies," Luke said huskily.

"I just have to grab my overnight bag," Hannah replied with a glint in her eyes. She walked up the stairs with Luke trailing behind her.

Ten minutes later, they had loaded the pies and rolls. Her bags had been placed in the cab, and Hannah's make-up and hair had been touched up. The grin she wore seemed to be plastered to her face. In the car, Luke leaned in close to her. "You look like the cat who ate the canary." He teased in her ear. Hannah just smiled wider and said nothing. "It's my first Thanksgiving with a family other than my own. Maybe you could help me out a little, so I don't look like I am about to steal their daughter upstairs for dessert instead of a piece of pumpkin pie." He smiled nervously. "I want to make a good first impression on your sisters."

She squeezed his hand tightly. "They will love you." Hannah tried to readjust her face to a more relaxed smile, and Luke laughed so hard he almost swerved off the road.

They made their deliveries, had to decline three sit-down invitations, and made it to dinner at her parents' on time, barely. Her parents greeted them at the door with genuine happiness. Just as Hannah had predicted, her sisters were in love with Luke before the dinner was over. Hannah was thrilled to spend time with Piper and Gage and was extremely impressed with how good Luke was with the kids. He had an innate sense of play, and Piper took to him immediately. Dinner was delicious, and the pumpkin cheesecake was everyone's yearly favorite. Her mother beamed at Luke's repeated compliments about the turkey. They said goodnight as the clock was turning nine, and the little ones started to fuss.

Hannah, her sisters, and her mother had a black Friday shopping date in the morning. Every year the men would watch the babies and prepare an annual brunch that they had to plan in its entirety without any help. One year they had made a surf and turf style lunch. Another year they had mac and cheese and last year they had made pancakes and bacon.

The women would wake before dawn fill their travel mugs full of coffee to the brim and wait in lines for stores to open. They sipped their coffee and laughed together. It was the only time all year they could be together, just the three of them. It was as if Hannah and her sister were all kids again. When the stores would open, they would rush around and find the best deals. This year, along with Christmas presents, they had a newborn and Hannah's new place that still looked a little on the empty side. The girls welcomed the challenge.

They arrived at Hannah's parents exhausted and hungry. "What's for lunch?" Katherine called as they entered the kitchen. Hannah could smell warm tomato sauce. "Spaghetti and meatballs, garlic bread with chocolate pudding." Her dad answered wearing the corny "Kiss the Chef" apron he wore every year with pride in his eyes.

"Which part did you make, babe?" Hannah asked Luke.

He smirked. "I buttered that garlic bread."

Hannah giggled. "I'm sure the bread will be the best part." They all enjoyed their feast with warmth and happiness. Hannah felt thankful. *This is what the holidays were all about.*

Chapter 23

Small Business Saturday proved to be the biggest doughnut day of the entire year. Hannah had made pumpkin, apple cider, and cinnamon sugar doughnuts, and which far outsold anything else she had made that day. She closed down at noon to give herself enough time to finish baking the goodies for the feast and arrive early enough to deliver them.

When Hannah drove up to the barn that sat nestled in the woods, she couldn't believe how magical it appeared. The barn was an aged grey with large white lights strung over the steps that led into the entrance. There were fall leaves on the side of the building and planters of mums covered the steps. The inside was just as stunning. Turkeys stood throughout the place and red and orange tablecloths covered the tables in an alternating pattern. Each table had the soft glow of red cinnamon candles and a giant chandelier that hung low in the center was draped with more leaves. Pumpkins of all colors were scattered around the room. Cornucopias sat at each one of the tables stuffed with different combinations of fruits and vegetables. She placed her baked goods at the designated end of the long table and stared in awe.

The dinner went off without a hitch and was completely sold out of tickets as usual. A few high schoolers were paid to serve the food, and everything about the dinner was perfect. Hannah spent a lot of time chatting with Molly, Luke, and the boys. Everyone around them treated them like family, and his parents seemed to know each one of the farms that had donated produce for the event intimately. Hannah was proud to be a part of this beautiful group of humans.

Luke

Luke's family had always attended the town Thanksgiving dinner for as long as he could remember. He had always seen the town as a part of his family. His parents loved seeing their different friends from around town. He looked around to see the people around him mingling. He watched Molly and Hannah interacting and saw a new friendship that was forming. Matt waved to him from across the room, but he ignored his greeting. They hadn't spoken since their argument about the paper, and he had ignored him at the Halloween party. Despite him doing his best to retract the article and print some positive things about Hannah's bakery, Luke was still angry that Matt had even thought for a minute what he had printed was okay.

He walked over to Steele's dad, and they chatted about how fishing had been that year and how the fall bow hunting season was going for him. He was always impressed with how little he allowed the stroke to slow him down. When he returned to the table, Noah caught him up on hockey. He had high hopes of being a coach at the collegiate level upon graduation. Luke was proud. Noah had grown into a fine man. Molly had done so well raising them both.

Logan had told Luke every detail from the camp he had attended this summer. Although their interests weren't as similar as his and Noah's were, he was still proud to have such a smart cousin. Even though Logan was quiet, he was stubborn and bold at heart. Luke loved that energetic side of him he rarely showed and knew it would serve him well as he grew into a man. When he entered college next fall, he would be more ready than Luke had ever been. Molly was just as proud and beamed as her boys talked about their passions. He worried that when Logan left, Molly would be left with a gaping hole in her life.

Luke watched Hannah shine among the crowd as she chatted with customers, his family, and friends. He was so grateful that she was an extrovert like he was and could see her cup overflowing with happiness from the power of the love that this community held for each other. He knew they were lucky.

If Hannah had received the same type of defamation in any other town, things might be different. The talk had changed from rumors to what Hannah may have done to illicit such horrible things to be said about her, to everyone watching over her for her safety. They loved having Hannah enrich the community and were happy to see Hannah and Luke together. If not a bit nosey about the whole thing. Sometimes, he felt like a museum display. He had been congratulated no less than ten times this evening. They were quickly becoming the town's golden couple.

There were rumors that whoever had been threatening her was a man who had been heard from around town, and Luke had been watching for him. The problem was that men tended to stare at Hannah. She looked impossibly gorgeous, and it appeared like she was glowing everywhere she went. It was extremely hard to say if anyone was acting odd because of this everyday occurrence.

Dinner was delicious, and he had told everyone who would listen to try Hannah's pumpkin pie. The sound of moaning was audible in the room when the desserts were brought out, and it was followed by the volume rapidly decreasing in the room. Everyone was happily stuffed, and sleepy. Luke prayed that every Thanksgiving would be like this for the rest of their days.

<h1 style="text-align:center">Chapter 24</h1>

Hannah

On Monday, Hannah was exhausted. She had been working long nights and early mornings to make everything happen the way it had, and for the next two days, she planned on doing very little. She had begun swimming at the local YMCA in the same building that the ice rink was located in since the lake had frozen over. She made a point to take time to swim each one of the days she was off and still painted when she got home.

Luke had to work both of these days, and she wasn't expecting to see him until Thursday that week when they were going to get a Christmas tree for Drury Lane and her apartment. She had painted a wintery scene on Monday night and spent time on Tuesday taking down her fall decorations. When the evening fell, she decided to run over to the grocery store to get ingredients for chili, so she grabbed her hat, jacket, and purse. She slid on her boots and walked across the street stepping through the dusting of snow that had fallen. She was feeling content with life and full of the hope of the season. Hannah made quick work of choosing her items and was soon checking out with the cashier as they chatted about the new puppy that she had mentioned the last time Hannah had seen her. She walked out the door and stepped across the street to her building.

When Hannah approached Drury Lane, she could tell immediately something was wrong. She reached for her phone in her pocket, but her pocket was empty. She quickly checked the other. It was empty just like the first. "Shit!" She shouted. She had left her phone on the counter in her kitchen. She didn't expect to need it just walking across the road into the grocery store. She jogged to get a closer look. Glass was shattered and littered the ground both inside and outside the building. Both front windows had been completely smashed. Her beautiful winter scene lay in shambles out in the snow. Jagged edges were left covering the panes. Hannah opened the front door and walked inside.

Her heart sank lower and lower with every step. Each display case that Zack had poured his heart into was destroyed. The lights that Emily had created just for Drury Lane had been crushed as well. The entire row left a trail of debris beneath it. It seemed that whoever had been here had broken things that could be broken quickly and easily, mostly that had included everything glass. She wasn't sure if anything was missing, but she didn't want to spend any more time wandering around without calling for help. She ascended the stairs quickly to her apartment, picturing the spot where her phone lay waiting.

When she reached the location where her phone should have sat, she was surprised it wasn't there at all. Her mind raced as she tried to remember if she had moved it and where it could be. At that moment, she saw a figure move in the opposite corner of the room. She had been so focused on the damage downstairs, that she hadn't even looked around the place when she entered. "Well, well,

well if it isn't little Miss Sunshine." Said the eerie voice from the figure. Hannah recognized the voice, but her brain couldn't put together the face and the name.

He moved into the light and the glint of the giant kitchen knife he was holding caught her eye. It was at that moment that for the first time in her life, Hannah was truly afraid. It was a deep and all-encompassing fear that made her pulse quicken and her vision tighten. The figure continued speaking. "You thought you could refuse me, leave me, and destroy me, while you run around this place muddying the waters like a filthy whore? I will not be denied. It's time to teach you a lesson that you don't seem to be learning."

Hannah's brain sparked more familiarity. "Pierre?" She asked. "What on earth are you talking about? You have the most successful bakery in the city, if not the entire state. Why are you putting all that on the line to be here?"

"Don't act like you don't know you condescending little bitch."

Hannah didn't have a clue what he was talking about. "Know what?" Hannah asked. She didn't know how she was going to get out of this situation. Luke had been working long hours the last two days, and he didn't know to know she needed him. Her eyes darted around the room as she desperately searched for her phone, but she didn't see it anywhere. The only prayer she had was to keep him talking.

"After you insisted you were leaving, I had two more employees leave. They claimed the atmosphere was too toxic. I couldn't hire and train fast enough to meet the customer's needs. I started to get poor reviews, and it led to fewer orders. Then, my building was repossessed to be sold on default of my loan. Now I have nothing, and it's all because of you. You always walked around that place flaunting your body at me and everyone else. I can't believe you had the audacity to refuse to sleep with me. You are a tease and a hoax. I tried to get people in this town to treat your business exactly the way you deserved. None of the reviews I left online seemed to make a difference. Everyone just adored you too much. The only person who I could convince is that spindly man who runs the coffee shop. No one else would agree not to ignore you and your business. You don't deserve to have any of this, but now it's time for all of it to come full circle."

This man was delusional. He had been leaving the reviews and trying to destroy her business. He was the reason Brett had been ignoring her. He must have threatened him to make him behave the way he had. Hannah realized he didn't plan on letting her leave. *But what could she do?* She couldn't call for help without her cell phone, and he would kill her if she attempted to escape. He stuck the knife to her throat and pushed her into her bedroom. He immediately hooked her wrists in handcuffs to the bed. As he fumbled with the handcuffs, Hannah began to scream. She called Luke's name over and over, hoping she could will him with all the forces of the world to her side. She knew it was hopeless, but if she was going to lose her life, she wasn't going to give up without a fight.

He began hitting her as she flailed and screamed, yelling obscenities at her while he demanded she be quiet. He reminded her that no one could hear her and all she was doing was making him angry. He hit her so hard that her lip split, and blood stained her mouth. She swallowed with the taste of metal thick on her tongue. Then he ripped a sheet long enough to tie around her face to muffle her sound.

Hannah knew her voice wouldn't be audible through the walls anymore, so she stopped. She tried to make sense of what was happening and tried to convince herself that she would be able to get out of there. And if she couldn't, she would need to be fine with this being the end. Silent tears streamed down her face. Pierre seemed to be swept up in his own life drama and was babbling on about her being a devil and how women should know their proper places.

He started slicing through her layers of clothes and whipping her bare chest with a belt that had been lying in the corner. Each snap burned against her skin, and every slash would bruise. Mentally, she escaped to her parent's home. She saw herself in the living room surrounded by her family, Luke, and his family, and the peace and love and the power of everyone gathered together. She said a prayer that she would see her mother again, and the front door shook under the weight of someone banging on it.

"This is the police open up!" She knew it was Luke and could hear the panic in his authoritative voice. He knew she was in trouble and her body relaxed despite the terror that surrounded her. Luke wouldn't let anything happen to her.

"Be quiet you little bitch. You make a sound, and I'll cut your tongue off!" *He thought that being quiet would make the police leave.* Pierre had lost all sense of reality. The thought frightened her. He was a wild card now. If he wanted her to be quiet. She would. Luke wouldn't leave without seeing the whites of her eyes.

"I said this is the police open up!" Luke yelled louder. It was a beat later that she heard him open the door and storm the living room. She felt his shadow drift over the door despite not seeing his face as he approached her room.

"You are trespassing on this property and holding this woman hostage. Place your knife on the ground slowly and put your hands in the air." Luke's words were slow and steady as he moved closer to Pierre.

"I am doing a service to your community by removing this evil Jezebel, so she doesn't infect you like the plague."

"Unfortunately, the pureness of her sexuality doesn't change any charges in the eyes of the court," Luke responded with tightness in his voice.

Suddenly, Pierre had moved from across the room and held the knife directly to her neck. Luke moved in a counteraction so he could see Hannah now, his gun drawn and body steady.

Hannah made eye contact with him and then shut her eyes as tears streamed down her face. She could feel the cool blade resting against her skin, and Pierre grasped her hair and yanked her head upwards. "Drop the knife," Luke demanded. Pierre stood unmoving. He defiantly spit towards Luke. "I need you to drop the knife," Luke repeated. The pressure of the knife seemed to increase just a hair, and whether it was intended or not, Hannah felt the knife nick her skin, and blood began rolling down her neck. In the next instant, she heard Luke fire one shot, and the knife and pressure on her neck abruptly stopped. Pierre slumped to the floor. She was too afraid to open her eyes, so she squeezed them tighter. She heard the jingle of keys and the sound of Luke moving towards her.

Luke knelt down checked Pierre's pulse, and quickly moved to Hannah. "Hannah, please be okay." He whispered as quickly unlocked the cuffs. "Hannah baby, look at me." He pleaded. "Say something." Hannah opened her eyes at his face filled with worry as tears continued to stream down hers.

He wrapped her into him and let out a sob. Holding her tightly, he scooped up the blanket lying off to her side and wrapped it around her to cover her unclothed torso. He used his radio to inform the dispatch that a man had been shot dead and an ambulance was needed for the victim. Hannah could already hear sirens in the distance. "Did he hurt you anywhere else?" He said as his fingers brushed near the spot of her neck that was still dripping wet. Hannah nodded and pulled the blanket down to reveal the bruises that were forming on her chest and stomach. His body stiffened, and he once again pulled her close.

"Thank you for knowing I needed you." She said with a hoarse voice and rested her body against his as they waited for the paramedics to enter her apartment.

Luke

Luke had been patrolling Main Street and noticed the mess inside Drury Lane. He immediately knew something was wrong. He checked his phone and had no missed calls from Hannah. There were no panicked text messages asking for help, and Hannah had no plans to be anywhere other than home. He had jumped out of his squad car after radioing for backup. Luke quickly walked through Drury Lane yelling for Hannah. There was no sign of her, so he bolted out the back door. He saw Hannah's Bug in the back and quickly climbed the stairs to her apartment. He tried the knob, but it was locked. He immediately banged on the door insisting he be let it. He knew Hannah was in trouble, and after no answer, he used all of his strength, and some he didn't know he had, to break the door down.

The sight of Hannah being held against her will fearful and hurt, had made Luke behave robotically. He had given the preparator orders but had refused to engage any further with him. All he had thought about was getting Hannah away from that madman and back into his arms. When he saw the blood, he fired without any feelings of fear or regret. He was grateful for the excuse to kill the man who had managed to cause Hannah pain for too long. He had followed protocol to the letter but didn't hesitate for a second when it was time to pull the trigger.

After making sure the scene was safe, he pulled Hannah into him. He was afraid of what injuries she might have, but she was breathing and responding to him. He wrapped the blanket that he knew that she loved around her and held her until someone arrived who could make sure she was truly okay.

<h1 style="text-align:center">Chapter 25</h1>

Hannah was kept in the Emergency Room overnight at Luke's insistence. He was terrified she might have other injuries that Hannah just couldn't remember. He called Molly to pick up a completely new bedding set for her room and his parents went over to clean up the blood. Luke called her parents, but Hannah told him she didn't want them to come. He assured them she was safe, and he wouldn't be leaving her side. Policy stated a discharge of his weapon warranted an investigation, and he would be off for at least a week while they launched their inquiry.

Hannah didn't say much that night. She had grabbed Luke's phone, they had discovered that Pierre had broken hers, and researched what had happened to the Golden Goose. Apparently, late orders and a drop in performance had lowered his standing in the city to another up-and-coming bakery, one in fact that she had opted not to compete with. The Golden Goose's building had been foreclosed upon. Pierre had been arrested on a few assault charges and public intoxication. He had been on a downward spiral that had seemed to coincide with about the time that Hannah had left. He was insistent that it was her fault that he had lost everything. The reality was that he was so intent on ruining her, that he had lost sight of the things that he had in front of him. A business can't flourish without consistency and leadership, and those were not his best qualities. He had caused his implosion.

When she was discharged in the morning, Luke brought her home. Hannah entered the apartment and instead of feeling the fear and seeing replays of the awful situation she had endured; she saw that her entire apartment had been transformed into a winter wonderland and looked almost unrecognizable. Molly, Becky, and Hannah's mother and sisters had gotten together and hung all of her decorations and added new ones. They had chosen a tree and somehow had found a Scottish pine, her favorite. They had simply hung the lights leaving it a blank canvas for Hannah to finish as she saw best. It glowed peacefully in the corner with boxes full of different colored ornaments set around the tree.

A new brightly colored knife set was on the counter along with various Christmas baking signs and gingerbread families. Christmas towels were hung in the bathroom and kitchen. Christmas rugs were set up throughout. Lights had been hung along the arch of the hallway, and candles had been lit and added to the ambiance. Someone had set new speakers up on the counter so she could fill the house with her music.

Molly had bought her a velvety rich red comforter with matching red sheets. There were Christmas green throw pillows that hadn't been there before, and a gray cable knit blanket that was plush on the backside was draped over the corner. Her winter scenes that she had painted on her canvases had been hung in a series on the left wall and garland had been draped around the windows. The entire house smelled of cinnamon and pine and Hannah burst into tears. Luke wrapped himself around her immediately.

"What is it?" He asked softly. "Is this place full of bad memories now? We could go to my place if it's too much." Hannah shook her head. "Are you worried about Drury Lane? I've already spoken with the local glass guy, and I called Zack. He and Emily are coming over tomorrow to replace the lights and anything else that is broken. They came to survey the damage and help with cleanup while you were in the hospital. Hannah started crying even harder. "Hannah? Talk to me beautiful." He stroked his hand gently through her hair.

"I can't believe everyone did all this for me. It's completely transformed the place. I don't know if I deserve to have all these wonderful people in my life."

"You know that exactly how everyone feels about you. You are the kindest and most welcoming human I know. Don't let this change you."

"Pierre tried to break me while I worked for him, and I didn't let him. I can't let him now either."

Luke

Luke had seen fellow officers in duty experience some horrible things and never quite be the same again. He could see each and every one of them and picture in his mind exactly the people they were before in stark contrast to the people they became after. He was worried sick as he sat by the hospital bed of the most important human that had ever entered his life. He was frightened she would be affected in the same haunting manner. The flashbacks that frequented his mind on repeat starred Hannah with her eyes closed and the knife pressed against her neck, made him want to vomit. He wished he would have known something was off earlier in the day. He had tried to keep an eye on her property and the defamation that kept showing up everywhere. He had spent his nights at home searching and had pleaded with his supervisors to continue to press on into the investigation, but they had simply not had enough to go on. They had been outwitted by a madman. He had failed to protect the one he loved the most, and it killed him. He prayed that Hannah's light would still burn brightly and that she wouldn't give up on the dreams that she was living.

He had called Hannah's parents to give them the news, and the grief and worry was thick on the phone. He heard the shock and panic in her mother's voice. Luke did what he could to reassure them, but Hannah was asking for space, and her mother just wanted to hold her baby. There was nothing more he could do but reassure her that he would be at her side and would call him the second she was ready. He hoped that her father could be strong for them both.

The next call he made was to Molly and briefed her on what had occurred. Molly was furious and offered her help immediately. Luke asked her to work with Hannah's mom to get Hannah's apartment cleaned up and do what they could to transform her home from a place of torture back into the place that Hannah loved. Molly assured him that she would take care of the apartment. "Just be with her, buddy. We love you guys. Let me know if there is anything else, I can do to help."

"Pray for her Molly." He had pleaded as tears filled his eyes as it all became too much to bear.

"I'm praying hard. She has the soul of a warrior and the pureness of a child. I know she can move through this, and she certainly won't have to do it alone."

After having the responsibility of her apartment taken care of, he returned the phone calls that he had missed from Steele who had been calling regularly to check on them since the news had become public. He insisted that he be allowed to help. Hannah was a part of their group now, and he loved her like a sister.

Luke had asked if he could coordinate the cleaning up of the glass that had been shattered and covered the hardwood floor. He didn't want Hannah wading through the wreckage losing faith in herself and what she had begun to grow. He suggested Steele call Emily and Zack for help. They would know exactly what Hannah would want done, and he knew how special their work was to her. If Hannah was going to pull herself together and reopen, she would want Emily and Zack to be the ones helping rebuild. Steele had promised he would do everything he could to help and have a plan in place for when she was ready to make those decisions. After he hung up with Steele, he prayed like he had never prayed before.

The crime scene unit had processed the scene promptly. Because they were investigating his authority to discharge his weapon, and because Woodsburrow was a safe community that rarely had violent crime, they had shown up as Hannah was being wheeled out the door. It hadn't been long before they were given the okay to return to the building.

Everyone had been ready to get inside Drury Lane by the time those vehicles had cleared the scene. Luke continued to get updates as the cleanup ensued and let out a giant sigh of relief when he received confirmation that everything was ready just in time. Hannah had been discharged hours later.

Chapter 26

Hannah and Luke laid low the next two days as Hannah's cuts and bruises ached. She slept, took baths, and ate the food and goodies her friends and family had lovingly made for her and streamed Christmas music on repeat off Luke's phone. She had directed Luke as he decorated the tree and had managed to show a few laughs. It was cute watching that burly man hanging dainty sparkling ornaments. Once or twice, he shook his sexy butt to the Christmas songs and glanced back at her to see if he had made her smile.

Hannah's mother had called multiple times a day to check in, and by the end of day two, Hannah finally felt up to a small conversation with her. "Hannah baby, I'm so glad you are okay! I am grateful you have had so much help around you. I love you so much." She could hear her mother's relief on the phone as panic filled her chest. Her mother's heart would have been absolutely broken if she hadn't made it out of Pierre's grasp.

"I love you too, Mom. Thanks for your help with cleaning up the apartment. It really looks great, and it's helped to have a cheery place around me. I don't feel up to talking about how I'm doing though. Do you think we could try again tomorrow?"

"Of course, love. You let me know when you are up to having Dad and I visit, and we will come up."

"I will, Mom. Talk to you tomorrow." The reality of all the pain that Pierre had caused through her stung like the knife he had placed on her neck. She had been to a mental place that had accepted her unwanted demise, but the people who loved her would have only hurt. The confusion of it all spun in her brain.

On the third day, Hannah's pain had subsided, and her brain had started to clear the fog or at least begin to put the pieces back into place. She put herself together and went downstairs to check on the progress. Somehow, everything had been cleaned up. New lights hung from the ceiling and a few new chairs had been added, but everything essentially looked as if nothing had happened. Hannah, Luke, and Marg hung snowflakes, gingerbread families, snowmen, and Santas from the boxes in the back that Hannah had been waiting to unbox. She drew a winter scene on the new front window as Marg and Luke made sure every last bit of dirt and glass had been removed. Marg gave her an extra-large hug and told her she would see her tomorrow. "I'm so proud of your strength." She had told her.

Luke and Hannah grabbed their coats and hats to drive out to the tree farm. Brett met her by the sidewalk. "Do you have a minute to talk?" He said quietly not meeting her eye. Pierre was right, he did look spindly. He was a skinny small man with thick black glasses and sandy curly hair. Hannah nodded her head and held eye contact with him, staring him straight in the face despite his inability to look into hers.

"I need to apologize. I had been ignoring you on purpose and had started a few of the rumors that were swirling around town."

"But why?" Hannah asked. "I didn't do anything to you. I wasn't competing for your business. I was only kind to you."

"I know. Pierre showed up and threatened to have my business shut down, and I was afraid. Woods and Brew is all that I have."

"You could have at least warned me he had been coming around. You had more information about who was trying to come after me than anyone else around here did. Even the waitress at the diner had the common courtesy to tell me someone was acting oddly. She didn't know who it was. If you had given me the information you had, it could have prevented this from happening." Hannah said angrily.

"I know. I was a coward. I feel so guilty. Not only that but your business increased my sales this year by fifteen percent. People chose to visit Woodsburrow this fall over other local cities because of your bakery. In return, they headed over to my coffee shop to get a cup of coffee. You have done amazing things for this town in the short amount of time you have been here. I can't say the same for myself. I want to make it up to you. I am truly sorry for the way I behaved."

"I might find it in my heart to forgive you, but today is not that day. I take back my offer of doing business together and don't see that happening in the near future."

"What can I do to make things right?"

"I don't know," Hannah replied. "Right now, I would just like it if you left."

Luke stepped forward as if to enforce what she had just said, and Brett immediately scurried away.

Hannah took Luke's hand and walked towards his truck. She would not let these weak men keep her from everything she had built and the beautiful things that were to come. She needed to thank her customers for their patience and prayers and get back to business. She would be open for business-as-usual tomorrow. She wasn't going to miss out on this holiday season, not professionally or personally. She was headed to the tree farm with Luke. Despite the horrible things that had happened the last few days, she felt a bright future ahead of her. Sure, her spirit was injured, but no one could put out the light of the amazing Hannah Jones.

Epilogue

Hannah

The past year had been the best year of her life. Hannah had loved each season in Woodsburrow, and Drury Lane had increased in popularity among the tourists. The farmers' markets were still her favorite, and the people and culture there made her feel like she was absolutely in her element. Whit and Bri met her on Tuesday nights for Ladies' Night at Gearshift. She had been able to go camping with Emily and Zack. She was so proud of how much their business had taken off from the work they had done at Drury Lane. In the fall, she had been interviewed by Travel and Country magazine after being named the top bakery to visit this Autumn. Hannah had celebrated with a special dinner at Gearshift with Luke's family, and hers, along with her friends Emily, and Zack, and Marg.

Molly had become one of her closest friends, and they had frequent girl dates both in Woodsburrow, and the city depending on how her relationship with Travis was currently going. Things had become civil with Brett, but she kept her distance from him. She didn't want to do any type of business or life with a man who she couldn't trust. She had been attending therapy sessions to deal with the PTSD and although panic hit her from time to time, it had become infrequent and was manageable when it did. Winter had returned, and Luke was coming over tonight to go to the tree farm. Hannah was excited. It was the best part of Christmas, and last year it had felt like a blur from the events that had preceded it.

Luke

Luke picked her up when the sun had set. "Are you ready for the most magical night of the year?" He told her. He had been wanting to make this up to her since last year. Hannah smiled. "I've been waiting for this all week. I don't think you can drive fast enough for me!" *Me too.* He thought. He held her soft hand while they drove to the tree farm, Hannah speaking excitingly about their holiday plans. They pulled into the parking lot at Treetop Farms. It looked like it had stepped right out of a Hallmark movie. Last year, it had been daytime when they had come. This year, it was dark. The entire area around the Christmas shop and precut trees was lit up in lights. A bonfire burned brightly with benches set up around it. Speakers were playing Christmas music and a horse-drawn sleigh sat ready and waiting. Hannah looked around. It was odd at how few people were here. She looked at Luke.

He grinned. "Sleigh ride my dear?"

Hannah grinned back. "How you set this up, I don't know. There weren't sleigh rides available last year."

"I'll never tell." He replied pushing his nervousness down deep into his chest.

They climbed into the sleigh with hot chocolate and the majestic horses pulled them around the property. At that moment, it started to snow. It was a light and airy snow that sparkled brightly in the moonlight. The sleigh ride was straight out of a dream. They circled the property until the driver stopped to let them off at the field that was available for tree cutting this year.

Luke grabbed his saw and Hannah's hand. They wandered around until Hannah decided on the perfect tree. It was a bit harder to see in the light of the Christmas lights and moon instead of the sun, but the magic of the moment made it worth it. "This is the one Luke. I'm sure this time. Are you going to cut it down? It's starting to get cold." She turned around anticipating he would be laughing at her. This was the third tree she had chosen tonight. She couldn't make up her mind on such an important decision.

Instead, Luke was down on one knee in the snow. "Hannah, my life has been nothing but better with you in it. My family loves you. I love you. I'll never get tired of your light, your smile, or your spirit of adventure. I'd like to live the rest of my life with you by my side. There is no woman in the world who is more suited to be my partner."

He opened the tiny jewelry box and a magnificent oval stone sat in the center with dozens of small stones surrounding it set in all different directions, so it appeared similar to the petals of a flower. The band was rose gold, and the diamonds shined brightly. "Hannah, will you be my wife?"

Hannah threw her arms around Luke tackling him over into the snow. "A million times yes!" She said as they kissed with snowflakes falling all over them. "Now about that tree.."

Meet the
Author

J.R. Cook is a wife and mom who has been a lover of books since she could read. She has a great love for all things UpNorth, and making the world a more beautiful place to be.